STRANGERS IN PARADISE

For Ashley Alsup —
who asked the hard
questions and for whom
my laundry was down.

Thanks,
Lee

STRANGERS IN PARADISE

Lee K. Abbott

Lee K. Abbott
4-6-88
Houston

G. P. Putnam's Sons / New York

G. P. Putnam's Sons
Publishers Since 1838
200 Madison Avenue
New York, NY 10016

The following stories have been published previously, some of them in slightly different form: "The End of Grief," *The Atlantic;* "The Beauties of Drink: An Essay," *The Iowa Review;* "Living Alone in Iota," *fiction international;* "X," *The Georgia Review;* "Time and Fear and Somehow Love," *The Georgia Review;* "Category Z," *The Atlantic;* "The World Is Almost Rotten," *Mid-American Review;* "Rolling Thunder," *Memphis State Review;* "Youth on Mars," *StoryQuarterly;* "Notes I Made on the Man I Was," *The Indiana Review;* "The Valley of Sin," *Carolina Quarterly;* "Where Is Garland Steeples Now?" *Sonora Review;* "I'm Glad You Asked," *Ascent;* "The World of Apples," *Nit & Wit: Chicago's Literary Arts Magazine.*

Library of Congress Cataloging-in-Publication Data

Abbott, Lee K.
Strangers in paradise.

I. Title.
PS3551.B262S8   1986   813'.54   86-8139
ISBN 0-399-13196-5

*The author gratefully acknowledges
the help and support of the
National Endowment for the Arts.*

For Noel and Kelly

CONTENTS

THE END OF GRIEF

T HE worst thing, in many ways the only thing, I heard about when I was growing up in the late fifties and early sixties concerned the horrible death of my father's brother, my Uncle Gideon, on the Bataan Death March in April of 1942, an event that for those of you who, like me, were absorbed by the pictures and news reports of the Vietnam War must now seem as peculiarly dated as the times of knights errant and fire-breathing dragons.

"Remember this," my father would say when I was small. "We human beings are capable of some real nasty behavior."

Every family has its own history of heartache, its private record of betrayal or misfortune; but when I was a youngster—and probably because we live so far out of the way, in Deming, New Mexico, in a desert white and scorched and flat as one hell I've heard described—I believed, stupidly, that this infamy, a march of 78,000 native and American troops on a no-account Philippine peninsula, had touched everyone in our own safe world. From my mother, before she became a drunkard who would be carried off one day to live quietly and ever after in a private hospital in Roswell, and before she and Daddy divorced, I had learned about the other tragedies we Bakers and Hopcrafts (her people) had suffered: bankruptcies, disasters associated with weather or automobiles, paper fortunes that blew away like leaves, a drowning, a stillbirth, a black sheep or two. Yet if my mother could look backward for centuries, to the first of my ancestors who settled in the American Southwest in the early 1800s, my father, smart too, and just as familiar with our personal lore, could see only from the beginning of the Second World War to what was its mortal end for the young man I am said to be the spitting image of—my uncle.

Now, at thirty-seven, I remember clearly how Daddy, in his odd fashion, used to wish me good night with stories from a past that was no more important to me personally than money is to a rock. When I was in the third grade, he'd tell me—sitting at the foot of my bed, smoking a Pall Mall, an ashtray balanced on his knee—about the diseases the men in II Corps, and my uncle, suffered: dysentery, beriberi, night blindness, hookworm, diarrhea, mysterious swellings. When I was in the fourth grade, a time when I thought only about Little League baseball or swimming meets at the Mimbres Valley Country Club, he was taking me into his office, the newest outbuilding on our ranch, to show me his Department of the Army maps and geological surveys.

"They marched from here," he'd say, pointing to a crosshatching of lines identified as Balanga, "on the East Road to Lubao on Route Seven." His finger would trace the route, sometimes a path of gravel and packed dirt. "They would go from Capas by train and walk the next nine miles to Camp O'Donnell."

Yes, these were the names I heard through grammar school and into junior high: Bagac and Orion, the Marvilles Mountains, the island of Luzon, Manila Bay. In the year of my first kiss (with Jane Templeton at an FFA fair in our National Guard armory), he forced me to memorize the titles and honors of the Japanese commander, Lieutenant General Masaharu Homma, and several of his officers, including Colonel Nakayama and Colonel Takatsu. While my friends Dub Spedding and Bobby Hover were collecting memorabilia about Ted Williams and Hammering Hank Aaron, I was reading *Back from the Living Dead,* by Major Bert Bank. My father had sent to Alabama for it, had read it so thoroughly that the pages became creased and soiled and clotted with his notes, and by God I was going to read it, too, just as I would read, when he was finished, books like *Zone of Emptiness,* by Hiroshio Noma, and the documents published by the Allied Translator and Interpretor Section (ATIS), General Headquarters, Southwest Pacific Area. Once, when I was a sophomore at Deming High School, brainy enough to be on the debate team

and beefy enough to play varsity Wildcat football, he even gave
me a quiz.

"Before the surrender itself," he began, "what were our soldiers eating?"

We sat in his office, its many shelves laden with charts and
papers and file folders, his desk a clutter of books and writing
materials. On one wall hung a pair of khaki trousers and an
Imperial Army battle sword; on another, a partial order of battle.

"Who surrendered, by the way?"

"General King," I answered, a name I knew as well as my own.
"On April ninth, approximately fourteen hundred hours."

The room was full of smoke already, and, owing to the glare
from the floor lamp behind him, he seemed not so much my
father as an old, sly stranger—a wizard, I thought, or an Indian
medicine man—whose tests I had to pass in order to live as an
adult.

"The food, son," he said, "the meat first."

I recited the list: carabao, pack mule, lizard, dog and monkey,
even the meat and eggs from pythons.

"How much did black-market cigarettes cost?"

"Five dollars," I said. "Regularly they were five cents a pack."

He shook his head. "It kept changing," he told me. "Remember the situation: one day a certain price, the next day another. This is vital."

On it went. Name the military hospitals and the officers in
charge. How close was Corregidor? Why wouldn't Major General
Jones take off his sunglasses? Who was the commander of the
65th Brigade of the Japanese Fourteenth Army? What American
college had he attended? Describe the symptoms of malaria.
What is Article 3, Chapter 1 of the Japanese Army regulations for
handling prisoners of war? Translate *Bushido. Rikutatsu.*

At eleven I stopped him. We'd been at it for two hours. "I got to
study," I said. "Physics."

He was shuffling documents, and I wanted to be elsewhere. In
my room, I thought. In dreamland. Anywhere.

"Okay," he said. "Tomorrow we'll try something else."

I was at the door when he called me back.

"One more question," he said. "Why wasn't I in the war?"

A wind had come up, from the south and warm as breath. Tomorrow, while we classified soldiers according to sector and probable cause of death, we would have rain.

"Married," I told him.

He was rubbing his forehead, looking into space. "What else?"

"Medical deferment," I said. "Punctured eardrum, flat feet, pulmonary stenosis."

This sort of exchange worsened as I grew older and, in his mind at least, came to resemble more clearly his brother. We had the same forehead, he'd insist, pitching me yet another curled, yellowed photograph he filed in his fireproof cabinets. We had the same hair, too, coarse as thread and more brown than blond. The same watery hazel eyes. Our cheek structures were virtually identical, high and pointed. We even had, my father claimed, comparable habits of mind. We liked puzzles. Within reason, we took risks: embraced speed, high places, darkness. We hated bullies, dishonesty in our friends. We were nimble, alert, sensitive to climate changes. Gideon had traveled—Palm Springs and Chicago—and so would I. He preferred tall women, so mine, inevitably, would be tall. We were readers but not sissies. When I graduated, Daddy took me out to his office, made me sit, and told me to open the box on his desk.

"It's a present," he said. "You'll like it."

It was a gold Longines, a wristwatch I wear still, and I realized immediately that Daddy had wrapped it himself, maybe a dozen times before he was satisfied.

"Look at the inscription." He leaned across his desk, pointed.

Still in my cap and gown, the tassel tickling my neck, I could hear my mother calling us to the dinner table. The ceremony had been over for an hour.

"Read it," my father told me.

Engraved on the back in small Gothic letters was this: "Gideon

Alan Baker. Graduation: 16 June 1940. From his loving brother, Lyman."

"Gideon left it here before he enlisted," Daddy said. "He thought somebody might steal it."

I said thanks and stood to shake hands as I had been taught, firmly and with the palm full.

"You take care of that," he said, coming around his desk; and then I understood, more in my bones than in my brain, that he was smiling as he had smiled in 1940. To his mind, the hand he was holding, long-fingered and too soft, was less mine than his brother's; for him this was an instant of joy he had rescued, as boldly as if it were a person, from a past black and permanent as death itself.

"Gid liked expensive jewelry," Daddy said. "You will, too."

—

We would break eventually, my father and I, but for three years, while I was at the University of New Mexico, we continued our strange collaboration/review of Bataan, and torture, and my uncle. Within the week of my arrival, even before freshman orientation concluded, my father began writing me, filling his letters with facts I was to confirm in Zimmerman Library. "Find out," he'd scrawl, "who was responsible for the massacre of the 91st Filipino Division." A month later, he asked me to see if a Major Pedro L. Felix had been at Fort Benning, Georgia, on or about 12 October 1941. "What for?" I wrote back. By return mail I had an answer: "Gid mentions him twice. Maybe they met in the National Rice and Corn Corporation warehouse. I'm trying to establish a connection. This man survived four bayonet wounds, including a gash in the intestine."

Even when he admitted himself to Providence Memorial Hospital, in El Paso, to have his gall bladder removed, Daddy wrote— and I imagine now that he did so between visits from his nurses and doctors or after my mother had fallen asleep in her chair. "I need a complete list of General Parker's II Corps headquarters staff," he said once. "Maybe you could try the War College people for me. They stopped acknowledging my inquiries last August." Those letters, his penmanship bunched and tinier than you'd expect from a large man, were wrinkled and stained, as if he'd kept them in his pocket like Kleenex, or under his mattress; and rare was the note that would say, as one did, "Disregard previous request, found info elsewhere. Now have names of stationmaster and Lubao political officer."

Near Christmas that year I told him I wouldn't do any more research. "I'm done with this," I wrote. "You can't expect this of me anymore. It's not fair."

Never had I challenged him on any issue—not what vegetables to eat, nor how a young man treats a lady, nothing—so I spent a week waiting to see him pull up in front of my dormitory in his pickup, his face alive with the rage of betrayal. Instead I got another note, this one typed and arranged as if for business: "All's fine here (except Mother, who wants nothing more to do with me). I hope you're getting out some. The big project with me is to find somebody who knew Gid over there. Do your homework. I am proud of you. Love, your Dad."

As it happened—because of the co-op program I entered (I'm an oil engineer now) and because being away from home seemed to have given me license to explore the large world far from here—I didn't get home much. When I did, it was only for a weekend—hardly long enough, I see now, to note the effect this obsession (if that's all it was) had on my mother. She drank, but everybody I knew drank—Dr. Weems, my father's golfing partners at the club, our trust officer, the cowhands working for us. Alcohol was as much a part of home life as laundry or breakfast; and alcoholics, after all, were other, less fortunate people: the poor, the lonely, the ignorant—not one's own mother. If I had been smarter, I might have seen the effect during my senior spring break, when I came down to tell them I was planning to marry Deborah, now my wife, but for years what I most remembered about those two days was the food my dad ate and the five-thousand-dollar check he forced on me.

"Do you know what your father's favorite flower is?" my mother asked that last afternoon. "The bachelor button. You wouldn't expect that, would you?"

If she was drunk, I did not know it. My thoughts concerned getting back to Albuquerque before dark, and the O-Chem mid-term I had to take.

"His favorite composer is Mr. Bobby Worth," she said. "You know, 'Tonight We Love.' But he likes Ray Austin too."

In a housecoat, her hair flyaway and dry-looking, Mother was cleaning the silver, the candelabra and serving dishes, even my baby cup; most of her days were like this, I think, hours that she hoped to fill but never could. Hours that, finally, had shape and color and density. Then she got up, went to the kitchen and returned with an Army messkit, metal and cleverly self-contained. It held a scoop of something like papier-mâché.

"Take this out to your father."

He was eating, I would discover, less than six ounces of over-boiled rice once a day, the diet my uncle had survived on for two weeks before the surrender.

"It's an experiment," Daddy told me. "Don't worry, I'm not crazy."

The office was as I remembered, jammed floor to ceiling with documents, and I watched, fascinated, as he arranged himself cross-legged on the floor like a Buddha, the metal messkit under his chin as he ate with his fingers.

"No couches in the bush," he said. "Here, you try it."

He held out, balanced on his fingertips, a lump like wallpaper paste, and without thinking I let him put it in my mouth.

"The strong had to feed the weak," he said. "Carry them, too. Sometimes they carried dead men."

The stuff was gummy, as tasteless as sand, less food than pulp.

"They'd drink from shell craters, once in a while from a stream. A couple pesos got you milk, maybe a turnip."

The rice sat in my mouth like paper. Like ash.

"You want some more?" he asked.

I didn't move, just watched him eat and listened to him describe events nearly twenty-five years old. The violence wasn't all of it, he said. The heat, heavy as wool and thick, contributed, along with the terrain—blackened tree stumps, wallows, rice paddies, dust: a jungle that had become the moon. There was humidity like saddlecloth, and foot sores. Some men ate cane bark. You saw corpses everywhere. In the towns—Lamao, Lubao—the civilians might sneak you a mango. You marched eighteen hours; maybe you got salt, maybe you didn't. Some of the Nips had bikes; you had to run double time to keep up. You went crazy, entered mirages. You died. In the boxcars, narrow gauge and so low you had to stoop, you were packed so tight that the sweat ran down your legs and left your shoes soggy. If you had shoes.

"I can only eat this mush for about three days," Daddy said. "Then I get the runs."

Had my father experimented in other ways to put himself in my uncle's place? Without either a hat or a shirt, had he taken several long hikes in the desert, trying to recreate the exhaustion and pain Gideon must have felt? Had he emptied the tack box in our horse barn to spend a day inside it, cramped and sweaty and alone? I didn't know, didn't want to know. On the afternoon I am writing about, I was frightened—my heart in my ears, my breath ragged and hot, for it was easy to believe, though he kept telling me otherwise, that he had lost his mind, that he did not know this was 1967, or that he lived in America, or that he was a cattle rancher, not a prisoner of war. It was possible to believe that he, like those victims of religious rapture we read about in the papers, had slipped free of himself by a truly black magic. I thought that here, in the familiar quarters of his office, he heard voices, the wet groans and shouts and nightmare whimpers of men dying around him. Here, I thought, between one window that opened toward the Mimbres Mountains and another that faced the blank, shimmering horizon that was Mexico, he saw captains and sergeants without heads or arms, or privates and majors bloated black and left to rot.

"What's your position on this Vietnam thing?" he asked.

On the floor sat his tin messkit, clean as if our dog, Raleigh, had eaten there, and it struck me that I had no position on anything, nothing at all.

"I have a position," Daddy said, "and my position is that you steer clear of it, you understand?"

His eyes remained on me as they had when he began telling me about Gideon—about our skinny-boy thighs, our dumb respect for mechanical contraptions, our rail-stiff spines—but now his eyes were saying, as eyes can, that enough was enough. A brother had died, a son would not.

"They change your classification," he was saying, "you let me know. File for CO, take drugs—I don't care—but you tell them no deal, you hear?"

I heard; yes, I did.

"From now on, you're a Communist," he said. "You're a Russian, a Chinese, anything."

Years later I learned that he had gone to my draft board the day before, in his belt the Colt pistol he took as protection when he strung barbed wire at our section line. As I heard it, Daddy told Mr. Phinizy Spalding, a lifelong friend and the board's part-time director, that Scooter Baker was not going to die in some cesspool half a world away, that Lyman Baker, Sr., himself would see to it that Scooter showed up in panties and bra if it came to that. "I tell you, Phinzy," Daddy is supposed to have hollered in our post office, "you come after my boy, and I'll shoot his goddam foot off myself. You know I will." What I heard is that my father, his hand on the pistol grip, stood for several minutes, trembling with anger, not two paces from Mr. Spalding, muttering again and again, as if he would for a year, the one word that seemed to make the most sense in the world he knew: no, no, no.

But he was standing in front of me now, calm as the day itself, and I wanted to say that I was twenty-one. I was in love with a brunette economics major from Grants. I wasn't a registered voter yet. I was a kid, I was stupid.

"You listen to me," he said. "I'm going to give you some money—a lot of money, buddy—and when the time comes, if it does, you get out, you hear me?"

He was speaking to me, I realized, as he wished he had spoken to Gideon—big brother to little, wise man to dumb.

"You go to Sweden," he told me, his voice full of iron and the working life he loved, "go to Canada, Africa—makes no difference. You just go, you understand?"

We looked at each other, seriously and carefully. He was my father, he expected something of me, and there was a part of me that should know it. From his bent-forward shoulders and his narrowed eyes and the quiver in his cheek, I understood that all this Bataan stuff, the horror stories and the painstaking attention to detail and the grainy, timeworn photographs, had been an expression, unmistakable as slaughter itself, of nothing so much as love and memory and death and my relation among them.

—

As it turned out, I received a high lottery number when I graduated, so I missed the chance, as my father saw it, to define myself morally, to say what sort of son he'd raised. And in time, I admit, I tried to forget most of this. Deborah and I married, I took a job with Sinclair Oil in Texas for a time, and then, in 1976, just about the month our son Brian was born (he, yes, looks enough like me to look like my uncle, too), I came back here, to Deming, to work for a wildcat gas outfit named Mimbres Drilling, and to help Daddy with the ranch. Though my mother's drinking had led to her removal to Roswell, almost 250 miles away, these were good times: Deborah and I bought the split-level brick house we have, joined the club in our own right, made friends again with those I had grown up with. In the years after he stuffed his check into

my shirt pocket and gave me a breath-defeating hug, I tried to
believe that my father kept his Bataan studies to himself, more or
less. I assumed he still pestered the Defense Department and the
Records Division of the National Archives in Washington; but I
also assumed—at least until a few years later when he called to
tell me to drive out to the ranch to meet somebody—that his
studies were no longer so dire, nor so mad. He was a man with a
hobby, I had told Deborah, like coin or stamp collecting, or knowing the Latin names of desert plants.

"I want an hour of your time," he told me that night. "Just a
little unfinished business."

He was crazy, I thought. He was lonely.

"Please, son. Don't fight me on this."

I have said that we had broken, my father and I, but the break
was clean, not spite-filled, and could be fixed to the moment I
took his money and left. We had parted, I thought. He had gone
one way—backward, toward the past, toward grief—and I had
gone another; and we had agreed silently, I thought, that there
was an era, begun and ended in violence, that we neither would
nor could talk about again.

"You found somebody, didn't you?" I said. "Somebody who
knew Gid."

"Yeah," he told me. "An officer."

"After this no more," I told him. I felt slumped inside, as if all
there was of link and snap and hook had crashed loose and lay
ruined at the pit of me. "I mean it, Daddy."

"Sure," he said. "Just tonight."

The man Daddy wanted me to meet was Colonel Redmon A.
Walters, U.S. Army, Ret., who, before serving in Honduras and
in the Republic of South Korea, had been in the Philippines. On
the march from the West Road to San Fernando he had be-
friended a twenty-year-old PFC named Baker, Gideon Alan.

"They were in the same regiment," Daddy said, "the Thirty-
first Infantry. Both knew Brady."

I guess Daddy already realized that Colonel Walters—"Call me

Red," he said, "I'm a civilian now"—had in fact not known any uncle; or, rather, he had known my uncle in the same way you and I know the dead whose ages we are or whose places we see. Yet Red Walters was no liar; he was only a man—like my father—who had felt and heard too much, and to whom truth wasn't a thing of records and graphs and testimony. Truth was the simple elements: light and nerve, fear and hope.

"What kind of a guy was Gid?" Daddy was saying.

Red Walters sat where I usually did, so I leaned against a file cabinet and looked out the window to the part of our toolshed I could see.

"He was tough," Colonel Walters said. "Lots of guys weren't— they caved in right away—but not your brother. He was a son-of-a-bitch, is what he was."

I was hearing them, Red and Daddy, describe an old world they regarded from opposite ends of experience, and I felt nothing. Air was air, earth earth, and way off—in time if not in place—I stood, as alien to this as I would be to affairs on Mars.

"Where exactly did you meet him?" Daddy said.

Over his shoulder I could see a copy of General Homma's personal notes, which had come from the Office of Military History in Tokyo. Near it was the volume General Wainright had submitted to the War Department in 1946, *Report of the USAFFE and USFIP in the Philippine Islands, 1941–1942.* I had read them in another life, it seemed. In another world. With other eyes. With another brain.

"It was in Balanga," Red was saying. "Gid was part of that group in the field beyond the jail."

"Here?" Daddy had pointed to a spot the size of a fingernail. It represented twelve unfenced acres in which thousands of men had been bivouacked during the march.

"Even the Japs didn't know what was up," Red said. "It was pretty confusing."

"I heard it was crazy."

"Filthy," Red Walters said. "No medical facilities, guys dying, flies everywhere. There was a kind of cloud over the place. At night it was incredibly cold."

"He looked pretty bad, I bet."

"We all did," Colonel Walters told us. "Thin like scarecrows, and stupid-looking. Some guys couldn't remember their names. Their units. You just wanted to lie down mostly."

"What about the brutality?"

"You got used to it," he said. "You didn't complain. You shut up."

At this point I realized that Colonel Walters had not met my uncle—the odds against it, and my father's hopes, were too great—but the realization reached me slowly and without real shock, the way bad news must come to the chronically unlucky. It was old news, really. Maybe it was the news God sees, our human story told so often that it has lost its capacity to amaze or to instruct.

"He looked like me, right?" I asked.

At that moment Colonel Walters, gray-haired and now too fleshy at the neck, came alive for me. I could imagine him as he'd once been, hollow-eyed and feeble and broken.

"Hard to tell," he said. "He could've been big once, like you."

"He had my face, though?"

"It's been a long time," he said, "I don't remember faces much anymore."

He was talking about all of them, I think. Clifford Bluemel, Alf Weinstein, Lieutenant Henry G. Lee, Reynaldo Perez, Lieutenant Colonel William E. Chandler, the living and the dead—he was saying that he had known these and more, including the uncle I look like. Gideon was that boy there from Springfield, Missouri, and that one there from Pittsburgh, and that one way over there from Los Angeles; he was the staff sergeant hiding in the thicket, the noncom collapsed at the Blue Moon Dance Hall in San Fernando, the captain weeping in Orani, the one sore or dehydrated or sleeping forever. And so, after I understood this, I had a glass of whiskey with Colonel Walters and my father, and tried to be very quiet. They discussed horror and time; they discussed suffering and where the mind goes during battle and what a creature man is. They used words like "delirium" and "ruthless" and "hunger"—a vocabulary that seemed more appropriate to certain melodramatic books—and then, when the Johnnie Walker was gone, my daddy asked me to see Mr. Walters to his car.

"Hope I've been some help," the man said. His hand was meaty, his grip firm like a gentleman's.

"Yes," Daddy told him. "Invaluable. Thank you very much."

Beside his Ford station wagon, our night black as the cape a witch wears, I asked Colonel Red Walters how my father had gotten in touch with him.

"At William Beaumont," he said, "in Fort Bliss." Twice a year Colonel Walters was driving down from Carlsbad for checkups by the Army doctors. "There was a note on a bulletin board," he told me. "From your dad. Said he wanted to talk to Bataan survivors who'd known his brother. The name rang a bell, so I came up."

As I watched Red Walters drive down our two-mile dirt road toward the highway, I thought about Dr. Hammond Ellis, our Episcopalian minister, and what he says about burdens—a word, as he uses it, that describes what we carry or put aside in time. We can be this or that, he preaches. Good or bad. Generous or stingy like Scrooge. Upright or craven. In any case, we have the option, gotten from our Creator (or from your own self, if that's what you believe), to change. We can be a drinker one day, a teetotaler the next. We can go from dumb to wise, wrathful to peaceful; we can believe or not, trust or not, succeed or not. But always we have that choice. So, standing beside my old empty and dark house, I wondered about my father. He could be crazy now, I thought, or not. Sad, or not.

"Lyman Baker, Junior," I said to myself, "you go in there right now."

I must have sat across from him, in my customary chair, for an hour, watching him—betrayed by the lights in his eyes, and by the way he stubbed out his smokes or tugged at his earlobe— take up his life, piece by piece, his examination of himself as patient and thorough as those given to the livestock that have made him rich. I saw him, I tell you, lift up the burdens Dr. Ellis preaches about, take their measure again, and then, one by one, lay them aside. It was slow, I saw, but it was not painful; and in time he had put aside his boxer's temper and his banker's concern for numbers. He was a man with a plan now, I thought. A before B. Work and play. Then he got up, stretched, rubbed his hands, and a dozen free breaths came back to me.

"I think I'll cut down on the booze," he said. "That would be a good thing, wouldn't it?"

I thought it was and told him so.

"Maybe I'll visit your mother," he said. "It's been a long time." That was true, too.

"I'm hungry," he said. "Let's go into town, get us a steak."

He was moving now, putting on the leather jacket Deborah had given him for his sixtieth birthday, so I asked him, "What about this?"

I pointed to the books, the charts, the records, the maps—the millions of words and thousands of pictures he knew by heart. I wanted him to sweep them away, I suppose, set the whole mess aflame.

"What about it?" he said. "Just leave it."

I had my hand on a folder, one of thousands that were covered with his notes, and a thought, swift as love, came to me. So this is the end of grief, I thought. Of all his burdens, grief had gone first.

"We'll burn it tomorrow, okay?"

"Sure," he said. "Turn out the light, will you?"

THE BEAUTIES OF DRINK: AN ESSAY

THIS essay concerns intoxicating drink—arguably the misunderstood subject of our era—and starts with my first, when I was eleven. The occasion was a party with dual purposes: to celebrate my daddy's fiftieth birthday and, a week earlier, his latest hole in one at the Mimbres Valley Country Club—for which Allie Martin, the club pro, had given him a gallon of Johnnie Walker Red. In point of fact, the person who gave it to me was Mrs. Hal Thibodeaux, and what she said was this: "Scooter, what're you looking at?"

I was looking at booze, of course, those decanters and bottles and crystal pitchers my mother had set up in the den near Daddy's trophy case. It was near midnight, I suppose, and everybody was quite instinct (a word I picked up much later at UNM) with madness. Mr. Levisay, for example, had Mrs. Dalrhymple collapsed atop the ottoman, and from the patio you heard a Fats Molydore harangue about pissants and such mossback peckerwoods as were tending toward Congress that year, 1958.

"A. C.!" Mrs. Hal yelled for my daddy. "Should I give this boy something to drink, or what? He says he's thirsty."

I had been yanked out of sleep by noises which are elsewhere described as common to apocalypse. I heard the words "fernal" and "wayward," plus a commotion in regard to games of chance, then my daddy, A. C. Le Duc, appeared from a dark region in the direction of the utility room, his hair flyaway and naughty. He wobbled, held his hands toward heaven, then said to give his son any goddam thing he wanted. So, while Judge Cleve Pounds was dancing the Cleveland Chicken with Ruby, our housekeeper, Mrs. H. poured me what I now call three fingers of redeye.

"Well, squirt," she said, heaving her bosom for effect, "here's mud in your eye."

How nice it would be to report, dozens of years from the event itself, that drinking whiskey had an impact on me instantly profound and disruptive as war. It did not. Instead, my mouth stinging and hot, I sipped, sat on a cane barstool Mother had bought in Miami Beach, and, like a late-movie spy, kept to myself.

Across the way, a cocktail balanced on his forehead, Goonch Ilkin kept referring to himself as one slick hombre, while behind him E. Terry Long was shifting his watery eyeballs in and out of focus. In the living room, I could see Alberta Turner showing Dottie Hightower her garter belt; and behind them, slapped against the wall like Christ, stood Mr. Harvey Kinnebrew, whose face had the stricken, inflamed look of catastrophe. Beneath the music—which was Paul Whiteman and din itself—you heard voices, harsh as cigar smoke, on a thousand issues: Sherman Adams, the AFL-CIO and Elvis Presley, as well as opinions on where taxes ought to go (down), what ought to be done with Lucille Ball's red hair (burn it), and how to get rid of Chinese hordes and their evil ways (bomb 'em!).

It, this party, was what I know now as life itself—a dreamland of ghosts and emotions and willy-nilly ideas—and, fixed on my stool, I had one thought: Lord, I like this.

—

Everybody talks about the horrors, which are real enough, but not about drink's beauties. For one thing, time disappears. As I once said to the second of my wives, Darlene, "Without drink, you're at the mercy of minutes." We were in divorce court, I recall, within gavel-throwing range of Judge Pounds himself. "With it, you can be here one second, drink for a while, then wake up in another land, months apart from the person you were and the place he lived in." You could wake to discover, I said, that you had missed any of a million terrors—including pestilence, drought, blight or cosmic decline. Drink enough, and you could ease into another, mistier world, one composed around the soft depths of sleep.

For another thing, pain also disappears. Once, for example, on my way down here years ago to teach civics at the same high school (Deming, New Mexico) where I had learned much, as possessed by drunkenness as the woebegone are nowadays clutched by God, I flipped my VW off a highway overpass, flew eighty yards—a six-pack of Buckhorn whizzing about my ears like grenades—crashed and tumbled to a crunching stop, doors crushed, interior a blizzard of clutter and clothes. The first to approach me, I am told, were two Buckeye tourists, who peeked in, saw the mess I was, and gasped (in a single voice, I like to think), "Lordy, will you look at that?"

I was upside down and facing backward, everything of substance—cracked window, horizon, earth itself—running west and out of sight. I felt nothing, neither welt nor bruise nor open wound; and a time later I spilled out of that vehicle and lay next to it like a puddle.

"Howdy," I said, "my name's Albert Le Duc, Junior, but everybody calls me Scooter. What's yours?"

Those good Ohioans stared at me as if seeing a nightmare come to life. The man, particularly, seemed ready to bolt. "What's the matter?" I said, and the woman, perhaps someone's mother, pointed: "Your ear."

Sure enough. What used to be ear was now a pulpy flap, no more sentient than dried fruit. I fingered it carefully, more stupefied than frightened, then asked the lady to sit down, here, next to me.

"What for?" she wondered.

I was looking at our vast desert sky and feeling right tolerant of those without it.

"Well," I began, "I'd like to put my head in your lap."

For a second, I was convinced she might spit or kick me a little; she said, "Why?"

I took a deep breath.

"Comfort," I confessed. "I'm about to pass out."

That fall I took up the business of pedagogy, wore my hair long to hide my hearing-hole, and undertook in earnest fashion my higher calling to drink.

—

What you should know, now that this is being written, is that I am thirty-seven years old, no more debt-free than the majority of my fellow citizens, a regular voter, father of two (by the first wife, Jo Ann), and currently a resident of the Hot Springs Hotel in the scrub-covered hills above Hatch, New Mexico. This is no hotel at all, really, but that place addicted Americans like Betty Ford and Elizabeth Taylor might visit were they more middle-class and not so camera-shy. I am here at my daddy's expense, in an effort, he said, to "dry the hell out," which means bland food, rigorous exercise and a Marine Corps approach to mental health. Mostly, my story is not one of high drama—me being that vulgar Protestant many are or aim for—but I will, as part of my therapy, show you the good that drink is and how, sometimes, it makes us a better tribe.

Once upon a time, for example, I had a student named Butch in my eleventh-grade World Modern History class. This was during Vietnam, and Butch was a *West Side Story* hooligan who couldn't wait to be eighteen and an Army Ranger so he could whip the bejesus out of those foreign revolutionaries we were seeing on the *Nightly News.* He was as you are doubtlessly picturing him: slumped, bitter, and artfully tattooed, as well as expert in auto mechanics and most disenchanted by the charms of the Enlightenment. The only times, in fact, I liked the dirtbag was when I was drunk and then only because I saw him—and all of us, for that matter—for what he was: scared, weak and dumb. On the day I remember particularly, he was in the back row, making spit wads or arm farts, intending to diddle Mary Lou Feeny beside him; he was not at all attentive to the story I was telling about Diderot, about monarchies which are displaced, and about what a low-life species we'd be without the genius of Monsieur Montaigne.

"Scooter Le Duc?" Butch said at last. "What the hell are you talking about?"

It was a moment common in many places these days: old guy versus menacing younger version of himself. I was drunk too, which helped.

"Butch," I said, "c'mon up here a second."

It was late afternoon, our sun epic as always, and I knew that in an hour or so I'd be home, saying hello to my wife Ellen. By eight, I'd be orphic; by ten, asleep in a beer-hall never-never land.

"Right on," Butch said, pulling himself out of a slouch to commence that rolling walk he was famous for: hip, slide, lurch, idle, slide anew.

"Ladies and gentlemen," I told the class, "what you see crawling through the aisle is a bona-fide, triple-A, government-approved asshole." You could see the effect immediately: I might have been naked and roiling astride the busty Mary Lou Feeny. "Billy Jo De Marco, also known as Butch, is what you might call your basic ignoramus."

He was puzzled, not at all pleased, and I tried to watch his fists and lecture at the same time.

"What we got here is an American teenage dingleberry who likes food he can eat with his hands." That classroom, I swear, was alive with fear; you could hear, plain as gunfire, many adolescent glands at work. "But," I said, "he's gonna do us all a service soon, which is get cleaned up and be a hero." Butch was almost to me when I felt my last Coors kick in. "Of course, there is the outside chance that he might, uh, die." Saying that word in front of teenagers is like saying "pussy" in church. "And if he does, I want all of you to join me at his funeral and sob as you're inclined to."

When he reached me, I threw an arm around his shoulders, gave him a brotherly hug.

"That preacher, if he's the sort I imagine, is going to say some mighty unkind but true things. He's going to mention, for one, that Butch here was young and, as a young person, liable to slip any time into an outer, eternal darkness. Furthermore, he might say that ol' Butch was a virtually certifiable cretin. Maybe a nose-picker too."

I could see smiles, especially a wet one from Mary Lou F.

"But I want everyone here to know"—doubtless they expected me to cold-cock that boy—"that I love this youngster and do intend, on the occasion of his death, to weep abundantly and pitch myself into a pit of cold depression."

A bell was clanging somewhere, and in another minute I'd have thirty more live ones in here to entertain.

"Butch," I said, "pucker up."

Whereupon, quick as a cat, I grabbed that boy by the cheeks and gave him a movie-worthy smooch—a gesture of affection impossible in an otherwise sober man.

—

Another anecdote before we come to the big finish we're here for.

This scene comes from what is ostensibly the blue-hearted half of drink and concerns riot and Little League baseball. When I was married (to Darlene, number two) but separated, I went out one August night to Perkins Park to watch my youngest, J. E., play a little center field. Clad in Bermuda shorts and a ragged Lobo T-shirt (my legs a shade of landlubber white), I found myself sitting on a lawn chair beyond the outfield fence, my company those vagrants I am in continual sympathy with: pot-smokers, criminals of the mild sort, the lonely.

It was a wine night, I remember, brisk winds, heat swept south to Mexico, the clouds wispy and miles high; and the conversation in the twilight addressed the usual: moral concerns among the feckless, a lively discussion about taxes and who went where in the olden days of major-league baseball. Then, almost from the first batter, a man in the stands behind home plate started holler-ing, his speech that bray reproduced in our funny pages as "%$&**#$%!" According to him, what was happening on the field (and in the entire world!) was no less than blankety-blank with, for good measure, some so-and-so thrown in.

The third time he spewed forth—billingsgate, it was—a light flashed on in my soaked forebrain and I felt the presence of that which stands for principle in a drunk: outrage. I considered the fellows beside me—whiskered and wistful, they were, mottled and morose—then said, "I came here to watch a game, what about you?" You could see the idea catch them like a club on the chin, and when my nine-year-old took the field again, I called, "Hey, J. E., who's that sapsucker yelling?"

It took a second or two for him to find me in the shadows beyond the light standard.

"Ah, crap, Daddy," he said, "that's Bobby Hover's old man."

That inning I heard bile and foment, both; by the fifth, the warmth was gone from my heart. You could see old man Hover up there, the meager mom-and-pop crowd having fled from him as it would from rabies. Standing or sitting, he waved and yattered and spit, once racing down to rattle the chicken-wire backstop like a zoo monkey. "Yamma-yamma!" is what he screeched. "Fug, fug, fug."

The next inning, I'd had enough.

"Boys," I said, "let's mash that dipstick."

I was as brave on my Gallo Brothers diet as Charlie Atlas was on his regimen of iron and sweaty exertion; and, righteous with anger, we nonpaying sorts clambered over the chain-link to head for the infield. Euphoric and motley a mob as that which went after royal French mucky-mucks in olden times, our number included a dropout named Spoon, an older gent we called the Senator, two redneck grits who'd been to La Tuna for stealing railroad ties, and a guy who looked like cement on legs.

"Daddy?" J. E. said as we charged past. "What're you doing?"

I brought my troops to a jerky halt and, calm as Reverend Tippit is when he sends his devoted flock to perdition, told him, "J. E., we're going over there and rip that man's liver out."

We reached the screen as a group and, hooting and yelling, we tumbled over and crawled up the bleachers until I was wellnigh in Mr. Hover's lap. He was built like Bluto.

"Who the hell are you?" he said.

Around us, it was Xmas Eve, not even a mouse astir, and I felt as Hannibal must have when he and his beasts broke through the passes and found all of civilization lying meekly at his feet.

"Mr. Hover," I began, "may I introduce you to my colleagues." I pointed. Over there, I said, dressed in a gritty sweatshirt and in need of a shave, was Plague. Next to him, a being with dental problems, Venery. Behind him, and quick with a fist, Murrain. "These others," I said, "I'm sure you already know." They were, left to right, Sloth, Malice and Greed. "So what do you say?" I asked. "Are you gonna shut up or what?"

For a second his eyes looked like coal which had lain for ten million years in darkness. You could almost hear him thinking it over, his brain fractured and flat as a dry lake bed. Then he rose, fat man's belly a counterweight, and said that for all he cared I, and my confederates, could die.

"You're drunk," he said. "Get out of here."

At this point, each of us had a moment alone with himself: Hover, for his part, was convincing himself I wouldn't; I, for mine, was convinced I would. Hovering between us, as stark and painful as are all visions of our dreadfulness, was the picture of what, given the breed man is, we might become: a tussle of legs and arms, hissing and snorting and whaling on our respective stuffings. I considered our heavens: it was a night worthy of *The Little Prince*. I spoke, trying to shape my words to express a thousand things—love, seriousness, resolve, etc.

"Mr. Hover, sir, I am truly drunk, drunk enough to see the two of you, but what I saw and heard offended not only me but also them, these interested parents, our youth and—" I did not know, I admit, where this was going—"and, well, It."

He looked confused, suspicious. "It?"

Around us, the no-account crowd was shocked and aiming to sneak away; in the lights swarmed millions of insects. Yearning

for another sip of wine, I sought a gesture to include us, our
ballpark, our town, our nation, the whole widespread world.

"Yeah," I said. "It."

The light came to his eyes, left again.

"Oh," he said, "right."

—

What you have heard thus far is what my physician, Dr. Spellman, says is just quote tears, tears, tears unquote—the whole of
it attending to the shared theme of booze. "Scooter," he suggested the other day, "why don't you tell them about what
brought you here?" It was a good idea then, a better idea now,
and so, folks, I ask you to hie with me to a Sunday morning less
than two weeks ago when my daddy, who's aged but awfully
damn spry, rang me up to say that he'd put a foursome together
for that afternoon and did I care to play? I had one thought,
which may have been unspeakable, and another which brought
to mind links play and Sabbath-inspired fellowship.

"Shit, yes," I said. "What time you want me there?"

Until one o'clock, our tee time, I drank Oso Negro, which is
wetback rum and potent as TNT, polished my Spaldings to a high
shine, and stood in the back of my Olive Street duplex, whanging
a bucket of practice balls over Larry Aiken's house and onto the
parking lot of Fenton Riley's muffler shop. It felt good, I tell you,
to be out in the sunshine and wearing an outfit you might find
one day on Pinky Lee; I was especially pleased to discover that,
more often than not, I could still whack the ball with some authority and little grief.

"Gentlemen," I said when I arrived at the first tee, "ain't life
marvelous?"

Coots every one, they were as depressing a bunch as I one day
expect to find in hell.

"Scooter," Willie Newell muttered, "you drunk, or just crazy?"

I let them look at me for a second—my plaid slacks, my red

NuTonics, my stained planter's chapeau with pheasant feather in the hatband—then said something about the bear and the woods, the Pope and Catholicism.

"Let's play sport, boys," I hollered, and soon enough we were at it, each industrious as an old-fashioned bookkeeper.

By the fifth hole, and in accordance with our nassau, I was fifteen dollars in debt. "Hold it," I said at the top of Allie Martin's backswing, "let me figure this out." I possessed a pencil and a piece of paper and tried, while Mr. Hightower screamed at me, to bring order to this business of money and competition. "Okay," I said at last, minutes later, "let's resume." (I have had the opportunity, you should know, to see that paper since and what is on it is a sentence perhaps ninety words long, which begins in the arms of virtuous reason and ends, after several asides and trips to the hinterlands, in a heartening muddle of hope.)

At the turn—only a couple of holes before R. L. Crum started throwing his clubs and Mr. Newell started beating on my noggin—we went into the clubhouse for a sandwich and beer. I hadn't been to the club much in the last few years, so I hurried about, in the bar and dining room, saying howdy. I told George Dalrhymple how much I liked his new Biscayne and could I drive it sometime, my old Ford being nearly unusable now on account of disinterest and weak credit. "I'll get the keys later," I said, "thank you." I saw Mrs. Chubb Feeny, reminded her how much I missed those spaghetti dinners we had at their place when I was in junior high. I was arranging for a loan from Dillon Ripley when my daddy creeped up on my flank, clapped his horny hand on my shoulder and, in a doom-filled whisper, said I should get my heiny out to the tenth tee, pronto.

It was on the twelfth hole, a par five whose tee is set back in what passes for woods in this desert, that R. L. Crum fell apart like a three-dollar tuxedo and I was set upon. I had stroked a beaut and, hearty as Santa Claus, I told R. L., when he settled himself over his ball, to widen his stance a mite. "Pull that hand over, too," I added. "You look terrible." There was a sun worthy of

Brother Homer himself and birds tweeting in the distance, and I just couldn't keep quiet. "Hold that head down, R. L. I got great eyes." Drinking a Bloody Mary, I was trying to make contact with the soul of sport, which is perfection, and perhaps the soul of us as well. "Bend over," I told him. "Take some spine out of it."

What passed was a silence as honest as death: in slow motion I saw R. L. snatch that club back, grit, and fly forward. The ball blasted away; then, in an arc agonizing to behold, it dived to the right, smack into the core of a thick, thorny mesquite bush.

"Damn," I grumbled. "Ain't that a bitch?"

Here it was that R. L., spitting like a pressure cooker and thrown over into the underhalf of his spirit, whirled his club around his gray head and flung it thither. I was dumbstruck. "Whoa, now," I said. But in two giant steps, that old man, sputtering and making inhuman noises, had emptied his bag and was hurling everything—clubs, balls, his umbrella, a towel—into the plant life. I felt something let go in me—a muscle or comparable fiber. This was fury indeed, the sort, if it ends in carnage or conflagration, you read about for weeks; yet what was opening in me, near the heart or companion vessel, was a great flood of kindness.

I looked around. Nobody was moving. My daddy, a Chesterfield between his teeth, was as stiff as a fence post, nothing in his eyes about what a horror this was. Nearby, Mr. Hightower was picking at his thumbnail and maybe muttering to himself. And Willie Newell, otherwise glorious in his orange sport clothes, had the abstract, hooded expression of a snake.

"Wait a jiffy here, R. L.," I said.

He was now jumping on the bag itself, his voice part growl, part shriek. I tapped him on the shoulder, lightly, and he whirled around.

"Jesus," I said.

His face, normally blank and indifferent as sand, was crawling, patches on his cheeks red as sunset; so I tackled him. "It's all right," I said. I held that little man as you would a hysterical toddler, and tried to reach him as my mother had many times tried to reach me in a tantrum: "It's no big deal." He smelled as all these codgers did—dusty and not a little fruity. Take the long view, I told him. What did golf, or anything, really matter? We were just ooze, anyway, smarter and able to move on our own. "Think about it this way," I said, informing him of the billions we were, skinny, slovenly, robust—all of us fat for a larger fire. I said a dozen words to him—glee, mirth, salvation, etc.—trying to invest in each the entire weight of my person. "R. L.," I whispered, "this ain't so foul." I encouraged him to think of all, besides this immediate disappointment, which had not claimed him. Slaughter, for instance. Assault. Earthquake. And, well, diphtheria.

To be true, he resisted, scratching and slapping at me, trying once to gnaw on my neck. "You ought to be ashamed," I said. From my high, drunken perch, I was seeing him as woefully sore-minded, a poor loser who runs home to stew and maybe take it out on his furniture. "You stop that, now," I ordered, shaking him as more than once my daddy had wobbled me. "Grow up, you hear? What are you anyways?" You could tell he was lost, adrift like a castaway in his own despair.

"Aaaarrrggghh," he was crying. "Eeeeffff."

Big as I am, I held tighter and was reminded of times, mostly drunk-wrought, when I felt the world fall together as neatly as a deck of well-shuffled cards. "Well," I said, "what is it now?" In his face, now less than an inch from mine, was textbook apoplexy: the bug eyes of a frog, flared nostrils, lips quivering in a frenzy. "Listen," I began, "I want you to do something." For a second—or a minute—I didn't know what I thought, only that, warmed by vodka, I was as prepared as ever for the certain light of truth. "You get ahold of yourself right now, you hear?" We were on the ground now, him rocking in my lap. I made recommendations: Maybe he ought to fornicate more, I said, perhaps take up with one hefty as Mrs. Hightower.

"Second," I said, "get up a little later, you ain't missing nothing."

He was keening, moving toward the humble in himself, his voice a sobbing infant's.

"Third," I said, "throw off these expectations you have. Be firm in the present moment."

I had more to offer, but there was darkness somewhere, and something, bitter with ferment, was seeking to pass from my innards upward.

Then Mr. Newell, strong as a gorilla, clobbered me.

—

Two and a half hours later, Daddy and Sheriff Chuck Gribble came to fetch me; and, I'll admit, I was ready for them. What I told Dr. Spellman was that, once Willie Newell started thrashing on me, my whole frame of reference creaked, teetered, fell over and I leaped up, angrily.

"Okey-dokey, you old farts," I said, "the hell with you."

And I stormed off, my stride purposeful as that seen at track meets.

I went straight home, pitched open my front door and aimed for the icebox. In it was what I'd been living on: various pressed meats, processed cheese I couldn't toss out, greens to make my sleep easier, grape jelly I had a yen for, and liquor. My anger was largely gone; but what remained was a parched spot which needed drink as much as a bird needs song. I showered—no small achievement when you're barely upright and coherent as chaos—and changed into my finest outfit: undertaker's sport coat, the shiny wingtips of a banker, and a Juárez, Mexico, tie which suggested what women are here for on earth. At some level, I knew plans were being made in my behalf, and I intended to accept them as if they were wealth itself. So, smelling of Jade East, I sat on the porch, a tumbler of vodka between my legs.

What I'm going to say now will probably make as little sense to you as it did to Daddy and Sheriff Chuck; in any case, what happened was this: sitting there, heavy-lidded and numb, I had a four-alarm, wide-awake vision—one without fanfare or related trumpet work from heaven. I saw, from my aluminum chair, a world of shimmering elements and dancing lights and, suspended in them like angels, all the people I had known: Mother, my daddy, my Aunt Dolly, uncles, kids I had been schooled with. I saw my wives—Ellen, Darlene, Jo Ann—and, in rank beside them, my children. I saw, too, as if from a seam in our universe which happened to be on Art Monge's property, a file of strangers, each dressed for the big event of their lives.

"Well, I'll be," I said, and there they were, butcher, baker, etc., all lugging instruments of the loftiest kind: lyre, harp, flute. It was a goddam fashion show, what it was: formal wear and diaphanous gowns, arch headgear and glittery dangling rocks.

A couple of times I looked around. "Hey, Art!" I yelled at my neighbor. "You see anything?"

He was cussing his lawn mower and saying what havoc he'd like to wreak in this orb.

"Look out in the street," I hollered, "tell me what's out there."

He shook his head the way cops do over infractions of the mindless sort, kicked his machine to life.

I shook myself good then, closed my eyes and had a moment with myself. Okay, I thought. Relax. Think. What is this but another sort of pink elephant? I counted, as if playing hide-and-seek: one-Mississippi, two-Mississippi. I listened to my heart: lub-lub, lub-lub. I took a deep breath my mother says airs the brain, and returned to the real world.

"Scooter," I said, "when you open your eyes, ain't going to see nothing in the street but sticky asphalt and your beat-up Fairlane."

I popped open my eyes and, again, took in that tide of whosits and whatevers that was flowing from its world into mine.

"Holy moly!" I shouted. "Isn't this something?"

I was a poor man getting lucky; and, as I knew I would, I spotted other familiar faces. I saw Butch, now in the company of Mary Lou Feeny and a handful of grinning, pink offspring. I waved, they waved.

What was in me, in my very cockles, was that joy associated with triumph, an emotion dear enough to forgive that done without it. I saw, you should know, those Buckeyes, now loosened from their place in my past and moving in front of my door in a manner downright jaunty.

"Hail, Ohio!" I shouted.

"Hail, yourself," they said and were gone.

I took a drink. Light was everywhere now, being splashed about and showered like rain. I even saw Mr. Hover, his fury vanished, and saluted him as you would those heroes who march down your street. Important as a drum major, he was leading kids, and they were bound for a place more amusing than Knott's Berry Farm. And then, about the time my daddy and Sheriff Chuck rolled up in the old man's Continental, I saw that person nearest to me: Me.

Indeed, I could see myself as clearly as I now see this wall or that lumpy bed I dream on. Yes, there I was, shining and most benevolent, a bottle of booze in both hands, and a smile our white man's Easter Bunny would be woozy for. "How-do," I called from the porch; and, fetching as love itself, that Albert Le Duc, Jr., gleaming in the sunlight held open his arms and bade me enter. That Scooter who was in the street was bosom and lap and cradle—all those things we are inclined to fall into; and, in an instant, I struggled from my chair, as Daddy and his minion started up the walk, and exclaimed, "Virtue. Desire. Beauty. Splendor. Wisdom. Charity."

The words themselves were another wonder in this world, and as I uttered them—even as I tumbled face first into my father's arms—I saw them, like birds, rising, rising. And never coming back.

LIVING ALONE IN IOTA

TEN months after she left (he told the boys), he got the letter. "I am calling myself Ida now." Her penmanship was barely inside the margins of human communication. "For a time, I was a Louise, a T. Mama, and in Cisco a Velva." She was Harmonized, a Changed Lady, the Foul and Lackluster set aside for the satisfying Tinkle of Beauty (her caps). "I have seen Despair and licked it," she wrote. "Ill Humor, also. Plus, I am uplifted spiritually by my new man. His name is Chuck, but I call him King Daddy on account of his smile and many muscles."

Reese felt he'd been whanged with a tire iron. "Shit," he moaned, "why now?" When he'd known her, she was Billy Jean La Took—deep-socketed, complex, skin as smooth as quote the far-flung impossible unquote, foolish, bewildered, and astray, a body like stolen money. "She makes my ears bleed," he'd told the boys at the well site. "I mean, when she starts kissing my neck, I go off into a dark land. It's like death, only welcome."

Then she vamoosed.

"I don't believe it," he said, stumbling through the trailer, calling her name. All her stuff was gone—toothbrush, clothes, even a pair of mysterious, unlovely and fleshlike plants that looked like imports from Mars. "It was like waking up in a grave," he confided to the boys the next day. "You should've seen me crying. It was a humiliating spectacle, what it was. Severe and eternal."

The weekend passed before he found the note. It was in the refrigerator, but he hadn't been eating, just sitting in that gloomy living room, feeling the Panhandle winds rock the trailer, dust swirling mercilessly, thinking about dew fairies, the boogeyman, the whole terrible sad history of hurtful facts. TV wasn't a help— nor fantasy, nor memory. "I'll drink," he said, a path out of the pain coming clear to him.

The note was propped against a six-pack of Buckhorn. "Reese, honey," it read, "I am truly sorry for the evil way I have sneaked off. By now I am well gone, almost vanished. You could look for me in Goree. Even Olney. But I have fled Texas. I have talents and numerous dreams of glamour. You never saw me dance. Plus, I have improved my mind. . . ."

He read the whole letter to the boys. It was full of grimness addressed to a narrow-minded, slack, fearsome, idle and raunchy man. It mentioned Faith and Shared Duties, and, moving easily between the Hard and the Terrible, it drew freely from Science and the Modern Life, the last paragraph a touching mangle of tiny truths.

Reese was dumbstruck.

"I will write you again," she'd scribbled, "when I re-enter the world. For now, think of me as a pleasant memory and something soft you knew. Bye-bye."

Reese was love-sawed; and the drunk he sought that night was positively medieval. There was slop in his thoughts—as well as self-pity, sorrow, and wicked lessons in heartcraft. "I am without solace or affection in this world," he hollered. "You're looking at a man who *aches!*" He made all the bars around Iota—El Corral, Miss Lilly's Silver Slipper, E's Joint, etc.—marching into each, his shirttail flapping behind, his tearful eyes flashing with woeful and frenzied lights, shouting that he was a left man and full of doom. "Somebody hit me!" he cried, "I want to leave this vulgar planet!" Nobody obliged, of course, until he stormed into the Mile 39 outside Tatum. Pale and rancid with some kind of consumptive sweat, he was drunk-clobbered then, the world swirling without comfort, calm, or knowable center. "You're looking at a feeble and pained hombre," he said to the bartender. "I want black booze and a straw. Then loan me an ax so I can cut off your nose." The dude kept an Al Kaline Louisville Slugger behind the bar for hard cases like Reese. "I know your wife," Reese declared, swinging his attention to a pair of slick-dressed cowpokes at the bumper-pool table. "She's a lapdog. I know men who'd eat her hair. I know some fellas who'd—" Whacking the bar with his hand, steadying himself against a stool, he was just coming—"I am familiar with everything!"—to the smelly and splendid notions of Betrayal and Sin when the fellow clipped him, Reese spinning down with a smile and a shiver.

—

"I am laying aside trouble," he told the boys at work the next day, a lump the size of a tomato behind his ear. "I am reaching out for sense and duty. I have opened myself up to the fortunate future."

First thing, he fixed up the AirStream, bought new furniture, laid carpet (a gold thing with the fine texture of cat fur), got himself a self-warming and restful water bed. "May my dreams be colorful and babylike," he said. "If not, may I then forget them." He started taking guitar lessons. "Music lessens the tensions of the spirit," he told the boys. He was learning tunes quickly, his favorites melodious with melancholy: "You don't miss your water," he crooned, "till your well runs dry."

At the junior college, he went purposefully into a wrathful and morbid kung fu, working private and paranoid embellishments on the ancient art with queer bellywork, some toecraft of uncertain origin, and special desert words. "Chop-chop!" he'd howl, his face a moil of desire and grue, taking patient aim on a cinder block—"Evil and Wrong!"—and he'd cut loose as if forsaking everything humanoid; his face said, *Listen up, I am into mortification and the promise of a new life; without reason, I have been abandoned; I am twenty-eight, raised by ordinary mortals and profitably employed in the oil business; folks, you are looking at a sore and confused man.*

Then he started dating again.

—

The first lady answered the door in some kind of eccentric, flamenco emsemble, her shining and blank face a machine to crush hearts. Her name was Tucker. Tarvez Tucker.

"Reese," she began, "I am an adult, a Leo, and so cannot be hoodwinked. I do not respond to normal wooing."

"Nor do I," he said. "I appreciate hand-holding and gifts."

"You will like me," she said. "Even my interiors are irresistible."

They went to the Rocket Drive-In, and, sitting in the back seat of her Fairlane, they went round and round—"Speak to me, sweetness," she kept barking, "tell me I'm grand!"—ending in an athletic tangle of ears, hips and necks. The courtship was modern—loopy and subtle as chain. "You're wonderful," Reese insisted, going for her throat, "you remind me of a pearl." She was squatting on his stomach, her face breathtaking, pit-free and strange as heaven.

"You got any dope?" she said. "I like to be numb when I kiss."

The next one was Dorene, a Texas Tech Zeta in town for the summer. Her face a blaze of idealism, she talked about Ruin and Intrigue; and the heart went right out of Reese. He was for Goodness, he said. He was against dwelling in the grief-plagued regions of the human condition.

"I am for Light," he declared, "and Air and Friendship. You won't catch me being naughty."

"Shoot," Dorene said.

The next day he received the letter that said that Billy Jean La Took had reentered the world. "Jesus," he bawled. He stayed in bed, sleeping raggedly, thrashing, his toilsome and cheerless dreams a feast of sadness and regret. Hungry and unshaved, he once got up to watch TV, but the themes of the daytime shows were too familiar: Dread and Disappointment. Everyone—harridan, coquette, shopgirl, and wealthy patron of the arts—reminded him of Billy Jean La Took. On that one, he'd note her long, finely boned and lickable neck, on another her youthful legs. Here was a something anatomical—a pore, say, or a loose coil of hair—and there a gesture or a sympathetic word. She was the pretty ones and the ugly, both. The ignorant, the poor, the infirm, the fit, the stay-at-home, the innocent—she was them all. She was stomped love, expectation, reward and fulfillment.

Shaking and fevered, he searched the trailer all Sunday, hunting for something—a hairpin, a shower thong—she might have forgotten. He could almost smell her—something between ripe and medical, somewhere between soap and the outdoors. Under the bathroom sink, he found a knot of her hairs, so red and fine that speech left him and he found himself standing stiff backed and trembling in front of the mirror, sputtering, "Uh-uh-uh-uh." In a dresser drawer, he found lipstick. It was the shade, Peach Lustre, that did it, nearly smashed him.

On Monday, he merely walked through work, practically blind. You could have been talking to a wrench. It must've been an instinct for caution which got him through without injury, fitting pipe, doing the mud just so. "Boys," he said, "I am being sandbagged by memory."

He could see her sitting across from him at the kitchen table, lacquering her sharp and now worshiped fingernails or studying a romance that turned her good face dark in the contemplation of villainous but handsome heroes. "Reese," she'd murmur, "tell me again about your vandal days and petty crimes." And he'd travel the whole route of his average, reckless youth, from shoplifting at Woolworth's to shooting out streetlights with fence staples. He'd touch everything: adolescence, maturity, his minor achievements. "Tell me, too," she'd continue, "about your stern daddy and always fretful mama."

Then the idea hit him. "I will see her," he said. He got out the letter and looked at the address: Deming, New Mexico.

That night he settled into a profound sleep. It was a brave and simple picture he made, supine and stiff and snoring, his long fingers steepled over his stubborn heart, his face alive yet frozen in wholesome mirth—as if he'd touched, by accident or by design, a wild and evil beauty.

Before sunup, he hit the road, racing out to meet those two hundred miles between hither and yon with an expression lit by derelict joy. It was the hair and grit of life, what it was. He was singing—"Come back and try me again, Mama!"—his voice scaling all but the high, sissy notes; he was beating time on the steering wheel, the sunlight orange, streaming and glorious, the desert shimmering and speaking to him of Triumph and Virtue. You could tell that the Contrary, Curious and Puzzling were gone, and he was highballing in the realm of the Superb and Jaunty, his three-dollar Feed hat squashed low on his forehead, his eyes twinkling with vim and understanding.

"I am happy and elevated by knowledge," he told the dude who filled the pickup at the Standard station near Mescalero. The man was hangdog—grave, thoughtful and tragic, the very picture of failure. "My name's Meat," he said, "I gave up a long time ago. I'm into mongrelism now."

"You got to buck up," Reese told him. "You got to practice vigilance and patience. Trust me, you'll get what you need."

Outside Alamogordo, Reese picked up two six-packs, and, eighty miles later, liquored and popeyed and vanquished, he plugged into a surly interior dialogue with his subconscious. It was turmoil, what it was—doubt and the threat of failure. "Holy Jesus!" he hollered to himself, "I am hearing uproar and harangue." He'd grab hold of a thought, hang on for a frenzied instant, then see another. "She loves me, I know it!" He sang the Wang-Wang blues and, bouncing viciously down the highway, went eyeball to eyeball with his life story. "Billy Jean," he shouted, "I am going to fetch you away."

Near Las Cruces, his truck rattling and banging, the engine screeching, the cab a furnace of dust and heat and madness, he took a deep bite of some first-rate doodley-squat philosophy: "Son," he yelled at a Mercury with Arizona plates as it passed, "They should've never put the idea of love in the mind of a man!" So, by the time he blasted into Deming, his face yellow with hope, he was in a state as pure and unbecoming as loneliness, his heart thumping furiously, his well-folded brain crimped and throbbing.

"I am standing in a phone booth across the street," he said, "and I can tell you are sad and angry. Come out of your house."

She appeared in a flash, and Reese went manfully to the curb of Iron Street, his internal juices running hot, and told her that she'd gone to seed, was in a dire funk, couldn't live without his heedful care. "You're depressed and idle," he shouted. "Look at your hands, you're nervous. Jealous too. You're living in a mansion of pain."

"I'm pretty," she yelled back. "You ought to see my skin."

She showed him her hard and well-remembered tummy, and Reese felt all intelligence drain right out of him.

"I am missing you," he said.

"I'm strong now," she answered. "Useful also. You ought to practice toughness. King Daddy recommends crafts and daily exercise."

"You miss me," he said, "I can tell. I can see it in your hair." It was a magnificent and complicated pile, the product of timely tending.

"How's the trailer?"

He made up a story about selling it to the dead. He was just renting it, he said, from the raggedy-ass spirits of Hamlet and the Count of Monte Cristo. Those boys too were butchered by love. "Why don't you come back with me?"

"Can't," she said. "King Daddy would disapprove. He might break my arms. Plus, I love him."

"Could we kiss?"

She said yes, and he lurched across the street, weak-kneed and stiff-armed, zeal tugging him this way, dread the other. "My life is dandy," he said, "except you're not in it." It was a moment of supreme expectancy. "No tongue," she warned. "I'm keeping my eyes open, too." You could tell that kiss really ripped the spine out of him. She stood as still and icy and unyielding as a glacier.

"Say bye-bye to me, Reese."

"I'm melting inside," he groaned.

"Don't," she said. She gave him some advice: Stand up

straight. Be forthright. Avoid fat and salt. Choose yourself in all things. Never drink alone. Look on the bright side. "King Daddy told me those and now I am gorgeous and content. Adios."

All the way back to Iota, he kept going over it in his mind. Be cool, he told himself. You're a handsome creature. And tall. You got a whole inventory of good points and few low habits. You are a helpful co-worker, pay debts regular, and know how to eat with a fork. The only thing you lack is the woman you love. By Las Cruces, he was limp and weepy, his truck whipping all over the road. He was drenched with weakness. "Okay," he said to himself, "I will be strong. Watch my smoke."

Immediately, he surged into a new program—suave haircut, close-fitting shirts and new trousers. "I am an emporium of pride," he told the boys. "I am reading books about almost unexplainable concepts—space and such. I'm learning dance, too. You should see my routines." He went out with Tarvez Tucker.

"Sweet thing," he told her, "before I was swamped with loneliness. Now I want to swallow you whole."

Next night he called Dorene, the Texas Tech Zeta.

"You're talking to a new hombre," he said. "Look outside your window."

"Why?"

"In five minutes, I will be there. You will see by my gleaming face that I mean business."

But the gloom only deepened.

Everything reminded him of Billy Jean La Took. Instead of disappearing or shrinking from memory, she got bigger, tastier, more moral, stronger, slimmer, lovelier, smoother, more substantial. She was his heartbone and his tendons, all the grit that made him yelp and swell with fondness. She was nighttime, lovers' sunset, refreshing winds and soothing rainstorms. Everywhere he went, he kept seeing her: in the Safeway, her khaki short shorts riding up her cheeks; at the A & W, her voice husky and permanent; at the wheel of his truck, her arms golden and fragile. And when he lay on his water bed, listening to night sounds, the past atop him like a fat man, the night sweats hot and slick, he often imagined her standing on the edge of his memory, sweet and moist and without rival on this worthy earth.

"Dorene," he said one night, "I have stopped sniveling. I am upright in all things. I am courteous and control my temper. But you, honey, are still a cruel disappointment to my heart."

—

Another month passed before he told the boys what he planned. "I will see her once more," he said. "I been thinking about it the whole while. She is gone, true. But I am not convinced."

He didn't write, phone; nothing. Just one morning, flush-faced and tense with righteousness, he roared up the Chevy, closed the window to concentrate, and stomped on the gas pedal with a force that rippled the chassis and had the engine smoking and clanking and knocking by Ruidoso. "You remember me," Reese said to the guy who put in the oil. It was Meat, the same sour gent Reese'd seen before. "I came through months ago. I was talking knowledge and wisdom. My thoughts were fragrant."

Meat's face was pinched with suspicion.

"Well, forget that crap," Reese was saying. "You're looking at a man in awful condition. If I weren't healthy, I'd be dead."

This time he didn't buy beer in Alamogordo—just zipped through, headers banging, something greasy throwing off a shower of sparks, and yelled out the window that his name was Reese Joe Newell and the words that applied to him were *hard-bitten, driven, perilous, wasted, crazed, fitful, heartsore* and *within an eyelash of beautiful.* Not to mention *sad* and *well-intentioned.*

"I am desperate," he yelled at the DJ, Fast Eddie Morris. Bouncing, the seat springs going *boing-boing!*, he hammered on the dash, several plastic pieces popping loose, one nicking him, on the cheek. "Play me music that speaks to heartbreak!"

He clattered into Deming in a purblind state, mouth-breathing and jumpy like an abused animal. "Gimme green lights and wary drivers," he yowled, his head pounding. Twice he leaned on the horn, truly frightening the unobservant, before he slammed to a stop outside Billy Jean La Took's house. It was afternoon, and he peeked in her window.

"Jesus," he groaned, pounding himself on the breastbone. She was wearing a sporty and virtually illegal nightie—one so sheer and frilly that he felt crippled by despair. It was then that he felt her falling away from him. For keeps. The effect was swift, primary and consummate. "Who is that woman?" he wanted to say. "Is it true that she loved me once?"

"Hey," she said when she saw him, "I thought I was done with you. You're a lunatic, Reese."

"I am here to put you out of my mind," he said. "I want to get on to the next phase of my life."

Her face was earnest and sexy. "You should come back later. Meet King Daddy. He'd inspire you too."

"Open the door," Reese said. "I want to see your living room. Kitchen too. Think of me as a guest."

"You've seen enough already." She was pulling on a robe, in the process exposing generous and well-defined thigh muscles.

He couldn't believe it. She was as distant from him as he from his ancestral fishes.

"I am dismayed," she was saying. "You're an exasperating person, Reese."

"Did you love me?"

"You're a mistake, Reese honey." Nervously, she hustled around that bedroom, straightening knickknacks—teddy bears, glass doodads, even touching those two horrible plants—and fluffing the bedspread. "Yes, I loved you once," she said. "I love you no more. Now go home."

He saw himself as she must have seen him: sullen and lameheaded, grim and stupid.

"I am at the peak of my powers," she was saying, "I bowl, think well of myself and my neighbors, am charitable and take according to my needs. My love is elsewhere, sweetness. Now split. King Daddy is due in a jiffy."

"I will think of you always," Reese said, moving from the window.

—

All the way back to Iota, he was in a state of genuine peace, abstract and solemn, waving good-naturedly to truckers, humming a pleasant tune of his own creation and, every third mile or so, smacking himself in the head. "You can never tell about love," he told Meat. "It's a nice thing for many." His smile was as stiff as a clown's. "She wanted me back," he told the boys the following day. "From now on, I'm putting up a whole series of promises: be smart and go willingly to the end of a thing."

It was a lie, of course, but the boys accepted it as being as important to him as the memory of his first fight, and they hung with him until one day, three months later, when a look of real insight filled his eyes and he said, "Boys, I'm a fool."

X

Long ago now—but still as vital a chapter of my moral history as my first kiss (with Jane Templeton at the FFA marriage booth in the National Guard armory) or my first love affair (with Leonna Allen, now an LPN in Lubbock, Texas)—I saw my daddy, Hobey Don Baker, Sr., do something that, until recently, was no more important to me than money is to Martians. In an event now well known to the six thousand of us who live here in Deming, New Mexico, my father struck a man and then walked from the sixteenth green of our Mimbres Valley Country Club to the men's locker, where he destroyed two dozen sets of golf clubs, an act he carried out with the patience you need nowadays to paint by numbers or deal with lawyers from our government.

I was seventeen then, a recent graduate of our high school (where I now teach mathematics and coach JV football), and on the afternoon in question I had been sitting at the edge of the club pool, baking myself in the summer sunshine we are famous for. I was thinking—as I suspect all youth does—about the wonder I would become. I had a girlfriend, Pammy Jo (my wife now), a '57 Ford Fairlane 500 (yellow over black), and the knowledge that what lay before me seemed less future than fate—which is what happens when you are raised apart from the big world of horror and cross-heartedness; yet, at the moment I'd glimpsed the prize I would be—and the way it is in the storybooks I read— disaster struck: rushing up behind me, my mother ordered me to grab my shirt and thongs and to hurry out to the sixteenth green, our road hole, to see what the hell my daddy was fussing about.

"He's just chased Dottie Hightower off the course," she said. "Listen, you can hear him."

You couldn't hear him, really, just see him: a figure, six hundred yards distant, dressed in pink slacks, a black polka-dot sport shirt and a floppy panama hat to cover his bald spot—an outfit you expect to find on Las Vegas gangsters named Cheech.

"I don't hear anything," I said.

"He's out there being crazy again," she declared. "He's cussing out everybody."

We stepped closer to the chain-link fence surrounding the pool, and, my mother leaning forward like a sentinel, we listened.

"You hear it?" she said. "That was language in reference to smut."

I'd heard nothing but Dub Spedding's belly-flop and an unappetizing description of what Grace Hartger said she'd eaten for dinner last night. Daddy was stomping now, turning left and right, and waving his arms. In pain perhaps, he snatched his hat off, slammed it to the turf to charge at it the way he attacked the lawn mower when it would not start.

"Look at that," Mother said.

Daddy was standing in front of Butch Newell, who still sells us our Chevrolets, and Allie Martin, our golf pro, and pointing at Mr. Jimmy Sellers, who was sitting in his golf cart and having a beer.

"He's just missed a putt, that's all," I said. "Maybe it cost him fifty dollars."

But then, by the way she drew her beach towel around her and how her face went dark, I knew that what was going on out there had nothing to do with money.

"Maybe he's sick," I said.

His talk was vile, about creatures and how we are them. "Hear that?" she howled. "That was the word *wantonness.*"

I could hear birds, nearby traffic, and suddenly, like gunfire in a church, I heard my father. He was speaking about the world all right—how it had become an awful place, part zoo, part asylum. We were spine only, he was saying. With filth attached. We were muck, is what we were. Tissues and melts and sweats. His voice was sharp the way it became when the Luna County Democratic Party, which he was the chairman of, did something that made the Republicans look selfless.

"You get him right now," Mother said, shoving me onward.

At the pool nobody had moved: the Melcher sisters, old and also rich, were frozen; even the kids in the baby pool—the ones still in diapers, the toddlers—had stopped splashing and now stood as if they'd instantly grown very, very old.

"What do you want me to do?" I said. This was a man who, in teaching me to box, had mashed my nose and introduced me to the noisy afterworld of unconsciousness; and he was out there, pitching his clubs into the sky and ranting.

"Hobey Don, Jr.," my mother said, leading me by the elbow to the gate, "don't be so damned lamebrained."

—

I do not know now, twenty-five years later, what had ravaged my father's self-control, what had seized him as surely as devils are said to have clutched those ancient, fugitive Puritans we descend from. I can tell you that Daddy was well known for his temper; and, by way of illustration, I can point to the time he broke up Mother's dinner party for Woody and Helen Knapp by storming into our dining room, his cheeks red and blue with anger, in one fist the end of a trail of toilet paper that stretched—we soon learned—through the living room, over the petrified-wood coffee table my Aunt Dolly had picked up at an Arizona Runnin' Indian, down the hall, beside the phone stand which had belonged to my Granny Floyd, and into the guest lavatory.

"Elaine," he hollered, "you come with me right now." Mother had stopped chewing her green beans. "Woody," he said, "you and Helen too. I want you to see this."

Daddy stood next to me, waving that flowery tissue like a football pennant.

"And you too, young man."

What was wrong was that Mother (or Mrs. Levisay who house-cleaned Tuesday and Saturday) had put the roll on the holder backward so it dispensed from the front, not from behind as it goddam ought. We were a sight: the nearly five hundred pounds that were the Knapps squeezed into our bathroom with Mother and me, Daddy ordering us up close so we could see—and goddam well remember for the rest of our miserable, imperfect lives—that there was one way, and one way only, sensible as God intended, for bathroom tissue, or anything else, to be installed.

"You wouldn't drive a car backwards, would you?" He was talking to Mr. Knapp (napkin still tucked under his chin!), who looked as hopeless and lost as any stranger can be in a bathroom. "And Helen there, she wouldn't eat soup with a fork, would she?"

I could smell us: Mother's White Shoulders perfume, what the Pine Sol had left, the sweat Mr. Knapp is given to when he isn't sitting still.

"Things have a purpose," my daddy was saying—shouting, actually—and pointing at the john itself. "Man, creature, invention—the whole kit 'n' kaboodle."

Toilet paper was flying now, shooting overhead like streamers at a Wildcat basketball game. Mrs. Knapp, her shoulders and head draped by enough tissue to make a turban, was looking for a way out, slapping the walls, pawing blindly, and yelping in a squeak Mother said had been picked up at the Beaumont School for Girls in El Paso, "Woody, help me. Help me, now."

"Remember," my father was saying, "purpose." He had arranged himself on the closed toilet seat. "This may seem small to you, but, good Lord, you let the little things get away, next thing you know the big things have fallen apart. Toilet tissue one minute, maybe government the next."

Another time, while I was doing the dishes—just had the glassware left, in fact—he wandered past me, whistling the tune he always used when the world worked right ("I'm an Old Cowhand"), and flung open the refrigerator. It was nearly seven, I guess, and he was about to have his after-dinner rum concoction. I was thinking about little—the TV I'd watch or that History Club essay I had to write for Mrs. Tipton. And then I heard him: "Eeeeffff."

The freezer door went bang, and instantly he was at my elbow, breathing in a panic, hunched over and peering into my dish-water as if what lay at the bottom was sin itself.

"What the hell are you doing?" he hollered.

I went loose in the knees and he swept me out of the way.

"How many times I got to tell you," he shouted, "glasses first—water's hottest and cleanest—then the flatware, plates, serving dishes. Save your goddam saucepans for last!"

I was watching the world turn black and trying to remember how to defend myself.

"Here, I'll show you."

And he did. Not only did he rewash all the dishes, but he also—now muttering about the loss of common sense—opened every cabinet, drawer and cupboard we have so he could spend the next five hours washing, in water so hot we were in danger of steamburn, every item in the house associated with preparing, serving and consuming food. Chafing dish, tureen, pressure cooker, double boiler, candy dish, meat thermometer, basting brush, strainer, lobster hammer—everything disappeared into his soapy water.

"Scrub," he said. "Hard."

He was going at one dish as if it were covered with ink.

"Rinse," he said. "Hot, dammit."

A minute later he sent me to the utility room for the flimsy TV trays we own, and then he stopped. Every flat surface in the kitchen—the countertop, the tops of the freezer and the stove, the kitchen table itself, the trays—was piled high with our plates and such.

"See," he howled at last, "you see how it's done?"

There he stood, arms glistening, shirt soaked, trousers damp to the knee. His eyeballs were the brightest, maddest points of reference in the entire universe; and, yes, I did see.

He even blew up one time in Korea, going off the way shotguns do, loud and spreading. Mother told me that one day, unhappy with his duties as the I Corps supply officer, he appeared at the residence of his CO, plucked his major's insignia from his shoulders, threw them at the feet of that startled officer. "Pick those up, mister," he said.

The man looked startled, so my father said that, owing to shoddiness in the world at large and the preeminence in that cold, alien place of such vices as sloth, avarice, gluttony, backstabbing, and other high crimes he'd remember later, he was quitting—which he could do, he reminded that man, on account of his non–regular Army status as a reserve officer and his relation to my Uncle Lawrence, then a six-term congressman from the Fourth District of New Mexico.

"Colonel," my daddy is reported to have declared, "this is squalor, disease, violence and hunger, and I will have no part of it."

So he had blown up in the past and would blow up many, many times after the day I am concerned with here. He would go crazy when my cousin Shirley drowned at Elephant Butte and when the Beatles appeared on *The Ed Sullivan Show*. Later, he exploded when Billy Sumner won the club championship with a chip shot that bounced off the old white head of A. T. Seely. He blew up when Governor George Corley Wallace used the word "nigger" on national TV, and he beat our first RCA color set with my Little League Louisville Slugger when Lyndon Johnson, jug-eared and homely as dirt, showed America his surgery scars. As he aged, my father bellowed like a tyrant when Dr. Needham told him his gall bladder had to come out, and he raged like a Cyclops at the lineman from El Paso Electric who tried to string a low-voltage line across a corner of our ranch. When he was fifty, Daddy was hollering about calumny and false piety; at sixty, about the vulgar dimwits loose in the land; at seventy, about the excesses of those from the hindmost reaches of our species. Even a week before he died—which was three years ago, at seventy-four—he lay in his hospital bed, virtually screaming at his night nurse about the dreamland that citizens lived in. "This is a world of ignorance and waste," he hollered, "no bridge at all over the sea which is our foreordained doom!" Yes, he had blown up be-

fore and would blow up again, so on the day I trudged across our
flatland fairways I assumed he was loco this time because, say,
he'd caught Butch Newell cheating. Or that Allie Martin had
spoken unkindly about Hebrews. Or that Jimmy Sellers, whom
he seemed most mad at, had gypped him on the Ramada Inn
they were partners in.

I have told Pammy Jo many times that mine was the most
curious eight-minute walk I will ever take. I have read that in so-
called extreme moments—those that Mother associates with the
words *peril* and *dire*—we humans are capable of otherwise impossible physical activity. In emergencies, we can hoist automobiles, vault like Olympians, run at leopardlike speeds. So it
was with my father. As I drew nearer, my flip-flops making that
silly slapping noise, I saw Daddy spin, bounce as if on springs,
whirl, hop, and kick the air. He threw his ball onto the service
road. He windmilled his arms, stomped, spit on the putter he'd
jammed like a stake into the heart of the green. He even dashed
in a zigzag that from above might have looked like the scribbling
Arabs have. I was reminded of the cartoon creatures I see on
Saturday-morning TV, those who race over the edge of a cliff to
hang unnaturally in the air for several seconds, their expressions
passing from joy to worry to true horror. And then I realized—
almost, I am convinced, at the same moment he did—that Daddy
was going to roar headlong at Mr. Sellers, stop in a way that
would jar the innards, and cold-cock that man.

"No," I croaked, and when Daddy left off his tirade about
murkiness in the moral parts and the rupture that was our modern era, I felt something tiny and dry break free in my chest. To
my knowledge, he'd never struck a man in anger before, but as
he went at it now, like an honorable man with a single unbecoming task to do in life, I could see that violence—if that's all this
was—was as natural to him as fear is common to us all.

"James Edward Sellers," he was shouting, "I am going to tear
out your black heart."

I reached the green just as Mr. Sellers, fingering his split lip, was picking himself up. "Let's go," Daddy said, using a smile and a voice I never care again to see and hear. He seemed composed, as if he'd survived the worst in himself and was now looking forward to an eternity of deserved pleasures. "Grab my bag, son," he said. Nearby, Mr. Newell and Allie Martin had the faces you find on those who witness such calamity as auto wrecks: gray and why-filled.

"Where you going?" I asked.

He pointed: the clubhouse. "Now," he said. "This minute."

I hustled about, picking up his clubs, finding his two iron beyond the sand trap behind the willow tree. This was over, I figured. He had been the nincompoop my mother said sometimes he was, and now he could be again that fairly handsome elder who read books like *Historia Romania* and the biographies of dead clerics. He would, I believed, march into the clubhouse, collect himself over a mixed drink and then reappear—as he had done several times before—at the door to the men's locker. Into the caddy master's hand Daddy would place a written apology so abject with repentance and so slyly organized that when it was read over the PA, perhaps by Jimmy Sellers himself, those lounging around the pool and walking the links, as well as those in the showers or in the snack bar or in the upstairs dining room, would hush their chitchat, listen as librarians can, and afterward break into that applause which greets genuinely good news.

—

At the men's locker, I found the door locked. Twenty people had wedged themselves into the narrow, dim hallway; with amusement, I thought that, as he had done with Woody and Helen Knapp, Daddy had herded them here, mad and delighted, to show them the proper way to fold a bath towel or how a gentleman shines his wingtip shoes or what tie to wear with red.

"That was the trashcan," Mr. Hightower said behind me.

We had heard the banging and clatter that metal makes when it is drop-kicked.

Elvis Peacock was shaking his head. "Could have been the towel rack. Or that automatic hand-dryer."

You heard the crash and whang of doors slamming and a two-minute screech that Mr. Phinizy Spalding identified as the wooden rack of linen hooks that ran from the showers to the ball washers.

Patient as preachers, they listened and I listened to them. A jerky scraping was Dr. Weems's easy chair being dragged. Pounded. And, at last, splintered.

"What was that?" someone said.

We'd heard a deafening rattle, like gravel on a tin roof.

"Pocket change," Herb Swetman told us. "He's broken into the cigarette machine."

A glass shattered, Judge Sanders's starting pistol went off, and it was time for me to knock on the door.

"I got your clubs," I said. He was moving, spikes clicking and scratching like claws. I had the thought that this wasn't my father at all but the boogeyman all children hear about. It was nothing to believe that what now stopped behind the door, still as the stuff inside a grave, was the scaly, hot-eyed, murder-filled monster who, over the years, was supposed to leap out of closets or flop down from trees to slay youngsters for the crimes they sometimes dream of. "What do you want me to do with them?"

I was speaking directly into the MEMBERS ONLY sign, feeling as awkward and self-conscious as I would one day feel asking Pammy Jo to marry me. Crowded behind were Frank Redman and T. Moncure Yourtees, our assistant city manager. Behind them stood the Clute brothers, Mickey and Sam, both looking as interested in this as their Pope is in carnality. Last in line, silhouetted in the doorway, stood Mr. Jimmy Sellers himself. A muscle had popped in my neck and for a time it was impossible to breathe.

"You all right?" I asked. "Mother is real upset."

Here, then, hushed as Dr. Hammond Ellis says will be the daybreak of doom, my daddy, his face pressed against the door-jamb, told me he had something special in mind. I recognized his voice as the one he'd used ten years before when, drunk and sore-hearted with nostalgia, he had sat on the end of my bed to tell me how his brother, my Uncle Alton (whom I am supposed to be the spitting image of) had died in the WW II Bataan Death March; it was a story of deprivation, of fortitude in the face of overwhelming sadness, and of what we human brothers—in our yellow incarnation this time—are capable of in a world slipped free of grace.

"What do you want me to do?" I asked.

"You listen carefully," he whispered.

"Yes, sir." He was my daddy and I was being polite.

He said, "I want you to break those clubs, you hear?"

The news traveled down the line behind me and returned before my mind turned completely practical: "How will you know?"

Mr. Phinizy Spalding had lit a cigar, the smoke just reaching me.

"Junior," Daddy was saying, "I am your parent and you will do what I say." He could have been speaking to me as he had to that colonel in Korea years before.

"Yes, sir," I said.

My mother had given him these clubs—Wilson irons and Hagen woods—less than four months before, and if you know anything about golf, you know that a linkster's clubs are to him what a wand is to a magician. They had leather grips and extra-stiff shafts, and they felt, even in my clumsy grip, like a product of science and philosophy: balanced, elegant, simple as love itself. They were shiny, cost over six hundred dollars, and I told him I would begin with his wedge.

"Good idea," he said.

Snapping those clubs was neither physically nor spiritually difficult. I was strong, and I was dumb. To those folks in the hallway, my actions probably seemed as ordinary as walking a straight line. Indeed, once I started, Mr. Hightower began handing me the clubs. "I'll be your assistant, Junior," he said. He was smiling like the helpful banker he is, and I thanked him. "My pleasure," he said, "happy to do it."

There was nothing in me—doubt, aggravation, none of it. Neither fear nor joy. Neither pleasure nor satisfaction. This was work, and I was doing it.

"I have your five iron now," I said.

At my feet lay what I'd already accomplished: a gleaming pile of twisted, broken, once expensive metal. And then I heard it: the noise I am partly here to tell about. I understand now—because I have dwelled on it and because it once happened to me—that, despite what was happening, he was still angry. Angry in a way that fell beyond ordinary expression. An anger that comes not from the heart or the brain, or another organ of sense, but from the soul itself. An anger that, looking down, angels must feel. For what he was doing, while I wrenched in half his woods and putter, was speaking, in a whisper I shall forever associate with the black half of rapture, some sort of gibberish, a mutter I can only transcribe as funny-pages gobbledygook, those dashes and stars you see in newspapers when the victim of rage empties his mind. It was X, which in the tenth-grade algebra I teach stands for the unknown—as in $x - 2 = y$. It is everything and nothing; and that day, accompanied by twenty wiser men, I heard Daddy speak it, just as yesterday I heard Dr. Hammond Ellis, our Episcopalian, preach about man's need for fellowship and eternal good. To be true, when I had at last fractured his putter, I believed that Daddy was mumbling as Adam and Eve were said to mumble, in the language of Eden that Dr. Ellis insists was ours before death. Because I am old-fashioned and still a believer, I contend that my father, enraged like any animal that sleeps and eats, was speaking a babble so private, yet so universal, that it goes from your lips to the ear of God Himself; it is more breathtaking, I hold, than the wheel, fire, travel in space—all those achievements, we hope, that makes us less monkey than man.

On Daddy yammered, a phenomenon those in the hall with me found as remarkable as chickens which count by twos. Mr. Hightower said it was Dutch. "I heard that in World War Two," he said. "Or maybe it's Flemish."

Frank Redman suggested it was Urdu, something he'd heard on TV the other night. "Junior, how's your daddy know Urdu?"

Elvis Peacock, the only one besides my father to have gone to university, said it was, well, Sanskrit, which was speech folks in piled-up headdress mutter before they zoom off to the afterlife. "Listen," he said, "I'm betting ten dollars on Sanskrit."

And so, once again, we listened and were not disappointed. My father, an American of 185 pounds and bristly, graying hair, and a reputation for muleheadedness, was in there—in that shambles of a locker room—yapping, if you believe the witnesses, in Basque, in Mennonite, in Zulu, or in the wet yackety-yack that Hungary's millions blather when they spy the vast Whatnot opening to greet them.

"Let's go in," Dr. Weems suggested at last.

From their expressions, these men seemed ready to vote on it.

"Daddy," I said, "can I come in now?"

It was midafternoon and it seemed we had waited forever.

"It's open," he said.

I sensed he was sitting, perhaps in the remains of Dr. Weems's easy chair; strangely, I expected him to be no more disturbed or disheveled than our most famous judges.

"Don't make any loud noises," Frank Redman said. "I know that man, he's liable to shoot somebody."

Slowly, I pushed open the door, stepped over the rubble of his clubs, and made room for those following me. You could see that a hurricane—a storm by the name of Hobey Don Baker, Sr.— had been through there. A bank of lockers had been tipped over, many sprung open to reveal what we in the upper class dry off with or look at when doing so. There were shampoo bottles scattered, as well as Bermuda shorts, tennis shoes, golf spikes, bottles of Johnnie Walker Red and Jack Daniels, Bicycle playing cards, chips that belonged to Mr. Mickey Clute's poker game, and a nasty paperback Frank Redman wouldn't later own up to. In one corner was a soiled bundle of lady's frilly underclothes that looked worthy of ample Mrs. Hightower herself. And then Allie Martin noticed Memo Gonzalez, the janitor, who was leaning against the wall to our right, almost facing Daddy.

"You been in here the whole time?" Allie Martin said.

As a group, we watched Memo nod: sure, he'd been in here. He was from Mexico—an especially bleak and depressed village, we thought—and the rumor was that he had been a thousand things in his youth: dope smuggler, highway bandito, police sergeant in Las Palomas, failed bullfighter—before Allie brought him up here, on a green card, to sweep up and keep our clubs clean.

"We been having conversation," he said. "Where you been?"

Right then, you knew that all the rumors were true, even those still to be invented, for you could see by the way he smoked his Lucky Strike and picked his teeth with a golf tee that he'd seen it and heard it, and that it—war, pestilence, famine, plague—had meant less to him than books mean to fish.

"Memo," my daddy said, "come over here, please."

I took note of one million things—the yellow light, the smell of the group I stood in, and the rusty taste coming from my stomach. I felt as apart from my father as I do now that he is dead. I wondered where my mother was and what was happening in the outer world. I thought of Pammy Jo and hoped she still loved me. I saw that Mr. Newell hadn't shaved and that Rice Hershey was the sourpuss bookkeeper Daddy said he was. A thought came, went, came back—and again I heard, in my memory, the X-language Daddy had used.

It was prayer, I thought. Or it was lunacy.

"Let's go," I said. "Mother says we're eating out tonight."

Standing, one arm around Memo's shoulders, Daddy looked, except for the hair slapped across his forehead like wet leaves, as alert and eager as he did at the breakfast table. I wanted to grab hold, say I loved him.

"Gentlemen," he was saying, "to cover expenses, I hold here a check for ten thousand dollars."

There were ooooohhhs and aaahhhs and the expressions they come from.

"If you need more, there is more."

And then he was marching past us, me running to catch up.

               —

Now this is the modern, sad part of the story, and it is a bit about my oldest boy, Buddy—who, like me in the former story, is seventeen—and how I came again to hear that double-talk I thought remarkable so long ago. There is no Memo in this part, nor folks like Messrs. Redman, Hightower and Newell, for they, like Daddy and Mother themselves, are either dead or old and mostly indoors. Mainly, though, this section is without the so-called innocent bystander because our world is utterly without bystanders, innocent or otherwise; we are all central, I believe, to events which are leading us, good and bad, to the dry paradise that is the end of things.

Buddy is like most youth these days—by turns lazy and feckless, stupid and smart-alecky, fussy and apathetic. Tall, too skinny through the chest, he speaks when spoken to and has a girlfriend named Alice Mary Tidwell who will one day be a fat but always cheerful woman. He reads periodicals like *Sports Illustrated* and what is required in school as advanced literature (which is *Silas Marner,* verse by Shakespeare, and made-up mishmash by New York writers who haven't lived anywhere). I love him not simply because he is my flesh but because I see that in all things—his own adulthood, for example—he will be decent-hearted and serious-minded, a man who will want, as you do, to be merely and always good. More than once we have talked about this—mostly when he was an adolescent. I used to sit at the end of his bed, as had my father with me, to offer my views on issues like relations among neighbors, what heft our obligations have, and how too often the heart never fits its wanting. One time, but without the dramatics my daddy enjoyed, I took him around the house, showing him what ought to be, not what was; later, when he was ten and mowing our yard, I went out, watched for a time, then stood in his path to stop him.

"What's the matter now?" he asked.

It was summer, dry but hot as fire gets, and I was partly joyful to see him sweat doing something he'd been told.

"First," I said, "you have to wear shoes. You hit a rock and no telling what'll happen."

He looked at the sandals we'd bought him in Juárez.

"And no more shorts," I added. "Long pants for the same reason."

He has his mother's blue eyes, which were fixed on me as hers often are when I rise up to put things straight in this universe.

"I'm wearing goggles," he said.

I was pleased, I told him, but then described, as Daddy did for me, how grass is cut in the ideal world.

"Starting from the outside," I began, "you go around in a square, okay? Throws the cuttings to the center and makes raking up easier."

Here it was, then, that we had a moment together, a moment which had nothing to do with yardwork; rather, it was a passage of time that, to the sentimentalist I am, seemed filled with wonder and knowledge—the first things we must pass on.

"Can I have five dollars?" he asked.

He was going to the movies, he said, with Jimmy Bullard and Clovis Barclay. I was watching his face—what it said about his inner life—and when he took the money from me, I accepted the urge, felt in the gut, to throw my arms around him and lay on the breath-deafening hug I am notorious for.

"Come on, Dad," he said, "don't squeeze so hard."

Mostly, however, and embarrassingly, we are not close. Like my father, I tend to lecture; like me, when I was his age, he is obliged to listen. I have talked about responsibility, the acceptance of which is a measure of our maturity and not nearly the weighty moral overcoat another might say it is, and Buddy has said, "Yes, sir." I have talked about honor, which is often seen as too ambiguous to be useful, and he has answered, "Yes, sir." I have talked about politics, which except for voting he is to avoid; and debt, which he may accept in moderation; and cleanliness, which remains a practical concern; and trust, which he must reward in others. Other times, I have warned him against tobacco, drinking with strangers, carelessness with firearms, public displays of temper, eating undercooked or fatty foods, wasting time, rudeness, sleeping in drafts, and lying when such is not called for. I have said, in a way Pammy Jo finds most amusing, that there is hardness and cruelty, confusion and turmoil; and there is knowing what's best. To all he has answered, "Yes, sir."

I have, of course, told him about his grandfather's outburst at the country club; to be true, I told him during that father–son talk which becomes necessary when the son acquires body hair and the shoulders broaden toward manhood. I forget the point I intended, but somewhere during a too-clinical discussion of arousal and penis length and courtship, I said, "Did you ever hear the locker-room story?" We were in our living room, he holding the well-illustrated pamphlet, *Growing Up: A Young Man's Mystery,* that Dr. Weems had given me. Outside, the August light was gladsome, and in here, amongst palaver that made romance sound like sport among Martians, I unloaded, taking nearly two hours telling about one. Giving him names, places, and states of mind, I watched his brain, as betrayed by his eyeballs, figure out what coitus had to do with madness. I watched him imagine Daddy as more than the grumpy old man he knew; and sexual congress—which, I confess, was the phrase I used— as something more than flesh attached to funny Latin words. I told him about Memo's tattoos, which were as detailed and epic as Spiderman comics, and about Allie Martin's hole in one afterward, and about my mother pitching turkey bones at the clock that night; and then, twilight near and our neighbors home from their trades, I watched Buddy's forehead wrinkle and his hand fidget while he thrashed about in the events I had recalled, helpless as a drowning mule in his effort to establish a connection between the past and this present business of creation.

Which, in the roundabout way I think appropriate, brings us to recent hours, whose events feature a father, a son, a prophylactic, and mumbo-jumbo from the start of time.

—

It is early April now, rainy enough to be annoying, and Pammy Jo and our youngest, Taylor, are in the eighth day of their two-week visit to her sister in El Paso. It is an absence which means that Buddy and I eat hot dogs and Kraft macaroni too often, or we visit the Triangle Drive-In for Del Cruz's chicken-fried steak in white gravy. It is an absence I feel physically, as if what I am missing from my bed and my conversation is more body part than companion. There is a larger effect, too, specifically with reference to time—which seems to stretch forward endlessly to a future ever out of reach. Time becomes inconceivable: it is reincarnation or other hocus-pocus our wishing invents. What I am saying here is that when my wife is around I know where I am in America; and I can say to anybody that I am forty-two years old, a Scorpio (if you care), a cum-laude graduate of the University of New Mexico (B.S. in mathematics), a shareholder in several companies (IBM, for one), a father, a sportsman who does not care for hunting or fishing, a practicing Episcopalian, and heir to nearly one million dollars' worth of baked desert rangeland (and the cattle that graze there). But when she is gone—when she visits her father in Roswell or when she attends her social workers' convention in Santa Fe—my horizon shrinks and loneliness has such weight that I am pitched forward and ever in danger of wobbling to a stop.

The other day I felt this as a restlessness to see my neighbors, a desire to be moving, so I told Buddy I was going out.

"When you gonna be back?" he asked.

It was noon and there was no reason to be anywhere—here, this continent, this world.

"I don't know, maybe I'll go to the club."

He was watching Larry Bird and the Celtics make mincemeat out of the Bullets from Washington. Plus, he had a package of Hydrox cookies and most of the milk in the house. "Have a good time," he said, and I was gone.

Yet for the next few hours it was less I than someone else who drove around Deming. At one time, this man who was not me found himself stopped outside a shabby duplex on Olive Street where he had been violently drunk for the first time. He had been with Donnie Bobo and Dickie Greene and, in the company of Oso Negro and Buckhorn beer, he'd seen the night itself fly apart and burn. An hour later, he found himself on one of the line roads that head east through the scrub and brush toward Las Cruces. He had been here twice before with Bernice Ruth Ellis, and the sex they had had been fitful, not at all the hurly-burly described in *Penthouse* magazine—in part because he was married and because she was the confused daughter of our most celebrated Christian, Dr. Hammond Ellis. This infidelity occurred long ago, in the second year of my marriage, and is an episode I do not forgive myself for. It is one secret I've kept, and there are times, especially when I see Bernice and her husband Charlie Potts at the Fourth of July dance or at the Piggly Wiggly, when I think it did not happen at all; or that, if it did, it happened in a place—a crossroads of time and circumstance—in which there was no evil or eye looking down.

Around four, I found myself at the club, one of many husbands and fathers who seemed too bored or too free. My friend Leroy Sellers—Jimmy's son—was sitting on a camp stool in the pro shop, making sense out of our war with Nicaragua. Bobby Hover was there, looking like the rich real-estate broker he is; so were Joe Bob Newell, Spudd Webb, Archie Meents and Ed Fletcher— all fellows I'd grown up with or met through my exploits on the football field. In time, aided by the Scotch whiskey Spud brought from his locker, we fixed civilization up fine. After eliminating

poverty, we took the starch out of the diets of fat men, dealt with
such dreams as are suffered by tyrants, turned winners into
losers, fired two county commissioners, and agreed that in humans we liked muscle, the eagle's eyesight, voices you can hear
across the room, and what they teach in Sweden about freedom.
Joe Bob told us about his brother who was building jet fighters
for LTV in Dallas, Ed Fletcher suggested a cure for flatulence,
and Spud himself took the high ground in defense of intergalac-
tic communication with, say, Venutians—a point he made by
drawing our attention to the ten billion stars and planets which
were said to be out there.

He was standing, I remember, and his workingman's face had
taken on a blissful shine, red and wet the way yours would be
were you to win ten million dollars in a lottery.

"They're up there, I tell you," he said, daring each of us to
contradict him. "You got to be less narrow-minded, boys."

For a moment, it was possible to believe him—to understand
that out there, where light is said to bend toward time, lived
creatures, like ourselves, who had our happy habits of wonder
and hope.

At six-thirty, while Ed Fletcher addressed the topic of loyalty in
Washington, D.C., I called Buddy to say I'd be a while yet. "No
problem," he said, "I'm going over to Doug Sherwin's." I know now
that he had already done it: that he had gone into our bedroom and
had opened my bureau drawer, finding the plain drugstore condom
Pammy Jo and I used for birth control. I know, too, that his mind
was filled with a dozen contrary notions—guilt and anxiousness
and excitement; and I suspect that at the moment we in the pro
shop were putting Mr. Nixon on his feet again, Buddy was bringing
himself to that point his *Young Man's Mystery* book calls "orgasm," which is defined as a matter of friction and fluids.

———

I got home late, finding eight lights burning and the TV turned
to a Sunday-night movie about, near as I can tell, greed and those

the victim of it. Buddy wasn't home, which was just as well because I was drunk. I have mostly forgone heavy drinking, a crutch (Pammy Jo's word) I leaned too heavily on after my father died. Nowadays, I have wine to be polite or take my alcohol mixed, for there was a time—nearly eighteen months, in fact— when I was addled enough to be drunk virtually every night; those in my family have said that they were truly afraid of me during this period, seeing me as a desperate sort who wouldn't watch his tongue and who heaped on others the misery he'd heaped on himself. So, unsteadily and ashamed, I made coffee and ate peanut butter, a remedy I'd heard on *Donahue* once. I tried reading the Raymond Chandler I like, but the words, not to mention the events and the people shaped by them, kept sliding off the page. I looked at *Life* magazine but could not figure out what beasts like giraffes and African elephants were doing next to the colorful vacation homes of the rich. I thought, at last, of calling Pammy Jo, but didn't. She would hear the thing I was covering up and she would be sad. So, believing I would go to bed, I scribbled this note: "Buddy, I'm going to school tomorrow to do lesson plans; you, as promised, begin painting the garage."

My daddy claimed, especially in his rage-filled years in later life, that he'd developed the extra sense of suspicion, a faculty he likened to an awareness old-time oilmen have: roughnecks, it is said, know when a well is about to come in by a "harmonic tremor," a subtle shaking of our earth heralded by a noise that causes dogs to pick up their ears. I have inherited this sense, along with bony elbows and a mouth that can be set hard as a doorknob. In our bedroom, which is as big as a one-hundred-dollar-a-night hotel room, I knew immediately that something was wrong. My bedsheets looked too tight, and the clutter on my nightstand—a *National Geographic,* the Kleenex box, the clock-radio, plus a water glass—seemed unfamiliar, somehow different. That organ of suspicion, which is composed, I know now, of habit and how you are taught, was well at work in me. I compare it to my dog, a pound-bred beast named Raleigh, and how sometimes he becomes three parts attention, one part mud-

dle. I made my way around my room on tiptoe, feeling myself the
intruder here. I have fist-fought twice in my lifetime—the last in
the ninth grade with Billy Joe De Marco, which is when I broke
my wrist—but, counting the change on my dresser and opening
my jewelry box, I was ready. I heard what nighttime has to offer
in these parts: Poot Tipton in his backyard next door hollering at
his brother; a car going too fast on Iron Street; our air-conditioner
taking its own pulse. Who was here? I was thinking, and pictures
came to mind of robberies and the serious prowling we suffer
around here. And then, arms held as I had been taught, tight to
the body, the fists on either side of the head, I went into the
bathroom.

For several moments I didn't see the used condom on the water
tank for the toilet. Rather, I was studying the man in the mirror
who is me. It would be a cliché to say that in my face—particularly
the way the cheekbones lie and how the nose goes flat at the
bridge—was my father's; but there he was, at forty or fifty, gazing
at me from a mirror my wife had paid too much for at the White
House department store. It is also possible to believe that in his
face lay the images, as well, of *his* father, who had gone broke at
least twice. In a way quite natural under the circumstances, I let
my heart and breath go free, flipped on the lights, and looked at
that room as Chuck Gribble, our sheriff, looks at places that are the
scenes of small crimes. I report to you now that I found the
condom immediately and took note of it as in past years I have
taken note of bad news that happens in big towns far, far away.

"Yes," I said.

It was a word which then meant no more to me than what is
muttered in Paraguay. Yet I muttered it again and again—as if an
official with important-looking documents had knocked on my
door to say, "Are you Hobey Don Baker, Junior?"

—

That night I behaved like an ignorant father. I phoned the Sherwin house, but Betty, Doug's mother, said Buddy wasn't there.

"You okay, Junior?" she said. "You sound funny." For the most part, my voice was coming from my chest and, yes, it wasn't her friend talking; it was Buddy's father.

"You see him," I told her, "it's time to come home, all right?"

Sure, she said, and reminded me of the barbecue on Wednesday. "You haven't been drinking, have you, Junior?"

I watched my hand shake and attended to the rasp my breathing made. "I'm fine, Betty, thanks."

I called Clovis Barclay and put up with Earl, his father, scolding me about how late it was. Afterward, I stood on the street, watching our neighbors' lights go off after the late news. It would be a cool night, the clouds racing up from Chihuahua, and I hoped Buddy hadn't gone out without a jacket. I was not angry, just dislocated—as unhinged as I was when I tried to quit smoking. I heard the same noise over and over: a fierce ear whine. I regarded heaven, which was up and far away, and hell, which was underfoot and near; and then I went indoors to make myself a camp in Buddy's room.

It is a truism that teenagers have the collector's spirit. In my time, I'd hoarded baseball cards and kept statistics on the Aggie basketball I listened to on the radio. I had trophies (swimming), drawings and photographs of jet planes that Grumman had sent me. I had saved coins for a while—nothing special—plus books on oceans. Buddy was no different. He possessed a Zenith record player and at least one hundred albums from Fed-Mart: Mötley Crüe, Devo, and foreign-looking groups whose lyrics were about love, or what passed for it. On the walls—ceiling too—were charts ("Generalized," of time and rock units) of Canada and the USA. The rocks we stood on, I learned, came from the Silurian Age. From his desk I discovered that apparently he'd never thrown away a single school assignment; you could see him, represented in thousands of pages, go from one unable to spell "garage" to one familiar with what Euclid had achieved. I am not proud of this snooping, but I had to know, and isn't knowing—

even if it is painful and frightful and small—better than not knowing? And then, after I'd counted his shirts and pants, he was standing at his door.

"Hey," he said, "I read the note."

I took a second, trying to strip the age out of my voice. "Who was she?" I asked. "Was it Alice Mary?"

He stepped backward, shaking his head as if he'd run into a cobweb. He was wearing a shirt like the checkered flag at the Indy 500 and pants that are too expensive and too tight.

"You had a girl in here tonight," I said. "I want to know who."

It was a shameful question, but I had to ask it again before I realized—my organ of suspicion, I guess—that there had been no girl, or woman; that, instead, he had indulged in what my 1949 edition of *Webster's New Collegiate Dictionary* calls, stupidly, "self-pollution," which is masturbation and is as normal to us as flying is to birds.

"In my bathroom," I said. "On top of the commode."

He went to look and while he was gone I, in my mind, began putting his books in order. Large to small. Good to bad.

"It was Francis Greathouse," he said when he returned. "You don't know her. Her old man works for the state police, a sergeant." Buddy looked defeated, as nervewracked as the time his Little League team was beaten and the world to him had gone topsy-turvy into chaos.

"Stop," I said. "I don't believe you."

It was true, he insisted. She sat behind him last year, in fifth-period chemistry. She had brown hair and was tall. "They live on Fir Street. It's a white place, I don't know the number."

The rocks we have in the world are these: Cambrian, Ordovician, Devonian. And they go back six hundred million years or more, to times that were dark, silent, and wet.

"Go to bed," I said, "we'll talk about this in the morning."

His face was flushed and open, and I could see that it too was mine and how I looked a generation ago.

"You're right," he said.

A fiber had snapped in my stomach—a muscle or link between nerve and bone.

"It wasn't Francis Greathouse," he was saying, "it wasn't anybody."

And then, as it had been in that men's locker, I heard it again, our X-language, a tumbling rush of speech that if put down here would be all *z*'s and *y*'s and *c*'s, the crash of tongue-thick syllables and disordered parts that everywhere is laughed at as madness. It wasn't anger I was experiencing—that word can't apply here—but sadness. Sadness that had to do with time and love. I was in the hall, several paces from Buddy's door, next to the water colors of trees and distance we have bought as art, and the world—as it had for my father—fell away from me. Piece by piece. Element by element. A wind had come up, freezing and from twelve directions, and there was nothing hereabouts but your narrator and his fear. I wore the cotton shirt of a civilized man and the long pants of a grown-up, but I could not think, as I am doing now, of how I came to be in this century.

"What's wrong?" Buddy said. "Dad?"

My arm, as if on strings, went up. Down. Up again.

"Dad," he said, "you're scaring me."

I think now I was speaking, as Daddy had spoken, of deceit and miserable hope and craftiness and forfeiture and my own ignorance—and of, especially, a future too weird and horrible to ponder. I was speaking, using but controlled by X, of the mud and ooze we will one day be. If I had to translate, I would assert that, victim of a grammar composed of violence and waywardness, I said this: *We are flesh and it is fallen.* And this: *This way is the way, and there is an end.* And this: *We are matter, it must be saved.* And this: *There are dark waters all around.* And this: *Please stop, please stop.*

In those minutes in my hallway, in a home I still owe eighty thousand dollars for, while my oldest son trembled as if I had struck him, X wasn't unknown any longer. It had hair and teeth and ancient, common desires. I knew X.

It was him.

It was me.

It was all of us.

—

Twenty-five years ago, Memo Gonzalez, to whom my daddy had given his ten-thousand-dollar check, stood unmoving next to Dr. Weems's splintered chair. Jimmy Sellers, who told this to me, says there was nothing at all in Memo's face. It was stone, with the impression that the nose, mouth, and eyes had been added later. He was strong, built like a toolbox, and nobody—not even Mickey Clute, who'd wrestled heavyweight in school—thought to go over there and ask for the money. Several minutes passed—the way they do in the dentist's office—before Memo walked (lumbered, Jimmy says) toward Allie Martin. He set himself in front of Mr. Martin, and twenty pairs of eyes stared at the tattoos on his arms— inky, clotted designs which were of ideas he held sacred and the women he'd known. Death. Conception. Maria. "I got to be moving along, Allie Martin," he said at last. "I quit." Whereupon he went out and, as in some fairy tales, was never seen again.

I like that moment. I like, too, the moment I had with my father in his Biscayne in the members' parking lot. I did not feel like a teenager then; rather, I felt myself to be the trustee of a dozen secrets, none of which had a name yet but all of which would be with me until there was no more me to know them. "You drive," he said. But before he gave me the keys, he touched me, squeezed me at the shoulder, and in that touch, man to boy, was the knowledge that we were the same: two creatures made blind by the same light and deafened by the same noise; that his dismay was the thing I'd grow into as I had already grown into his hand-me-down trousers; that we were harmless in water, or air; that we were put here, two-legged and flawed, to keep order.

It is a moment, so help me, that I intend to recreate for Buddy when he gets home from the picture show. It will be brief, like the original, but I hope it will remain for him forever as it has remained for me.

TIME AND FEAR AND SOMEHOW LOVE

SINCE, as she conceived it, the letter was to be the final word on the subject, she endeavored to start slowly, then lead up to, as fine drama does, those moments of lamentation, those periods—always potent and manifold—of ruin and dismay which are like, her daddy had said once, mangy wildcats with wings. She would begin with how it was in those olden days, when the man who would be the Colonel, her husband, used to drive straight to her home in Portland from his father's hotel in Old Orchard Beach; he would take her dancing on the pier where Count Basie, Ella Fitzgerald and the Dorsey Brothers played, and where he had a circle of pals with names like Digger and Fuzzy, and from where it was impossible to imagine that now, forty years later, she had neither him nor any of it, and that one day she would be sitting at her typewriter, writing to her son, and saying, as if speaking of another, "Elaine was a drinking woman."

Which was, really, not the way to begin at all, for, despite the bad stuff—being divorced, for example, and having come scarcely an hour from death—this letter was to have its share of happy times, times which made you think of laughter, of swimming parties at the country club, of driving home backward from the Moderns' house. Yes, she would mention the lovely house in Panama, three stories with a maid on each floor, and those trips by boat to Havana—which is pronounced Ha-*ban*-a, by the way, and calls to mind Major and Mrs. Geist, and nightclubs and people gay as Ricky Ricardo—as well as the phone call from Harlingen, Texas, with the electricity which shot through her when he said, "come on down and let's be married"; and the trip by train with those other WW II soldiers, each a gentleman, who watched over her and played bridge with her and protected her privacy as she slept through Ohio.

Yes, she conceived of a letter to her son which began: "Kit, you are ignorant and unfeeling as stone, and thirty-four years of being alive haven't taught you the least about me or my life." She imagined a letter, alive with all the truth she had, which wouldn't go away or sink harmlessly into memory or get mistaken for the confession it was not. She meant to show that living remained a difficult enterprise, moilsome with hoopla and hurly-burly, the whole of it insensible as chaos yet dear as love; and she wanted her letter to possess the authority of that elephant gun the Colonel had forced her to fire when they were stationed in Peoria, Illinois, a weapon which went *Bang* like the word of God Himself, shook her insides like dominoes, and did seem to ring even now like the first note of doom. It was to be a letter about love and suffering, which would leave him standing alone in his kitchen, as she had stood alone when she learned the Colonel was dead, saying, "Shit" and "My God" and "What now?" It was to start with this line: "Here, Mister, here is the hurt and how it lasts forever."

—

At first, she tried to put everything in—how, for example, she was only a Virginia girl, taught well how to comport herself as a lady, who had been brought north by a daddy who sold Hartford insurance and played a gentleman's billiards; and by a mother, Elaine had now to admit, she did not remember too clearly because of alcohol's effect on memory and Mother's being finally a figure of shadow and secret, always elsewhere, never here. On those early pages, she recalled her favorite songs—"Tonight We Love," by Bobby Worth, and "Angel with the Laughing Eyes"— and where the Colonel had gone to college (Dartmouth), and her fondness for the Episcopal litany, particularly the verse which said "we have left undone those things which we ought to have done," so the Lord was to have mercy on us, miserable offenders. She made a list of bric-a-brac she retained from her marriage: a vase for bachelor buttons (the Colonel's favorite flower), his por-ringer, his silver baby cup, a card tray, an embroidered hanky he'd bought in Korea, and a charcoal iron she now used as a doorstop. She quoted Mr. Henry Van Dyke on time, which was "too slow for those who wait, too swift for those who fear." And then, because she could avoid it no longer, she recalled again that place—a crossroads of time and character—where, even without drink itself, drunkenness had begun.

"I dwell on it now," she wrote, "because it is full of despair." In 1942, this man who was to be her husband was in Harlingen, Texas, over a thousand miles away, at gunnery school. "My beau-tiful wedding gown hung in the closet, the invitations had been mailed, the reception planned, and I had been busy writing thank-you notes for our gifts as well as working at the law firm daily." She was happy, life no more fragile than rock or steel from Pennsylvania. So it was here—when she was most deceived, she said—that the phone rang one night and her mother called up-stairs to hurry, it was Lyman. "Remember," Mother said, "it's long distance." A big deal then, when all distances seemed novel and fraught with peril. Breathless, Elaine flew down two flights of stairs, taking several steps at a time, and squatted near the phone. Mother was in the kitchen, doing dishes, and Daddy was in his library working on his new accounts. And she remembered clearly, as if hearing anew Lyman's scratchy New England voice, how the bottom fell out of her when he said he couldn't get home for the ceremony; instead, he was wiring money for plane fare, and arrangements had been made with the base chaplain. A Lieutenant Borders, he said, would be his best man and some-body named Joyce who worked at the PX would be her brides-maid. What is happening in me? she thought. I should know that thing sinking down.

"Elaine," he said, "did you hear me, it's all fixed here." She said yes, she heard, her voice choked and suddenly older than the twenty-one she was; and then Mother—"for such a tiny woman, she had the dignity of a queen!"—was beside her, holding the receiver, saying, "Yes, we understand" and "Please, don't worry" and "Oh, she'll get over this." Yet now, decades removed from the event but again in that house she had enjoyed so much as a girl, she still had not gotten over anything. After all, there were plans to change, apologies to offer—to dear Mrs. Sweem, the organist, to Dr. Butler, the priest, and to Wendy Smythe who was traveling all the way from Vassar. And there was Texas itself, out there was a horror of outlaws, whiskered galoots, and their tarts. The state had endless vistas, Lyman had told her, big and strange as color movies. Plus storms, winds that could heave aside houses—not to mention ignorance and squatty towns without paved roadways or dependable telephones. It was a place of guns and drought and public figures named Cooter or Joe Bob—not the place at all for one who had dined with Mr. Cole Porter and the president of the Boston Shoe Company.

"I can't do this," Elaine said; but her daddy said this was wartime, allowances had to be made. Sacrifice was the hallmark of her ilk, she heard him say. "So I bucked up," she wrote. "I got myself up like Mrs. Astor, with a Bonwit Teller suit and my sister Dolly's hat with the veil and feathers and a proper lady's gloves, and put three weeks of apparel into an eighty-dollar Gladstone bag that had buckles and straps enough for Harry Houdini himself." There were no planes for civilians in Portland at the time, nor in Boston; and it was by a mix of fortune and force of will— like an episode from *The Unforgotten Prisoner,* by R. C. Hutchinson, or *One Light Burning*—that she found herself aboard a troop train, a girl among hundreds of men, terrified of their poker, their Mr. Kelly comic books and their songs ("What the Wolf Did at the Ca-Ca-Castle"), but most of all frightened of their sprawl, their violent laughter, the smell of an army rattling in a single direction toward death.

"Then a most curious thing happened," she wrote. "They treated me like a movie star." They said, "Hey, lady, sit over here" and "Don't get off, ma'am, we'll get you something." It was like one of those Mickey Rooney musicals where everybody, from yokel to snotty bluenose, is composed of good nature and sense, talented enough to dance the Cleveland Chicken or repeat a memorable joke. A boy who said he was from Tufts University but actually looked sly enough to be an artful liar juggled oranges; and another, this one imitating a Tidewater bumpkin, did a trick with the ace of spades, which was so much more than sleight of hand it appeared sinister. They treated her as a kid sister, fetching USO goodies at every stop and telling her their life stories, all of which involved the infuriate and featured folks like herself, she would admit—foolish, bewildered, and astray, folks with an outstanding defect like withered limb or romantic habit of mind. In Missouri, above the rumble and squeal of the train, one private, saying he was a poet, read several stanzas titled "Bolts of Melody," which had, as its hero, a devious person-age named Mu Mon Kwan; in Arkansas, another said his favorite from history was Batygh the Tartar, a villain renowned for murder and such savagery as blasphemy. "Best of all," Elaine wrote, "they gave me advice." One who seemed too stunted for even Uncle Sam said, "Don't never trust someone who smiles overmuch. They are back-stabbers and what my old teacher calls minions." And another, this one standing in the cluttered aisle, erect and sincere as virtue, declared, "Lady, what do you think of jazz? I think it's money, almost, for those of us without." Where-upon there was such good-natured hooting and brotherly punch-ing of the thick parts as you now see at sport when the home squad triumphs.

"I slept, too," she wrote, "hours and hours in those five days. I had dreams in which there were noises like dogs make coughing up a bone, and dreams full of pictures I suspect you find in Chicago police stations, and dreams in which I was a moll named Judy French or Marjorie from Downtown and spoke like a hero-ine invented by Frank Slaughter—all of which you must not make too much of, there being in this world already too many excuses for the evil we do."

Then she was there—in a place of dizzying sunlight, heat, and

apparently mutinous activity, a train depot so full of coming and
going and hubbub that, in the banging and clatter, it took several
minutes to find him, Lyman, standing by a jeep, waving. He was
dressed in spotless suntans, his silver lieutenant's bar gleaming,
a wilted gardenia in one hand, his garrison cap in the other; and
though he did seem like a prince to her, she knew now that this
was merely another charade of memory, for he was already, even
as he hugged and kissed and grinned like Little Jack Horner, the
Colonel he would become—full of temper and rage, knobby-
kneed, given to intolerance, with a bad heart and a dark slice of
lung that would have to come out, and a Chinaman's belief in
dark powers, a man made mournful by sentiment.

"Hurry," he was saying now, flopping her suitcase into the
jeep. "I got the chaplain waiting."

She was shocked. Her dress was shabby with wrinkles, her
gloves were as filthy as a hobo's, and her hat—which over a
thousand miles ago had been, well, jaunty—drooped like a sock,
its feather greasy and wilted.

"Lyman, you take me somewhere to clean up," she said. "Don't
they have a hotel here? I need a bath."

He looked befuddled. He said, "You look gorgeous. They won't
care." *They,* this Fergus who was chaplain, and the sweethearts
Frank Borders and Joyce—they'd understand.

"Nobody understands me but me," she said. "These people
don't even know me."

It was not here, she wrote, that the despair she was thinking of
overtook her. Nor was it on the ride which she remembered as
bumpy and windblown, through a town which looked like what
the carnival leaves behind. Lyman was talking like crazy—not
closemouthed as he would become, but chattering. War talk.
What that far-off cannon might do and what a lummox the DI
was and how orders were cut. He'd heard from his father, who
was going blind, and his brother who was already in England,
working top secret for the Signal Corps. "You know how he's
getting around in the blackouts?" Lyman said. "Holding hands,

that's how." There was little funnier, according to Lyman, than the idea of his brother, the biggest of the big track stars at Hebron, holding hands in the dark with a bunch of men.

"No, I suppose not," she said, noting how in the heat, which had the density of a fat man, the buildings seemed flatter and weaker, as if the chief materials of construction in this corner of the world were straw and mud, the whole of it held fast by hope.

Nor did the despair she was addressing grip her when they reached the base chapel, the jeep skidding to a stop. A border of whitewashed rocks marked the road, and the chapel—itself white and covered with silly, fussy gingerbread—looked like a structure thrown up by Las Vegas hoodlums.

"C'mon," he said, "let's get a move on."

It was here, then, that she began to feel it—the quake in the underhalf of her heart, the numbing shiver like a lance through an organ she imagined was thick and heavily veined—as he hustled her inside a building that was not St. Paul's with its spires and shiny woodwork. He introduced her to Lieutenant Borders (who, in another life certainly had been a felon preying on the feeble-witted) and his girlfriend Joyce (who wore a red Elvis Presley hairdo long before the advent of the so-called King of Rock and Roll). And then, in an instant which seemed to be the penultimate stroke of an epoch, they were walking her forward, with a dour figure, Major Fergus, chaplain, USA, waiting on them.

He had, she wrote, that face you expect to see the day after Mardi Gras, dark with turmoil and excess, and she knew, well before he said, "Hello, how are you," that his was the God of the Baptists, fugitive and slack-minded, that parlous shade which gave us talking fish and centuries of carnage.

"I had my heart set on Dr. Butler's God," she wrote to her son, "that one I still advise you to believe in—that one of books and manners and reasoned faiths."

But then, in these merry olden times she was concerned with, she said, "Lyman, could I have some water, please?"

She was scared. She felt nerve and fiber giving way inside her, swelling or shrinking or stiffening to stone.

"Here you go, honey." It was Joyce, bosomy and smelling virtually fertile. "You learn to drink a lot down here. The dust and all."

After many deep breaths, each of which seemed the first following years of paralysis, Elaine said, "All right, I'm ready."

They stood—for an hour, she swore—while Major Fergus, florid and smiling wide as a pumpkin, read a hodgepodge of dos and do nots; and Joyce, misty-eyed as a schoolgirl, breathed with her mouth open; and Frank Borders puffed himself up like a William Makepeace Thackeray roué; and Lyman held on to her elbow as if he expected to topple over and disappear.

Then it was over, except for that noise.

Who's crying? she wondered. That person does need some help.

And then she realized it was she herself crying—a remote, sad wail which involved time and fear and somehow love.

—

The next four pages she filled with random events, parties foremost. She was approaching one soiree in particular, that one of consequence in which she got a hard glimpse of her future, but she would come to it, she said, as she had come to these other truths about herself: by indirection and by surprise, its method its point. "It's as my daddy says," she wrote, "I am going in that back door of insight, that one approached through bramble and dense thicket, along a disordered, overgrown path."

Lord, there were parties—for occasions slight and grand. In the fifteen years she meant to ignore, there were parties everywhere: in Defuniak Springs, Florida, and San Diego (where the Colonel bought the bungalow on Pacific Beach), in Illinois and again in Old Orchard Beach when he went to Korea. The parties had booze, of course, rivers of it, which were aids for those with horselike behinds to do the cha-cha-cha. Booze made the befuddled eloquent; the loutish, lovely. There were parties for George Washington and Black Jack Pershing, as well as for St. Valentine, Army–Navy football and Armistice Day. One party mourned Adlai Stevenson, another the bearded bumbler Fidel Castro. "In those days," she wrote, "parties were as common as dollar bills; be it birthday, anniversary, promotion or national holiday, they were a chance for us to do mischief, to come near catalepsy."

Oh, life was as fine as grade-school arithmetic. "I was meeting folks from the larger world—generals and their wives who read more than recipes; and I was seeing life as it was meant to be led; and though I was drinking Bacardi and real Russian vodka, I could, at any time, say that rhyme about seashells at the seashore or hold up my end of the conversation about, say, Mr. Dulles's unseemly connection with the United Fruit Company or what to do about Bishop Sheen." Which, to be true, should have alerted her to what she knew now was the principal certainty of her age: life is rampant with folly and misdeed, and no number of Japanese lanterns or ice sculptures or paper hats can make up for the fact that man is a jackass; and belief in higher powers which reward sense and privilege is no more attractive than hair on a woman's lip.

"I am referring," she wrote to her son, "to New Mexico, where you were born and where, I do imagine it now, everything comes to an end." She remembered all the details of the Colonel's letter from Seoul—its tissuelike texture, his cramped boarding-school penmanship, those Kodak snapshots of him looking as overwhelmed as a child in front of a dozen jack-in-the-box temples. She remembered, too, reading over and over that line which said he'd been transferred to White Sands Proving Ground, in the desert, but they could live in a little town called Las Cruces in a civilian house, and that she wasn't to upset herself, because Frank Hollar—did she remember him from Camp Crowder?—was already there and said the place, though small, had its virtues. Neighborliness among them. She imagined that if this had

been a movie or the product of the slumped brain of one like Ed
Sullivan, there should have been a thundering upswell of background music—notes the hero never hears when doom portends,
a boom-boom-boom on the drums which say, in effect, *Don't go
into that room, please, just stay out here where all is light and
sweet air.* "I don't have to do this," she said, realizing immediately that she did; and she remembered, at last, opening the
Rand McNally Atlas and seeing a place as empty as map space
itself, a place of six thousand people with a college of agriculture
and mechanical arts, where there was no spring and no fall,
neither snow in winter nor rain in summer. She could hear, as
she stared at the negligible black dot which she feared would be
her home forever, a voice, mirthful and deranged, crying, "Here,
you won't need that leg, nor that eye, nor that beating foolish
heart."

They squabbled when Lyman arrived home, and on the trip
down, their belongings stacked atop and stuffed into his
Chevrolet. And once—was it in Oklahoma?—when what sat at
the horizon looked as vast and featureless as melancholy, the
Colonel (who was a captain then) jerked the car to the shoulder
and jumped out, grabbing her door, his lips narrow and blood-
less, his eyes furious with fatigue. "I could slug you," he said. He
was shaking her by the shoulders, whispering as if beyond, in the
shade of a scrawny tree or in the lee of a no-account hill, huddled
thousands of upright, fearsome sodbusters each of whom would
be offended by his angry, endless talk. "Why are you doing this?"
he said. "I could hurt you. Just shut up." To which she, stiff-
necked as a schoolmarm, said, "No, you couldn't. Not you and a
million like you." Which is how, this son of hers was to understand, drunks speak when they feel courageous, mighty, and
righteous to their soaked souls.

There was a party when they arrived. Another when they
bought the house on West Gallagher. And more when they joined
the country club, when the son was born, when Lyman made
major, and when he won the club championship by beating

Willie Newell three and two with a putt that was part miracle, part guts. They met the Bissels, the Georges and Dalrhymples; the E. J. Akers and Mrs. Sally Brickman; Alice and Johnny Ostriker; Nelson Popp and his first wife Vivian; Professor Beeker and Allie Martin, the club pro; the Blairs, Joan and Harvey, plus their cousin from Fort Worth—168 folks ("Honest," she wrote, "I counted them once!"), all of whom, from time to time, did like to throw off their current selves and, charmed by liquors, sport about in the truth. A terrible and inward tribe, these were folks who dressed up like slatterns or Dracula or mayors of desert towns to indulge in hijinks; made honest by booze, they would sashay right up to you and say that your eyes were mismatched or that your gown from the White House in El Paso was a most unbecoming shade of aquamarine or that Republicans knew how to run this universe, which they would do wonderfully, your backbiting and carping notwithstanding. They were citizens who hollered when they ought not and made scenes few forgot and bruised feelings which grew sorer over time; folks—"I am thinking of myself now," she wrote—who one evening, despite Fourth of July merriment, the marvelous notes from Mr. Albert Grady's clarinet and the toothsome chitchat from Betty Turner, said to themselves, I will not have this anymore, I am going home.

Elaine couldn't find the Colonel immediately—not in the ballroom, which was dark and smoky, nor in the pro shop, where the stuffed shirts went to prattle about life and its meanings, nor in the men's locker, which she searched like a sneak-thief. Ed Keating, who fetched her a Bloody Mary, thought he'd seen Lyman at the bar; Peyton Miller, with whom Elaine drank rum and grapefruit juice, said she'd seen him and Frank Papen banging practice balls into the tennis court from the first tee. And then she saw him, by the pool, with the Clute brothers, Mickey and M. L., and what's-his-name, the Bulldog coach who always looked sweaty and unstable—all of them in swim trunks which looked as silly as boxer shorts.

"Give me the keys to the car," she said. "I'm bored."

He heard it, she knew—the note in her voice which hinted she
might, as she had done before, stomp her feet and curse and
throw her purse at him.

"Where is your hair?" she wondered when he came to the
fence. "You used to have hair on your chest, and now you don't."

She should stay, he said, it was early. The Clutes were planning a pancake breakfast at their place.

"You are so collapsed," she said, looking at his stomach. "I
mean fallen down. I like men with—what?—pectorals!"

"I'll get dressed," he offered. "I'll go with you."

So she said to him, quietly, to protect his vanity, "If you try, I'll
throw this glass on you and you'll be embarrassed. Now stand up
straight."

"Why are you doing this?"

She took a drink. "Why am I doing what?"

Which led her to tell a joke to those men while the Colonel
went for his pants—a joke they couldn't appreciate because they
were such poops, such clodhoppers, like the Colonel himself,
who had the big mitts of an ape and big feet and smoked like a
coal house and swore at Gary Moore on the TV.

"Don't you worry about me," she said, snatching the keys.
"Daddy said I was a big girl, and I believe him."

So we are brought, she wrote, to the thing we goddam Anglo-
Saxons know rapture is not: mishap, when the world's music is
clamor and din.

She remembered marching across the squishy practice green,
first throwing away those shoes with heels too high to drive with,
and coming to the parking lot, weakly illuminated by one bulb
above the members' entrance to the pool snack shop. The cars
had been parked, it seemed, by the same spirit which controls
Ouija boards and water-witching. "This is what I'm looking for,"
she said, "a brand-new Ford Fairlane 500." She imagined it took
her twenty minutes of wandering through the aisles to find it
wedged between an Oldsmobile and a boat of a Dodge which—"if
objects and possessions in this world do imitate their owners, as I

believe"—belonged to Dottie Hightower, herself windy laughter, ponderous as the tides.

"I had to climb through the window," she wrote, adding that the car still smelled new. She thought of fear, which had a head and a he-man's arms; and briefly she felt the world wobble, then tilt, light itself cockeyed and runny. "Calm down," she told herself. "Say those old-timey things you know: *Mary, Mary, how does your garden grow?*" Trying to start the car, she felt clumsy and sore-hearted, feckless as an orphan. A song came to mind: "Who Does It to You, Me?" There were, surely, one thousand keys to fumble among: for the steamer trunks in the utility room, the garage, the house, the glove box, the back door and one, from the Arrow Lock Corporation, which appeared to belong to a hole infernal and crooked as this life itself. There was a screech too, metal on metal, when she hit the accelerator and jerked the steering wheel, and then there was no sound at all except a lonesome lady's voice from the parking lot, hollering, "Jesus H. Christ."

Rocking back and forth, she swung the wheel wildly, at last ending up facing the wrong way, the front of the car aiming toward a cyclone fence; behind her, she could see the entrance now as dark and distant as sleep. "Okay," she said, "I'll do it this way," and jammed the shift lever into reverse.

"Imagine now," she wrote, "that you, highball in hand, are standing at a second-floor ballroom window and you see what I describe. You are likely to say, 'What the hell is going on?' for there is obvious chaos at ground level, a car going hither and yon at breakneck speeds, some squealing of tires and such horn-honking as is found every day in New York. It is a fascinating display, and maybe you are inclined for a second to think, 'My, this is comedy.' But if you are the kind I imagine, then you are apt, given a peek at the stricken, baffled face behind the wheel, to declare, 'This ain't funny at all.' For what you see is that newish machine, its lights off, swerving too swiftly toward a so-called Immovable Object."

She believed she hit the solid brick posts at thirty-five miles per hour—fast enough that the noise, calamitous and loud as mayhem, took an hour to reach her. She recalled flying backward, the stuff of the world liquid or air. Somewhere she saw a face and a dozen shapes sweep past, tall with the stemlike grace of jonquils. She could hear her heart, heavy with fear. And then, in an instant composed more of surprise than dread, the gate loomed upward, and every joint, from ankle and hip to neck, seemed to lock; and the noise began to reach her, *crunch* and *whang* and *thump* so profound there could have been giants outside pounding on the roof, plus a tempest of glass and something metal— chrome, perhaps—which went *whip, whip, whip* until the radio, glowing weakly, said, *"No more, no more,"* and the harps, the brass *oompah-pah-pah,* and the squeaky woodwinds poured over her like a flood.

Too drunk to be sore, she didn't know how long she lay on the front seat, the motor clanking. She saw herself explaining to the Colonel how this had happened: the late hour, the unwise mixing of spirits, the inconsiderate way the cars were parked, the downright stinginess of mucky-mucks whose responsibility it was to provide enough light so a person—most especially a person unfamiliar with the layout, and ragged of thought—could find her way home. She saw, too, the Colonel standing over her, his face like a martyr's. "I have had an accident," she would say, "and I know why."

So here it opened, that spook-house back door of insight Daddy had spoken of, and she could see herself, a generation older, shrunken as a corpse and whey-faced, curled on a couch as she was drawn up on this front seat: the hour noon, the curtains closed, this person she was to become no more fetching than misrule itself.

"It was an unadorned vision," she wrote. "I was swollen at the belly, glassy-eyed, wearing a nightgown not fit for the Wicked Witch of the West, with skin as waxy as paper."

Elaine was thinking—each thought impossible with wings and scales.

And she was hearing the whisper that eternity, beastly and common, had begun.

—

"So I became a homebody," she wrote, "either a slugabed or industrious as a coolie." Her hair wild with exhaustion, she developed the habit of shaking her fingers near her eyes. Early and late, she drank, and took shorthand from the TV, once hurling at the Colonel a dozen scribbled pages which, she claimed, were *Gunsmoke*, the tragic events especially bold with energy. One night she pitched chicken bones at the living-room clock above the desk. She wound up like Feller or Mr. Don Drysdale, saying, "Strike goddam one!" Hour after long hour, while the Colonel was out playing golf, she listened to Paul Whiteman and Platters records. Woozy with sentiment, she sat cross-legged on the floor, smoking L & Ms. She saw herself jeweled, heavily powdered and smelling of Je Reviens. "Life is better," she sang, "in France, Persia or Heaven." She wrote letters, too—hundreds of them: to Senator Montoya, complaining of injustice and blight in this orb; to her daddy, saying, "I am truly sorry that you are ill, but I can do little here and see where you are as a mist or shade, nothing more"; to Mr. John O'Hara, asking for more of that menace which passed for lust; to Lyman's parents, saying, "Your boy has made Colonel now and looks most splendid when he yells"; and once to Dr. Butler, at St. Paul's: "Maybe you are dead and, if so, how goes it up yonder among the winged many?"

In the summers, wearing a kimono and the overlarge straw hat of a woman named Ida or Fitz, she sat in a chaise in the backyard, drinking. "Oh, I was some gardener in those days," she wrote. She had a trowel and a garden rake and pruning shears; and she wielded them with the fury of defeat itself, snipping at rose and willow, studying seed catalogues and ordering ferns which withered immediately. She watered, and drank Cuba Libres and Screwdrivers, uprooting one bush a dozen times before it looked okay near the patio. Dry as dust, the heat came down hard and thick; and she drank Old-Fashioneds, trying to read about princes, rakehells described as "devilishly handsome" who embraced breathless, shortsighted females. When the Colonel came home, she'd say, "Look up the word *bilious* for me. And *thrall.* My vocabulary needs broadening." Then one afternoon, as she leaned against the back gate, staring into the yard, she said, "I want a swimming pool," falling in love as quickly as thought with words like *glistening* and *ripples.*

"This is how it was," she wrote. "I called up Frank Papen at the bank and said *gimme my money* and he said *what money* and I said *from the mutual funds and have one of your people bring it to me,* and he said *how much,* and I told him *fifteen thousand dollars, please.*" Which caused some fluster and white-collar sputtering, but there it was by midafternoon, a certified cashier's check, nubby as braille—which, she told a contractor named Dupard Epps, was all his if he and his equipment could begin within the hour.

"I want it shaped like a piano," she said, "a grand piano, no diving board, with black and white tile."

When they arrived—several burly sorts with two trucks and a digging instrument she knew now was a backhoe—they found her at the already disassembled gate, pounding happily on the cinder block with the Colonel's hammer. The wall was gouged and deeply hacked. She was a sight, she knew, addled and jittery, as if she'd emerged from a century of sleep. "Pull this old thing down," she ordered. "Which one of you is Mr. Epps?" A short fellow stepped forward; he resembled the kind who counted on his fingers or believed in UFOs. "Well," she began, "you fellows get started, then we'll drink some." Which was when—"As it was meant to happen," she wrote—that the Colonel pulled into the drive in his staff car, an ugly olive-colored heap, and told weak-minded Mr. Epps to go on home, there'd been a mistake.

"Wait," Elaine said, "what about my money?"

She had the check out, waving it, wondering what it took, if not money, to move men and machine to build something as simple as an itty-bitty swimming pool with stairs and rope and, now that she was thinking of it, a cabana so guests could change clothes without having to walk dripping into the kitchen to make a sandwich.

"What're you doing here?" she said. "It's only afternoon, so you're supposed to be someplace else."

He had a miser's face, such as you used to find on walking sticks or umbrella handles.

"Go on," she said, "scoot on out of here."

She could hear roaring from somewhere near, and a crack which sounded like thunder. "Don't mumble," she said. "I was taught to speak up. What'd you say?"

Again he told her: her father had died. A stroke.

And now, as she sat typing this whole story out, she thought, *How convenient, how tidy,* noting how fortune and circumstance had converged at this point to produce tragedy in the faraway place of her youth. Instantly, she became as clear-minded as a judge. She had these thoughts: this is 1967, I am almost forty-six, take me home now. She saw the Colonel standing in the brilliant sunlight. He expected something—hysterics or the rage of a Joan Crawford heroine.

"How do you know?" she said.

"Your sister," he said. "Nobody was answering the phone here."

She felt weightless and numb, fixed at the fierce center of a hundred ragged, freezing winds. Near the fence, on her knees, she began sweeping brick chips into a pile. It was amazing what a hammer could do in the hands of a wounded woman.

"I believe I am meant to do something in this life," she said. "Just what, I don't know."

The next morning, he drove her to El Paso. At the airport, he told her he'd be along in a few days; he was directing an exercise—was it Operation Climate?—he couldn't leave, and someone, maybe the Zants, would have to be found to look after this son she was now addressing. She said "Yes" for the millionth time and tried to ignore the nerve twitching in her neck; and then, while she stood at the gate, waiting to board, it occurred to her—the way, she believed, insight occurred to such genius as she had read about in history: swift as terror and with the same chill—that maybe she wouldn't be coming back to this place.

"Know where I see myself now?" she said. "Aloft and beautiful, that's where."

Which, this son of hers was to know, was the little ding-dong bell that the thing she knew as climax was beginning. It was the part, she wrote, where knowledge was revealed and you felt better facing it. "In the mysteries I read and wonder about, it's the part of shoot-em-ups and fistfights, and you know it's serious because everyone weeps; and what's left is hope or resignation or gob-bledygook only Harvard eggheads fret about. There is time, which is long, and it is filled with hugger-mugger, escapades which aim to delight. Plus, you have a creature to root for, who finds himself in jeopardy, as well as pauses for rumination—all of it unhappy as Christmas in Russia. Imagine. So organized and well said. You get angry words, folks tugging at each other's hair, then the treachery is over and you can go to sleep now—which convinces me that it does require drink to appreciate such neatness." She had figured out drink—which was not woe or pity or such. Drink was charm and magic and everlasting weal. "I know booze," she wrote. "Booze is love—cheap as death and meant for all."

Elaine didn't tell the Colonel she was through when he flew in the following week. She had Mother to worry about, as well as a myriad of details to discuss with the estate lawyer. Condolence cards had to be answered, calls made. Lyman tried to be helpful; he went to her daddy's office and carted home boxes of papers, most of which she threw out. One night he visited his own parents, reading to his father, who was virtually blind now. The Colonel was as polite as a bankrupt pasha, she remembered, begging her pardon and wearing a tie to dinner. He drove her to the pier one day, but the dance house was gone; and he took her on the road to Biddeford. She couldn't get over the trees, towering and plentiful and ancient. One day she went to the beach alone, sitting in the sand for hours, watching the waves. It was cold. The water was always cold.

So she told him then.

"I dressed up as I had for that train ride to Texas," she wrote. "I wore my finest hat and gloves with seed pearls, plus a dress Jackie Kennedy herself couldn't afford now, and I presented myself as Daddy said I ought. Which means that I went to my sister's room, which Lyman was using, and knocked before entering."

He was not sleeping, as she had expected, but reading. Except for the table lamp, there was little light in the room; for a second she believed she was speaking to a ghost.

"I have known you a long time, Lyman," she began. "And you are, mostly, a good person."

She felt as she had years before, when she was making thirty-five dollars a week in Mr. Gray's law firm and there were stars she knew the names of.

"Lyman," she said, "go on home now, please."

She had had a whole speech, at least five minutes of talking (not counting the hems and haws which would appear in the natural course of things), but it was gone now—as these times themselves, careless and omen-filled, were gone.

"In the morning he left," she wrote. "And a couple weeks later, my trunks began arriving from New Mexico, and in the time since then I have not been more than five miles from this desk I sit at now."

She was still a drunk, she wanted her son to know: "Indeed, I am drunk now." She was coming to the end of it now. "I shall be drunk tomorrow, too, and drunk always until I die, for it is by booze that I know myself best." It was booze—the charm and wiles of it—which had sprung her free of the times he was reading about; and it was booze which had given shape to her life, made it an enterprise of the elements he could look forward to in his own—namely, passion and want, and the darkness which imperils it all. "Mister," she wrote, "I want you to drink—and be content in its tender, adult arms."

CATEGORY Z

A T 6 A.M., the sergeant ordered us to board the bus. He spit a lot, called us pansies, ladies, queerbait. He wore his garrison cap like a hoodlum, was built like a hammer and had the whitewall haircut Uncle Sam preferred. He took away our lunches and radios, told us to shut up; this was the Army's day.

"For the next twenty hours," he shouted at us, "you're mine." I looked out the window. We would be going from Lordsburg through Deming and Las Cruces to Fort Bliss, in El Paso, almost two hundred miles of desert, lonely and stark as the moon. "Do nothing, girls, abso-goddam-lutely nothing to make me mad. Am I clear?"

This guy is a joke, I was thinking. He is John Wayne, Sergeant Rock, a dufus.

We were twelve, all Chicanos except for my pal Ray Reed, me, and Cooter Brown, a kid we knew from high school. For some, me among them, this was only "pre-induction," but for others, including Ray Reed and Brown, this was induction itself; we were all 1A, which in 1969, the year some of this takes place, meant what Cooter called Veetnam.

"I ain't going," he said. "No way."

He sat in front of us, and Ray asked what made him so special. The sergeant—Krebs was his name—sat by the driver, drinking coffee from a thermos.

"I got a note," Cooter said.

He unfolded a square of paper—from a Big Chief tablet, I think—and I took a peek. "Dear United States Army," it read. "Please excuse Master Wm. A. Brown from his draft physical. He has ringworm, tetanus, and a little polio. Yours sincerely, Dr. August T. Weems, M.D., Esq." It read like a tardy note at school.

"You wrote this," I said.

His was the smile of a first-time father.

"Damn straight," he said. "Pretty good, huh?"

Ray Reed and I were a lot alike, often excellent in the subjects we liked, and handsome enough to be in love every year, but this boy Cooter was what we called a dweeze, a word for which we knew no synonym in the English that teachers ask for. One month he was fat (put you in mind of the Pillsbury Dough Boy); another, he was skinny. He'd graduated a year before us and worked sometimes as a night irrigator for my father, Avis Buell, who's the pro at our country club. I had also seen Cooter a few times at the Elks lodge, playing drums for Uncle Roy and the Red Creek Wranglers. Cooter had the singing voice of a chicken.

"Between you and me," he was saying, "I gotta know."

"What's that?" I said.

"You scared?"

I'd been reclassified for two months, but this was my first physical and I had a back problem. Besides, I was going to college.

"What about him?"

Next to me, Ray Reed was asleep, his mouth open. He had the expression of a man dreaming about money. Or women. Ray weighed about two hundred, All District (AA) outside linebacker, and had fist-fought Coach Mirmanian during two-a-days last September. He rode cycles—motocross, mostly—and I could think of nothing that frightened him.

"What about you, Cooter? You scared?"

"Hell, no," he said. "This is political, man. I'm a peacenik, honest. What about you, dove or hawk?"

In those days, I'll admit now, I was nothing but a semigrown teenager, a B-minus student, fair in algebra and such world history as we had, a reader of books that made the brain race, and, best of all, a recipient of a full golf scholarship to the University of Houston. I was a lot like the fourteen-year-old son I have now: nice-minded as, say, your first barber and unable to see farther

than the hundred miles I knew here in my desert. I had a love of
the game, a girlfriend named Sally Whittles, a brand-new set of
Arnold Palmer irons, and no larger desire than to be one of those
tanned sportsmen you see on our country's most famous links.

"I'm conscientious," Cooter was telling me. "I'm tapped in—
SDS, Venceremos Brigade, YDF, the whole works. This is
protest, Buell. Jimi Hendrix, Country Joe, Abbie Hoffman, the
Chicago thing—it's a collective, man. We have a common soul."

Sergeant Krebs had turned around.

"Brown," he yelled.

Cooter waved his hand. "Back here."

"Shut your face."

In Las Cruces the bus pulled into the 70-80 truck stop near the
Palms Motel.

"You may use the latrine," Krebs told us. "You may smoke, you
may shoot the breeze. You have fifteen minutes."

In the men's room, Cooter described us as meat, fodder, dog
leavings. He mentioned Che Guevara, Emerson and Thoreau, a
California professor named Marcuse. We heard language like
"proletariat" and "serving class," and listened to what Cooter
knew about corporate crime and about the dread Du Pont was
doing to us.

"Where'd you get all this?" Ray Reed asked.

"Books," Cooter said. "*The New York Times*. I'm radical, man,
an objector."

"Cooter Brown," Ray said, "you're a dipstick."

In the toilet, I could hear Cooter telling a couple of the Chicanos about "the heritage of the oppressed." Like them, he said,
he was disenfranchised, fit for consuming only, a 3-D thing that
ate, slept, and lived in debt. "I'm displaced," he said. "Dis-
possessed, too." His older sister, Francine, was a waitress at the
Ramada Inn—"a victim of sexual politics!" His father, Tully, was
a working stiff, a mechanic at Ellis Lincoln-Ford. "No profit-
sharing," he said. "We're the underkind, boys. We want peace,
am I right?" In the next few minutes, I learned his mother had

died of cancer two years before. He'd had a dog once, a pound breed named Fuzzy, part collie, maybe part sheep—"a big sucker."

After I washed my hands, he dropped his jeans.

"Holy Christ," I said, "what's that?"

The two Chicanos were backing out the door, flabbergasted. I could hear Sergeant Krebs telling Ray Reed a war story that seemed to take place in a Baltimore slum.

"These, my friend," Cooter was saying, "are one hundred per-cent pure India silk, hand-sewn, reinforced-crotch ladies' bikini underpants."

Here it was that a thought came to me and I took one step backward. Indeed, Cooter Brown was scared; he was frightened for his life—and I liked him. There, in one of America's nasty men's rooms, a kid with the high forehead of a comic-book egg-head and the pinched lips of a milksnake, he had seen some-thing—himself, I guess—in a vision, in a nightmare. He had seen himself, I believe, as a smear of blasted flesh, a ruin of himself, a crawling, drooling, weeping thing; and I had this ques-tion: If he's scared, why aren't I?

"Those Army medics," Cooter told me, "are going to take one look at me and throw me out as 4F, count on it. I'm twenty million F, Buell. They're gonna put me in the Z category, as positively undesirable as a human can be."

Back on the bus, Ray Reed sat by himself on the seat behind Krebs. They were having a conversation that involved rope and what man is.

"What's *his* problem?" Cooter asked me.

"He's a patriot." I remember trying to make the word sound sensible. "He wants to get out of town, see other places. His recruiter told him he could go to Germany, Greece."

Just south of Las Cruces, where I-10 lay out flat and straight on the mesa above the Mesilla Valley, Cooter asked if I smoked reefer.

"Sure," I said. "A little Mexican weed."

"I had some this morning," he said. "Pure Colombian. Really screws up the coordination."

Up front, Ray Reed was laughing with Krebs, so I told Cooter about my back, how I'd had five vertebrae fused when I was in the ninth grade. I'd been in a car wreck on the way to the Phoenix Open with my father.

"I did some speed, too," Cooter whispered. "That's why I'm blabbing so much. My blood pressure's gonna ring bells."

I was thinking about my girlfriend, Sally Whittles, and where we might be in ten years, when Cooter told me what was in his overnight bag. Candy, he said. M&Ms, Mars bars, Three Musketeers. "Gets the blood sugar up," he said. "They'll think I'm diabetic. A certified vampire."

I'd heard they kept you overnight, I said.

"I'll be blind," he told me, rolling his head and slapping the seat. "I won't talk. I'll French-kiss somebody, a general."

For the next hour, Cooter went on about the things he'd do— spit in his urine sample, masturbate, grab ass—but I was watching the landscape, the scrub-covered Franklin Mountains on the left and that part of my world on the right that went on parched and white and lit up forever. I couldn't imagine Vietnam. The TV I watched made it seem unbelievably lush—too green and wet and noisy. It was Oz, I thought. It was old, and full of murder. Mr. Cronkite said its people believed in tree spirits. It rained, plants had souls, and in it were 500,000 young people like me that I was glad I would not join.

About nine-thirty, we reached the outskirts of Fort Bliss, and Cooter rose up in his seat. Outside stood ranks and ranks of barracks, wooden and identical, no place at all to live. We could see signs with official lettering that made no sense as language. We rolled by an obstacle course—hurdles, tires, barbed wire— and Cooter tapped me on the shoulder.

"I don't think I can do it, Archie."

He might have been ready to cry, and I knew what he was talking about.

"I know what's gonna happen," he said. "They're gonna tell me to jump and I'm gonna say 'How high?' I ain't political, Archie. I'm a wuss."

Sweat was running down his temples.

"What about the panties?"

He shook his head. "Took 'em off," he said. "They're Francine's, my sister."

We turned a corner, and a group of recruits—a platoon, maybe—came into view, marching and chanting about gore and how happy they were to be sons-of-bitches.

"Jerks," Cooter sighed.

It was uttered the way you and I say "Amen" in church, half swallowed and not at all encouraged; but I didn't hear any more until the bus stopped and Krebs, calling us females, told us to grab our gear and get out.

—

You could say my day turned out fine. A doctor with freckles named Finkel took one look at me, told me go away. I was putting on my sneakers when Ray Reed found me. "I'm in," he said.

"What about Brown?"

Ray didn't know. I'd heard Cooter's voice a couple times. He was saying "Yes, sir" with real enthusiasm.

"Here," Ray Reed said, a key in his hand. "You take my bike. "I'm gonna stay, they can have me now."

And that was it. I went home that evening, me and a few Chicanos who were missing fingers or had the misfortune to be deeply ignorant, and in time I put aside most of the foregoing. That fall, I left for Houston, playing three years on the golf team, then went to Florida for PGA school. I took a month qualifying, but got my A card, played on the satellite tour in Honduras and Guatemala, twice in Mexico City.

Only once did I hear from Ray Reed. In his letter, he spoke of Army Mickey Mouse and where he wanted to be in the next life. Every day, he said, was as lousy as the last.

As everyone expected, Sally Whittles and I married, and after my dad put together a syndicate of club men—Dr. Weems, Buzz King, Freddy Newell—I spent two years trying to make a living as a professional. At the Tallahassee Open, I won enough for a new Buick and real meal money; in 1973, I qualified for the U.S. Open at Winged Foot but didn't make the cut. Then, following my father's heart attack, I came back here, to Lordsburg, to be the assistant pro. I sold cardigans, NuTonic spikes, gave lessons, bought a house near the course and thought little about Ray Reed and Cooter Brown.

Ray must have been back about a month when I saw him at the Labor Day party at the club. He was working for his dad on their ranch north of town.

"Still got the Yamaha?" he asked me.

He was thinner, losing hair at the temples, no lines at all in his face to say what he'd seen, what he'd done.

"Yes," I told him. I hadn't ridden much but kept the cycle in good repair. "It's in my garage. When you gonna come by?"

"Soon," he said, "real soon."

He didn't turn up, of course. A year went by. And another. And sometimes, I'd go out in the garage, start up his cycle, lose myself in the racket it made. In high school, we'd been best friends. We'd partied together, cruised Main Street, even lost our cherries to the same Juárez whore. One summer we'd gone to Pacific Beach in San Diego, took Ray's old Nash. We had known each other since first grade, and now that was all gone. So one Saturday I bought a helmet, gloves, and steel-toed boots for my son, Eric, and took him into the desert to show him how to ride fast and not get hurt.

Then Cooter Brown appeared.

I was on the practice tee, trying to keep Mrs. Baird's right elbow from flying out on her backswing, when I saw a guy by the door to the men's locker. It was late afternoon, the sunlight sharp and white enough for the hell a bad God might have, and for a time, while Mrs. Baird flung herself at a bucket of balls, I kept my mouth shut and wondered who it was.

I thought about my wife, Sally, and how she looks waking up, sleep-soaked and radiant. I listened to the wind, saw the contrail of a plane miles overhead and wondered if I was cold and only alone.

Who are you? I asked myself. Who are you now?

I told Mrs. Baird she could finish by herself—"head down," I said, "tuck that elbow"—and walked toward that man in the sunlight.

"Cooter Brown," I said. "Long time."

He had the well-cut hair and square shoulders of someone who is very proud now.

"William," he said. "I'm called William now, or Will."

I had my hand out for a shake and he took it.

"Ray Reed said you'd be out here. You're doing all right, he says."

There were fifteen cars in the lot and I could hear Casper Lutz in the pro shop singing a ballad he liked. I felt awkward, stupid as a cow, and wanted to apologize for the too-colorful clothes I wore.

"I'm in Hollywood now," he said, "flying choppers." The Army had made him a warrant officer, given him a million jobs to do in the air. He had the touch, he said. The aptitude, the facility. A superior sense of equilibrium, good eyes, poise. Now he was flying stunts for the movies. TV and commercials too.

"You ever see *Reruns*? Or *Going Away*?"

I said no, then he told me Ray Reed was going to meet us at the Grange, a bar on Ormond.

"You knew Ray over there?"

"Some," he said. "Ray was at Tay Ninh for a time. We were tight."

At the bar, I called Sally, said I'd be home late.

"What's wrong, Archie? You sound weird."

Except for Cooter, me and the bartender, Jimmy Sample, the place was empty, and I had nothing to look at but the scribbling on the wall by the pay phone. I saw the names of some I knew, and I felt as I had when I stood over a five-foot birdie putt I knew I would not sink.

"You remember Cooter Brown?" I asked.

"The guy in the panties?"

He was standing by the jukebox. He would play something twangy, I thought. A tune a Nashville cowboy had invented about bad love.

"I'm having a drink with him now."

"Oh," she said, and that was all until I said goodbye.

Ray Reed walked in about eight, and he and Cooter made a little war noise saying hello. We had a table in the corner, from which we could see the Grange fill up and grow smoky.

"How's your dad?" Ray wondered.

"Good," Cooter told him. "Gonna retire in three years. Francine's in Albuquerque, married to a guy named Wilson. Got two kids."

We drank to that and to several other things in the next hour— good health, money, having women—then they told Vietnam stories. I heard about a black corporal named Philly Dog and a place called LZ Thelma. Some names I recognized: DMZ, Westmoreland, Saigon. But most were unfamiliar, private: First Corinthians, the Battle of Bob Hope, Firebase Maggie. Ray Reed told about life in II Corps, how the land lay, what you sweat when you heard the wrong sound in the wrong place at the wrong time. Cooter Brown told about his remarkable life in the skies—descent, rotor wash, skids, China Beach. Once they toasted a woman named Madam Q.

"Right on," Ray Reed said.

"You bet your ass," Cooter said.

Many beers later I told them I'd been a rabbit.

"What's that?" Cooter asked.

It was a golfer, I said, who showed up on Monday to qualify for the few open spots in the tournament that began on Thursday. "I played with Jack Nicklaus once," I said, "at the Kemper."

"I'll drink to that," Cooter said, and I went on. I liked being married, I said, being a father. And for a time, as I talked and in a way I can't explain, I felt the years had fallen away between them and me. It was practically spiritual, I think now, as if, as kids do, I could say anything and wishing would make it so. I felt dumb, too—dumb as are lucky men when the jackpot comes their way for the second time.

Then Ray Reed said he was going home.

"Take care," Cooter told him.

"You too," Ray said. "Good to see you."

Cooter's Chrysler was large and had every gadget he could afford—power windows, automatic door locks, a computer that figured how far you could go on the gas you had. On the way to my house, he played the tape deck, rock 'n' roll, particularly a song that rhymed, in a manner I thought wonderful, "docket" and "rocket." Cooter told me he knew lots of actors—Lee Majors, Fess Parker, the guy who played Batman.

"California," he said. "Party state, Arch. You ought to come out."

He was nervous, embarrassed, and I didn't want to say much until I said adios.

"Turn here," I told him, and in a few minutes we stopped outside my house. A light was on in the garage.

"I did the right thing," Cooter said.

A few doors down the block, the Risners were having a party, and for an instant I wanted to be there with the two men on the porch. They held drinks and were looking eastward with smiles.

"You want to come in," I asked. "Say hello?"

He held a cigarette he didn't seem to enjoy.

"Your wife's Sally, right?"

The two men on the porch were joined by another who looked just as content.

"I remember her," Cooter said. "You're lucky, Arch."

He had more he wanted me to know, and for the longest time, while the men went inside, I waited to hear it. I aimed to count stars and attend to what my heart was doing, but for some reason—perhaps because of the moon we had and the blackness everywhere—I thought about Sergeant Krebs and the war he'd be fighting next.

"I'm a prole, Archie," Cooter told me at last. "I do what I'm told."

Then he left, and I had my indoors to look forward to.

—

There is a moment in golf, as there must be in other sports, or what in life sports stand for, when you strike the ball with such authority and accuracy that you know it will be where you planned it to be. I have described it to Sally as a moment of purest intelligence—poetry, if you will—when nothing at all stands between you and what you imagine. It is more mystic than what gurus practice, and often more religious than the state of mind Baptists have. More than luck, it is a peacefulness—whole as we think love to be—and, for a time, it is able to spread its shine to all you do thereafter. It is the way I felt, in the year this occurs, when I walked down the hall in my house to find my son, Eric, in the garage.

"What's the matter?" I said.

Spread out, in a pattern that would make you say a Buell had done it, were dozens of parts from Ray Reed's motorcycle.

"It was misfiring pretty bad today," Eric said. "Besides, it needed cleaning."

"Kind of late, don't you think?"

He was scrubbing part of the clutch assembly with an old toothbrush and turpentine, and doing a good job.

"Yeah," he said. "I'll put this away."

"Never mind," I told him. "I'll do it."

I waited until he went inside before I sat in the midst of the parts of Ray Reed's motorcycle. The party at the Risners' was breaking up, nothing would be on TV, and it seemed suddenly that I had a lot of time. Working the rest of the night, I believed I could get the Yamaha back together. Then tomorrow—or the next day, or the day after that—I could take it south in the desert, toward Hatchita, maybe twenty miles. I'd have a helmet, work boots, a jacket, and I'd see how fast I could go getting back.

THE WORLD IS ALMOST ROTTEN

T HE man who killed my father was Tommy Cruse (middle initial R for Reese), but when I knew him years ago he was calling himself Mr. Birdie on account of ways Daddy once called divine but unseemly. He slew my daddy as sure as it was dirty Bob Ford who plugged Jesse James: It was a deed accomplished not with pistol nor shiny blade nor fine piano wire, but with, metaphorically speaking, a number-nine Wilson Pro Staff stiff-shaft, leather-grip golf iron and a swing my momma remembers even now as quote wanton with miracle unquote.

Lori Ann, to whom I told this story again last night for the ten thousandth time, thinks I am a bore on the subject, Daddy having died only last year and Tommy Cruse well out of my life for twenty. She said that, notwithstanding my Rice University BA in history (not to mention my decade as a legitimate adult, my half-dozen years as a member of the legal profession in the enchanted state of New Mexico, my tidy haircut, my overall handsomeness and holdings in useful real estate), if I believed there was any connection between Event A in 1960 and Event B in 1981, then she was a fool for having married me, and I a nincompoop you could find any day of the week picking at his earhole and listening for the galaxial whispers of Venutians.

She was the sort, she said, who believed that glory lay down one path, madness down another, and that if I didn't put aside the themes of golf, competition among linksters, disappointment, death and the poetic connection among them, then she was going to pack her nighties, gather up my daughters Beth Ann and Viola, hop into that Volvo I paid too much for and spend her remaining years of vigor and good looks in the company of her own daddy, E. G., and that tall work of manhood who lived in the house across the fence. Now, she wondered, how would I like that?

I was dumbstruck. "Once more," I said, "I'm working on the abridged version."

"Do you know what this is?" She had her little fist up under my nose and the light she gets in her eyes when the cleaning lady talks long distance to Panama.

I told her not to get worked up; that after this last time, I'd become, once again, upstanding in every regard, that sober-minded, dutiful, Presbyterian TKE she fell in love with during Greek Week. I'd be anything—lapdog, vigilant sentinel like the Queen has, baboon with a tie and human charm; we could go to Aruba as she wanted, buy that talking microwave, switch circle of friends, if she'd only, just this once, let me address again how it can happen in America, a land properly known for its plenty and righteousness and fair play, that a club-wielding Texan of considerable muscle and vast personal appeal can sashay into a youngster's home, win the approval of his momma, and then turn his daddy into a sniveling, sobbing blob on the fourteenth green of a country club inaugurated by Mr. Tommy Bolt himself and blessed by the commissioner of the United States Golf Association!

"Jesus, Lamar," she said. "Sometimes I'd like to pull your face off."

Then she stormed inside, where I heard packing and leaving noises.

———

Tommy Cruse waltzed into my daddy's home on one of those scorching afternoons that our desert in August is feared for. He shook my hand like a pugilist, called me "Tiger" and "Bub," said he'd heard all about me from the Colonel, and gave me a dollar to lug his suitcase into the guest room. I told him that my name was Lamar Michael Hoyt, Jr., age thirteen, a seventh-grader at Alameda Junior High School, where I achieved excellence in every endeavor, particularly fused English and Chinese tumbling.

"You don't say." He showed me wrestling esoterica which left a welt on my forearm.

He was wearing drugstore flip-flops, peachy-salmon golf slacks, and had the hairdo now worn by people who don't believe in such fundaments as work and steadfastness. Which put my middle-aged mother into a fit of girly affectation and flirtatiousness, Mr. Tommy Cruse being, she maintained, the first and best born of swarthiness and matinee swank. Oh, she was—figuratively speaking—all over him that afternoon, fetching him a Tom Collins and Fritos, admiring his teeth and pointing out, by way of conversation, the pedigree of certain knickknacks, including my grannie's collection of flatirons. She said how pleased she was that he was to be our house guest for this week of the Las Cruces Country Club Invitational, and what a distinct thrill it was to have a fellow Texan around so the two of them could discuss Mr. Royal's Longhorns and what she was calling the red-clay vistas of eternity.

"Good Lord," I was whispering.

She told him everything about us—how I'd had a birthmark on my back, which had to be burned off with dry ice; where my daddy really went on those trips to the Fourth Army Golf Tournament in San Antonio; which banditos her own father had killed when chasing that brigand Pancho Villa with Uncle John Pershing; what qualities she looked for in a helpmate, specifically forthrightness and no frugality of spirit; and how bridge was her game, but, if need be, she could deal canasta, poker, spades, her having (don't you know?) soft hands and a deft manner of fingering.

"Hey," I put in once, "let's eat."

Momma looked at me like I had an intestinal goober on my new shirt.

"Don't you have someplace to be, Lamar?" She smiled the

whole time, her teeth wet like an angry dog's. "Get Mr. Cruse a napkin, he's knocked his goody off."

It was like that for an hour, the three of us on the patio staring into a fierce and extreme sunset, my momma talking about Cuba and some Uruguayan buckaroos she'd met on a cruise ship named *El Fronterizo* while my daddy, the Colonel, was supervising the loading of a—what was it, Lamar?—yes, a deadly arsenal of war-making materiel. She mentioned my Aunt Tilly from Brownfield, the one whose dog Sylvester fell in the outhouse, and some cousins I didn't know I had who were in the employ of a Sells-Floto circus out of Ottawa, Canada.

Through it all, Mr. Cruse smiled and let fly with a profile or two, eating fish snacks with the industry of a coal miner. He had style, I'll admit, plus posture and a firm handshake and the well-shined heel of a gentleman; I'm sure that Momma thought that if I at Mr. Cruse's age—about twenty-six, I reckoned—had a smidgen of his confidence and maybe half of his savoir faire (which, I figured then, was French for smarty-pants!), then maybe there was a merciful God. Me, I wanted to vamoose, go to the club for the Calcutta, learn how much Daddy had sold for. Momma, of course, recalls none of this, but her face does grow pink at the mention of you-know-who, and you can tell that her thoughts are as tight as new thread.

My daddy came in around seven, having been on the missile range watching a splendid piece of Uncle Sam's technology rip the bejesus out of several used tanks. "Tommy," he yelled, standing at the sliding glass doors in his khakis, "you lowdown sumbitch!"

Mr. Cruse leaped to his feet in a wink, grinning. "Colonel, you asshole, you!"

I told Lori Ann once that everybody used to talk that way. Friends, especially. Why, I said once, at my daddy's fiftieth-birthday party I heard a roomful of his most bosom buddies refer to him and themselves as no-account, shiftless, rootless, bootless, butt-kicking, dick-stepping shitkickers. And the night of the Cal-

cutta, while I stood with Momma in the section reserved for
females and offspring, and the golfers and their syndicates
crowded around the blackboard which was used to record the
money amounts each man in the Championship Flight was auc-
tioned for, I heard the MC, Dr. Elwood Weems, refer to his own
brother, Woody, as a dried flapjack of cow vomit.

Around ten-thirty, my daddy was introduced.

"Gentlemen, if I could have your attention, please!" You could
barely see Dr. Weems through the smoke and the people standing on cocktail tables. "It is my pleasure to introduce a gent you
all know, four times Club Champion, an ace with the short game,
Old Automatic himself, Colonel Lamar Hoyt!"

Daddy was wearing his pink shirt with the black polka dots, an
item you're now likely to find on a dead New Yorker named
SuperFly or Spoon; but then he looked fine and omnipotent, a
figure which moved my momma, standing in the back, to open
the bidding at two hundred fifty dollars. ("Jesus," she's told me
since, "I dearly loved your daddy in that nasty outfit, made me
want to rhumba or something untoward.")

At six hundred dollars, my daddy did a hucklebuck to a tune
J. Wilson Newell played on the piano, a melody which ended
with a severe run of Chopsticky tinkles and boom-boom that left
my daddy's eyeballs thyroid.

"Shake it, Colonel!" Mr. Cruse yelled one time. "Can you believe it, folks, I am that uncivilized man's guest!"

In the back, between my momma and Mrs. Geist, I was hop-
ping and clapping with each bid, my heart banging like a fish in a
tub. At seven hundred fifty, Dr. Weems catalogued my daddy's
virtues, which were, namely, good sportsmanship, an accurate
drive, a lover's touch from the froghair, a funny way of saying
"car" and "far" (on account of his upbringing in the foreign country of Hanover, New Hampshire), ability to drive home backward—"And soaking wet!" Momma hollered—and a wooden
putter with a solid brass head and its own teeny-tiny knit cover.

"Show us that swing," someone called, and in an instant my

daddy was smacking a dozen pro-shop Maxflis through an open window into the parking lot.

"Anyone here," Dr. Weems called, "own a Chrysler sedan with four broken windows?"

At one thousand dollars, my daddy flung the window shade from his shoulders, hushed the crowd with a wave of his hand and begged to be snatched from this toilsome earth now that he'd glimpsed the promised land. Though he was only play-acting, doing an act Lori Ann has since seen me do a dozen times, he put a tear in his eye, threw phlegm into his throat and offered up a prayer to all the forces, wrathful and morbid, saying that the only thing which stood between him and the vale was the desire to be crowned champion of the entire English-speaking universe.

"Folks," Dr. Weems said, his voice squealing over the scratchy PA, "I am touched. Here, look." He had his shirt open, one pasty, hairless breast quivering and sweaty.

At eighteen hundred and sixty-five dollars—"samolians," Daddy called them—the bidding ended, Colonel Hoyt the property of a syndicate which included the Motley brothers, Onan and Dorcey, R. C. "Buck" Holloway, and the president of the First National Bank, Frank O. Papen (known to my momma as "Duke" on account of his affiliation with wealth and position). I was on my daddy's shoulders, having been brought forward by Mr. Cruse as proof of something, prodigiousness maybe. This was one of the three or four moments of consequence in my entire life (the others being the movie *Psycho* at age fifteen and my first dip into the comforts of a willing female), moments when everything past is revealed as gross and the future opens up to you as a thing of awesome delight.

So there I sat, holding my daddy's ears, Mr. Cruse's Ben Hogan golf hat flopped down over my brow, while in front of us, in front of the raised bandstand, everybody—merchant, linkster and comely companion—was shouting and clapping, shaking a fist in mirth, or hollering, that ballroom a place of frenzy and hoopla, smoke rolling like thunderclouds. It was a time, I've told Lori

Ann, of miracle and profundity, and I felt like another—a Mr. Dante, in fact—hunting for and suddenly finding his purpose in a lower circle of hades. Yes, I've said often, I was staring into the faces, multiplied many times, of Greed, Sloth and Envy. There, from my perch, my heart in a renegade flip-flop of joy and mystery, my ears deafened by bluster, I was eyeball to eyeball with Avarice and Lust, not to mention Dopey, Sleepy, Happy and Doc.

Unfortunately, I missed the tournament that year, being laid low by what Momma called Fevers and Fun, all in excess, but which Lori Ann still calls a goofy male hysteria, a malady fetched up by my subconscious—a sneaky thing, as she imagines it, which dresses up human disasters in either illness or ignorance. I was dizzy and nauseous for days, stuck in bed, my dreams full of moil in a Dark Land. That first afternoon, I lay shivering and sweaty, trying to read in the lives of Blackbeard and Davy Crockett, adventures on the bounding main and fearful frontier usually being enough for me in the way of finding and conquering.

I couldn't concentrate. I kept imagining Daddy on the first tee, quick and accurate, his backswing as precise as riflery. Before sundown, my momma came home in a dither, looking like she'd emerged from the sea bottom, her hair wild with exhaustion.

"What a day," she kept saying. "Sometimes you just can't understand the upper crust, you know?"

Plopping into my easy chair, she shook her head in that thoughtful manner movie heroines like Bette Davis use when they spot a human leaving the fine climate of the straight and narrow for the tempests of the wide and wicked. She told me there was a screw-up with the tee times, and Reverend Tilberry—the kind of Methodist a large dog might make—fired the starting gun too soon, which resulted in a pair of misfortunes: a panicky scramble among the duffers and a wound to T. L. Fountain's heiny runny enough to require Blue Cross.

"How'd Daddy do?" I wondered.

Plus, she said, there was an episode at the scorer's tent involv-

ing a strange Amarillo adolescent and the woman who was supposed to be, but was in fact not, his aunt. "Lorene Grady thought
it was incest," Momma said, smoothing my covers and plugging
my mouth with the thermometer. "I thought it was pure affection, May to September."

In the other room I could hear ice tinkling and related highball
noises. It was Mr. Tommy Cruse putting himself in front of the
TV.

For five more minutes Momma went on, telling me about
Señor Martin Mendoza of Carta Blanca beer, who found himself
in a mesquite tree on the dogleg of the sixth hole and, in the
process, revealed himself to be no caballero at all; and about
Frank Redman, who spit on a short dark lady who mentioned
something about J. C. Penney flatware during an achingly evil
cross-grain putt on the fourth; and about, finally, Judge Clarence
P. Sanders, strolling forth in Bermudas, his face inflamed with
George Dickel, who delivered a lecture about the future from the
lip of the ninth-hole bunker and who, when he came to the part
about reservedness and fecklessness and sudden dispatch,
turned a nearly Hebraic pink and pitched forward flat out, his
last utterances lost in the natural muffling of three feet of spe-
cially sifted Rio Grande bottom sand.

I plucked out the thermometer. "How'd Daddy do?"

"Won," she said, offering me a Saltine. "The man he played
was a disgrace, pure shame. Your daddy had—I believe the
phrase is—his mojo working."

I had finished a dozen crackers when my daddy came in.
Momma had straightened up, throwing open my cowboy curtains and bringing me two paperbacks she'd gotten from her
sister—torrid epics with cover art which suggested action and
male–female gristlework.

"Don't say anything." Daddy looked like he'd forgotten his wallet or his own birthday. "I'm thinking that today was not my day."

He went around my room twice, stopping at last at my dresser,
opening the top knickknack drawer, which was packed with kid

junk—gum and change, plus a couple pounds of baseball cards. He still had his spikes on, a mistake I'd never see him make again, and there was alarm in the air, as if the pressures which held all things fast were diminishing; I imagined that everything underneath me, floor to center of the earth, was shifting, falling away.

"I'm thinking about quitting," he said.

The other time I'd hear those notes in his voice would be years later when he'd tell me that Momma was divorcing him and moving to Dallas to be with her sister.

"I'm fifty-five years old," he was saying, "and I believe I shot my wad out there." Oh, he said, he hit the ball fine. Old Automatic, all right. But short—always short, his opponent a kid with heft and disturbing club velocity. He'd spent the whole damn afternoon running after this kid, Daddy said. Whacking and banging and gritting his teeth—"Dentures, actually," he said, showing me. Every hole was the same: thwack, then *boom,* the former being my daddy's polite way of winning championships, the latter being what happens when you give a Visigoth a college education. "Only reason I won," he said, "was on account of my intelligence." It was that old story, he said, of age giving way to youth, experience being nothing to those of beef and oomph.

Watching him squeeze my kneecaps, I felt confused. "How'd Mr. Cruse do?"

Immediately all the colonelcy returned to his eyes—which is to say he looked as smug as a young hood in a red Buick.

"The dumb shit lost," he laughed. "Let me tell you something, Lamar. Only two things a man shouldn't do on the eve of competition, and one of them is blind himself on Mossy Wade's private stock." He stood, grinning. "The urp which came out of that boy destroyed several square yards of expensive bent grass. You remember that."

I said I would; and Daddy left my room in that same state of animation I left Lori Ann years later when, after an hour of toe-scratching and bush-beating, she said yes and evermore and yes again.

—

As it happened, I missed the tournament the following year too, having been sent to the Church of the Covenant Mountain Retreat, a Baptist summer camp for youngsters which featured—in declining order of importance—swimming, horseback riding, nature trails, softball and a forty-foot concrete statue of a humble, semiblind Jesus. I was fourteen then, well into puberty, my body like a chicken, all legs and wings. I had pimples and bad breath and enough face hair to look sullen. Plus, I was rebellious, having developed a walk, a world view and a supercilious lip curl that all but guaranteed me a place, Momma was convinced, on the same bench with Richard Speck and those Latin hoodlums who drooled after Natalie Wood in *West Side Story*. I told Lori Ann once that this was the warm-up stage to college existentialism, me being the sort drawn equally to murder and love. "I was one of those melancholy, disaffected strangers," I said. "I was putting aside tradition and standard, taking up the cudgel of selfhood, me that lone figure on the horizon, dressed in black, my mind made simple by doom and the courage to act against it."

"Oh, Lamar," she said that night, holding my cheeks, her own eyes scornful and dark, "blow it out your ear."

So, there I was, on a mountaintop in northern New Mexico, pineyness and rusticness my companions, my days given over to brooding and outwitting the preachers and counselors, a group of vigilant hombres swollen with goodness. These guys looked like lumberjacks, their outfits woolly and checkered and ascetic, their campfire harangues holy-word ghost stories plot-heavy with miracle and subterfuge that always seemed to serve the needs of downtrodden tribes besieged by bearded and cloaked peoples led by men named Joachim and Levy.

"I'm miserable," I told my daddy when he called a few days

before the tournament. "I'm up at six—they play this hymn over
the PA, 'Come Unto My Bosom, Shepherds of the Meek'—and it's
washing with the Lord and toweling off with the Lord and putting your tennies on with the Lord—"

"You know how much I'm paying for that place," he said.
"Shit, Lamar, that's my Biscayne money you're living on."

I told him about my cabinmates, in particular Pee Wee King,
who could imitate the voices of Daffy Duck and Yosemite Sam,
and this Colorado teenager named Marty who preferred the
name Slick but had his heart set on ministry to the natives of
Bogotá.

"With him," I said, "it's nothing but Spanish—morning, noon
and night. He calls me El Poyo del Mundo. It's a joke."

"Buck up, Lamar," he said, then told me a Korea story which
featured gunfire, epic cold and a horde of unhappy yellow people—the point of which was to remind me of my good fortune
and how much my butt would hurt if I didn't shape up and fly
right.

A few days later, Momma called, saying Mr. Cruse was in
town, fresh from a victory in Borger, Texas, over an International
Harvester mechanic named E. P. Bullard. "Guess what, Lamar?"

I was taking the call in the administration building, around me
a bustle of religious activity. The camp was getting ready for a
guest preacher from Rock, Kansas, a man whose pictures, tacked
on the bulletin board, put you in mind of theft. Plus, I could hear
my roommate Marty standing at the door of our cabin a few yards
away, hollering for the advent of a new era of plague and disquiet.

"I can't hear you, Momma."

"Mr. Cruse," she was saying. "He got married!"

Next to me, waiting to use the phone, a kid with a criminal look
was beating himself on the chest, mumbling about earth, wind
and fire.

"Hold on, Lamar," Momma said, "I'll put her on."

Next thing I was talking to a woman named Bonnie Jean La

Rue who described herself as beauteous, bred for the ruling class and a recent graduate of the Beaumont School for Girls in El Paso. (In a month, I'd see a Kodak of her; she was a bosomy redhead with an Elvis Presley haircut, a face which would look fine in a Texaco girly calendar.)

"How they hanging, boy?" she said. "You're missing a big do. Last night it was Uncle Roy and his Red Creek Wranglers. Tonight there's a magician. I'm to be sawed in half."

In the background I could hear Momma telling the only joke she knew, about the blind Apache and his three squaws.

Mr. Tommy Cruse came on the line next, describing how he'd been hither and yon in the last year, played the sand greens of Nebraska and positively crunched an Iowa corn farmer named Marv Gaiterswell by playing lefty. "Oh, by the way, thanks for the loan of your room. I got Bonnie Jean in there right now."

You could hear screeching and maybe a sentence or two.

Beside me, that criminal-looking kid was muttering about vengeance and doom everlasting.

"I got to go now, Mr. Cruse."

"Okay, boy," he said. "We won't break nothing."

That week I called home every night, getting the news from Momma or the new housekeeper, Mrs. Ling. I was jubilant. Though removed from the action, lost in a herd of darksome Christians, I knew my daddy would do well. There's no explaining this phenomenon, no logic. Sometimes a person just knows: his hair stands up, he gets gooseflesh; life becomes sensible; and normal smuts and confusions, everyday doodahs, drop away like old skin.

I told Pee Wee King, on the night Daddy qualified for the Championship Flight, that over two hundred miles away from us, at that very minute, sense was being made where there had been none, order was being asserted and a bridge like the Golden Gate was being flung over the famous gulf of oblivion. He shook his head mournfully, read me a verse from Corinthians in the voice of Porky Pig, and backed out the door like a banker tiptoeing from a scene of carnage and outrage.

The next night, Mrs. Ling told me that Mr. Cruse had lost in the second round, but my daddy, playing in his Ricky Ricardo outfit of gold trousers and red NuTonics, was moving into the semis. I felt like virtue itself, shriven and charmed. Momma told me about Wes Hightower doing a half-gainer from the high dive and Mrs. Talmadge Best being stung by wasps and two Mexican caddies named Tito and Memo stealing Nelson Popp's four iron during the fireworks. "Tommy and Bonnie Jean are gone," she said. "I got your windows open right now. That place smells flat athletic." So, every night, while Reverend T. L. Fishback read us a sermon or played his harmonica version of "His Works Shall Praise Him at the Gates" over the PA, I lay in bed giggling with mirth. My mind, I've told Lori Ann, was a place of rare airs and tinkling waters, its musics martial and glorious.

The evening of the finals, when this visiting reverend (name of Irvin, Monte H.) was thrashing in the pulpit, his sermon having swept those around me up on a tide of fury and resolve, I sneaked out of the tabernacle and crept through the unlocked window of the administration building. You could hear Pee Wee King scorning pulchritude in the voice of Tweety Bird, the reverend himself hoarse with mightiness; and outside, vigilant and gray-faced, stood that four-story Jesus, lit by floodlights, the whole world at his concrete feet.

It took a long time for anyone to answer the phone, and when Mrs. Ling came on I had to tell her to speak up, there being in the background the kind of noises revelers make when the hale meet the fit and the hearty open their pocketbooks.

"Oh, big damn night!" Mrs. Ling was hollering. "Everything here all monkey and Chubby Checkers." There must have been sixty people in the house, she said, all fatsos with happy faces, plus women like Grace Kelly. "I get Colonel-san," she said. "Everything much gusto."

If there is a point to this life, I was thinking, it had to be about glee and those tidy machines, people, who thrived on it.

"Hello, son of mine," he said. You knew he had six hours of expensive liquor in him.

"You won," I said.

"It was sweet, Lamar. Your momma said I looked like General MacArthur wading out of seawater."

I knew it, I said.

"That fellow knew it was a pure pleasure to have his pants beat off by a work such as me."

I felt clean, wise and special, as if I had just been dropped from an advanced, more tolerant universe. I told him I was proud and I would go anywhere, prison even, live as an exile among a population of mean-spirited forgers and burglars, if it meant that every summer he'd spend a certain Sunday evening, in one hand a highball and in the other a gleaming brass trophy, celebrating what happens when the deserved reap their rewards. Send me to Leavenworth or old rat hole in New Delhi, I said, it was worth it to me. I was so excited, my heart in my ears, that I didn't even mind the Baptist dread bellowing up from the tabernacle.

"Honest, Daddy," I was saying, "I'll pay you back. You get that Biscayne."

"You're a fine person," he said. "And I do love you."

Then, as they say at the Rialto Theater on Saturday afternoons, it happened.

"Daddy, I'm gonna go now."

"What's wrong, Lamar? What's the matter with your voice?"

"Nothing," I said. "Honest."

Lori Ann thinks I have made up the following because it's a topheavy, symbolic moment which appeals best to the clumsy and aimless. But I am telling the truth; for it was at that instant, as I was peering up at that monumental Jesus, my thoughts warm and fragrant, that it moved—shimmered, almost—one of its huge eyes winked and kept doing so, even after my momma came on the line to tell me the gossip she'd picked up from Mrs. Levisay and Ella Sweem; it was winking, sly like a movie-magazine opium smoker, even when Mrs. Ling said bye-bye, hot damn party, all stuff on fan; it was still winking, even when the line went dead and the only voices I heard in that clear night

were Sylvester the Cat's on the theme of wantonness and the
Reverend Monte H. Irvin's on the dogpath to heaven, a place
without smite, murrain, or flies.

—

The next year Tommy Reese Cruse returned. Alone. "Divorced,"
he said. Bonnie Jean had been an impediment, something that
came between him and his gifts. He had a new diet, too: fruits,
berries, nuts. "Put that Falstaff away, Colonel," he'd say. "Hell,
you're an old dude, you ought to know better." He'd shucked that
female like a man avoiding plague.

That afternoon, he stood under the upright willow in our backyard, chipping nearly one hundred practice balls into a bucket
he'd set some distance away.

"What makes him do that?" I asked Daddy. We were on the
patio, me drinking a Nehi. "Something wrong with his face?"

After every shot, Mr. Cruse was slapping himself, saying,
"Uuuurrrggghhh!" and "Eeeeffff!" He had the face of someone
who'd waded out too far.

"Puts me in an unhappy place," Daddy said. "Reminds me of
war."

Every third shot, Mr. Cruse slumped to his knees, his eyeballs
adrenal and gleaming. If beauty were a place, I was to tell Lori
Ann years later, then he was a continent from it, lost and broke.
He had hair that brought to mind the words *felon* and *night soil,*
plus this way of standing over the ball that seemed not only
wrong but physically impossible—crouched, elbows thrown out,
chin plugged into his chest, the whole thing suspect and, as I've
said to Momma, instinct with doom.

For a long time I studied, my daddy snoozing beside me, while
Mr. Cruse mumbled and hung over the ball with dread. He
barked and yipped and twitched, one time drawing blood from
his lip. On a good shot, a chip that fell in or close to the pail, he
grinned savagely, eyes squinty with attention; on a bad, he went

bug-eyed and gasping, as helpless as a fish in a tub. I felt removed, as abstract as a cynic, no more curious about this display
than those involving, say, jungle folk on the far side of our
darksome world.

Around five-thirty, my daddy awoke with a jolt, jumping from
his chair and shivering. Under the tree, Mr. Cruse had been stiff
as a fence post for nearly forty minutes, his tongue sticking out
like a pink diving board.

"I was dreaming," Daddy said. He'd been in a scourged land,
like the missile range itself, a place of waste and epic sunlight,
the smoking things tumbling from the sky pointed and deadly.
"You didn't hear any boom noises, did you?"

Through the sliding glass doors, I could hear Momma telling
Mrs. Ling her crippled-Apache joke again, its punch line being
empty of sense or real zest.

"I got to relax some," Daddy said. "You see me fading again,
Lamar, it means I'm in need of some support."

"What you want me to do?"

"Punch me or something."

That night we went to the Calcutta, but it was less merry than
grim, everyone tight-faced and fitful. The lights had gone out,
and the ballroom, which I had last seen as a place of glee, was
nightmarish, lit by a dozen wobbly flashlights and a smelly ker-
osene lantern Ira Felts had found in the pro shop. My daddy, of
course, had qualified for the Championship Flight of sixteen.
Tommy Cruse too. The many in that room were edgy—"testy,"
Momma said before leaving—and the bidding was a slow,
complaint-filled enterprise. Ping Walker made a speech about
thrift and venery, Yogi Jones charged into the room with a pair of
California-inspired panties over his ears, and the Fayards—
Adele, Morgan and Tip—played mournful mongrel Caribbean
music on their accordions, music I want now to characterize as
homicidal. Daddy stood on the bandstand again, by the chalk-
board, but this time he looked feeble and meek, the kind of guy
who carries change in a teeny purse. Mr. Cruse stood near me,

breathing heavily. I smelled a thousand odors on him, among them oil and sweat.

At one point, a man named Zookie Limmer, supposedly Allie Martin's cousin, stood on the bandstand like a gent, Momma says, in the throes. He mentioned thwarted urges and, drooling and panting, he drew for us a picture to which the word *deranged* might apply. Then he collapsed in a puddle of shabby sport clothes, a flashlight turned on his pasty, possessed and stricken face. Nobody moved for a long time. You could hear glands going dry.

"Call an ambulance," Jimbo Fada said at last, "this man's, uh, cold." I saw our state farm agent, E. L. Felice, stand over this crumpled Limmer fellow. "Up from there, fool," he ordered. "Up." Then Mr. Felice reared back and kicked the man in the ribs, whereupon Zookie Limmer bounced up, smiled and swaggered from that room like a teenager with a fat wallet and a girlfriend named Roxy. I felt my teenage heart in my throat.

"Eeeefff!" It was Tommy Reese Cruse, staring at me like I was a hungry man's last meal. "Uuuurrrggghhh!"

This was 1964, you remember, a time much distant from the current flusters and excitements; but it is a time, if I may be profound, which formed the headwaters of that famous river up which we are now without those celebrated paddles. I see the truth of it now, just as I see a flickering rerun of *Mannix* on my Sony and the Colonel's shining trophies on the bookcase, and the instructions Lori Ann left on how to dispose of her belongings. I see it now, no doubt as my daddy saw it, that *there,* in that shadow-laced and gloom-soaked ballroom, was the beginning of that oft-mentioned paved road down which we are traveling in that handcart; for it was at that moment that Tommy Reese Cruse, moving like a smuggler, bounded to the bandstand, ripped the microphone from Judge Sanders, and, standing in a whirl of light and smoke, his face pinched and drained, hollered, "Do it, gentlemen! Crown me, for I have come, and it is mine!"

—

The next day, with me as his loyal caddy, the Colonel teed off at noon, Oscar Tweego of Odessa his opponent—a man whose swing and person were no more attractive than a flysore hound dog wearing teardrop earrings. My daddy would whip him, but it would be a victory without special thrill, conducted in a vacuum of disinterest; the news on our links that day concerned only Mr. T. R. Cruse.

He'd shown up at one, we learned, wearing a Hibbs and Hannon cowboy hat and hockey socks, plus an intriguing jumpsuit made from a lap robe. It was clothing, Momma said, that somebody in Hong Kong went blind making. She said he'd risen an hour after we left for the practice range, did something in his room that sounded like push-ups, then came out mumbling about quote trespass and personal injury unquote.

"I moved his bags out forthwith," she told Daddy. "Mrs. Ling had to help," she said, one satchel being a weighty, infernal item with the words THUG and FOLLY stenciled on it. "Feel my back, Lamar, that's strain."

At one-thirty, the story was that Mr. Cruse had flattened himself on the froghair of the second green, pawed the turf, pronounced it meet, and, with a murderer's cackle, stroked a putt that broke, yes, uphill, the ball trembling at the lip of the cup before it toppled in with a plop. On the next hole, he was talking about twilights and human melts, his cup of endurance having run over—an army of things, Hop Moody said, which were available in a slick pamphlet Tommy Reese Cruse had titled "Golf and the Higher Planes."

"Listen, to this," Hop Moody said, his eyes twinkling with wonder. He read us a passage which mentioned the I–It relationship. "What do you think of that, Colonel?" Mr. Moody looked like a man named Buell or Sinclair, ready to believe anything. I was standing next to Oscar Tweego, himself in a state close enough to defeat to be tearful.

"You say he's on the fifth hole?" my daddy asked.

"Who knows?" Mr. Moody was pointing toward a distant stand of cottonwoods. "He's moving fast, using one club. He gave his bag to Kirby Knott, said it was full of spit."

I knew it was coming then, the confrontation between the Colonel and Mr. Cruse—an insight which I repeated for Daddy the last time I saw him two years ago, after he'd sold his house and moved into an apartment. He'd been talking about dying—going out, he called it, throwing off coil and care and companions. He said his only enjoyment any longer was a Swanson's Salisbury steak in front of the Motorola, the things keeping him going being the hope that Joyce De Witt's top might fall off during *Three's Company* and a rooting interest in the little guy knocking the diddly-squat out of the big. "I'll get him," I declared at last. We were sitting by the pool, me in a pair of swim trunks Lori Ann thinks I look masculine in, my daddy in his Bermudas and sandals. He looked ancient, his skin like crepe paper, knobby-kneed, patches of psoriasis on his elbows like frost. "Honest," I insisted, "I'll take some time off, hunt him up." I mentioned cleaving, I believe, plus hacking and sawing and punching unto pulp. I said my gardener, Trent Tucker, had a gun—"a weapon, he calls it!"—that could make a satisfying hole in anything, man or beast. In addition, I knew a private detective, J. Berry Kiss. I reminded my daddy that I was a lawyer and had some intimacy with crime and the deserved fate of bad guys. "Lamar," Daddy said, "go home." The light in his eye was dim and flickering. Then, shaking my hand like a stranger, he said he was going inside, see who Cronkite was pissing on today. "You come back tomorrow, Lamar," he said. "If I'm still alive, you shoot me." You could tell he was despondent.

By the end of the ninth hole, when Daddy went into the clubhouse for a cheeseburger and a Coke, Mr. Oscar Tweego, his hair slapped across his forehead like a washcloth, was beside himself with gloom. He'd lost every hole.

"What's the Colonel using?" he asked me. "I'm so far out of this, even cheating won't help. I had considered it."

My daddy, whom I could see moving about in his outfit of green slacks and Florida shirt, was in the employ of wit and guile, making up in mentalities what he lacked in beef.

"Shit," Mr. Tweego grumbled, "that's what's in my mind right now. Shit and piss."

Several hundred yards away, on the seventh fairway stood Tommy Reese Cruse in a pose that was a fair duplication of backhanded well-knot, profound and complex. He'd slipped out of his jumpsuit a while back and was now disporting himself in trunks so shiny with satin that Mrs. E. L. Felice had sent her boys, Skipper and Mort, to the car for her sunshades. He had a crowd of dozens around him, including the dance band from the Holiday Inn, Ramon and the Night Moods, who, the story was, had been hired right off the highway—where it ran past the fifth green—and were supposed to sing backup for a tune Mr. Cruse had composed, music that started high, went higher, and ended with a note that made pain seem appealing.

"What's he doing now?" Daddy wondered, standing on the tenth tee, Mr. Tweego trembling beside me. "Reverend Shipwell mentioned an invocation earlier."

I told what I'd knew: that TRC had been overheard muttering to himself about the elements and the principles; that, according to Ruby Levisay, he'd taken on a bardworthy expression, his teeth the only points of light in a mouth so deep and dark it seemed to go for miles; that, finding himself in a fairway bunker, he stood aside for many minutes, obviously in study, then rooted himself in the trap so securely the sand was up to his knees, and, after a moment when his brow went dark and steam appeared to rise from his shoulders, he blasted away, the ball, nearly warped, shooting out with a snarl, rising almost out of sight and exploding, every little piece—cover and core and rubber wrapping—falling into the cup.

"There's a lesson in this," Daddy told me, happily. "Gimme a minute, I'll figure it out."

On the next hole my daddy eliminated Mr. Tweego, and the

three of us joined the gallery trailing TRC. He was on the green, using a whisk broom to sweep the leaves from his path, his hair—according to Judge Sanders—a statement about many things, among them squalor.

"I don't need to see this," Mr. Tweego said. He was shaking Daddy's hand, saying bye-bye. "In Odessa, we don't allow this stuff." Tweego looked like a man who would be mortally fat one day. "I'm going home now," he said, "refresh myself, get on Ruthie. Colonel, you come on down next year, see the delights which await you." He patted me on the head. "Here's a dollar, Lamar, you were fine." Then he hurried away, faster than he ought, shaking his head in dismay.

Tommy Reese Cruse ate his lunch under the cottonwood tree which overhung the porch to the club dining room, the folk around him frozen with astonishment at the volume and kind of food he preferred—food he spoke of as magic or biology. "You got any tubers?" he asked one of the waiters, saying he was moving in the realm of deferred repentance and had need for that which slaked and made his heart thump.

The Colonel and I watched, me in a state best called un-amused. I mentioned white trash and the low down, plus that snake's belly lower than which Mr. TRC was.

"I feel great," Daddy said. "Here, feel this." He was making a muscle of his bicep. "Look at this." He had rolled up one trouser leg to show me his calf. It was hard, too. "Listen here." He grabbed my head, pulled me to his chest. "What's that saying?" His heart was saying lub-lub, lub-lub. "Look at that sky," he cried. It was cloudless and vast. "Look at that grass." It was as thick as new hair. "Know what they're saying?"

Staring into his open, cheerful face, I shook my head.

"They are saying Colonel Lamar M. Hoyt, Champion!"

He was wrong—Heaven and earth were no more interested in him than in the trials and works of an old red ant in the Gobi, nature a thing without thought, wish or special talent.

The rest of the afternoon, TRC toyed with his opponent, Yogi

Jones. One time he bowed in front of Dee Ann Harrison, slipped
her scarf off, blindfolded himself and whacked a tee shot with as
much effort as you or I open a screen door. The ball went
straight, landing dead center on the fairway. "Run on down
there, darling," he suggested, "tell me what you find." She scur-
ried off in a flash, the skirts of her sundress flying. My daddy and
I were among the many who watched her stop, look, and lift the
ball as if it were a land mine. "There's something here," she
shouted, and in a minute she was back, clutching a sheaf of
papers, a shine high on her cheeks. "Read what it says," TRC
whispered.

Yogi Jones was behind him, twitching, all the lead out of his
spine. We were a hushed and respectful mob as Dee Ann unfolded those papers.

"Does it mention time?" TRC wondered.

She nodded.

"Does it mention space?"

She swallowed: it did.

Durwood Sherrill was fanning himself with yesterday's *Sun
News*. "That man is hurting me," he mumbled. "If I go down,
you revive me." The air was alive with magnetism and electricity,
oxygen as rare here as on the moon.

"Read me the rest, sweet chips," TRC said. My daddy was
grinning as if he knew a large secret while Dee Ann read through
that text, her lips evidently dry and sore. "From where?" she said.
The notes were margin to margin with tiny handwriting, the
letters like an arrangement of human bones.

"From the part that begins 'In an age which tends to dis-
parage . . .'"

Mr. Sherrill grabbed his chest, an unwholesome blue coming
to his lips. "Okay, people," he said, "push on me now, here." He
was indicating his heart spot.

Dee Ann read about ideas, governance and dominion in the
world, plus several sentences, each longer than four hundred
words, which addressed the notions of sacrifice and didactic pur-

pose. "Read me that part again," Mr. Cruse said, making her utter once more a phrase about exploit and humbug. Through it all, he gazed into the trees as if he could see in them a possibly intelligent animal making signs; then, when Dee Ann finished out of breath but clearly stimulated by too close a contact with language like "hugger-mugger" and "trespass," he told Yogi Jones to close his yap, grab his bag and come on, as there was some sport to be played.

"My-my," the Colonel said, "he is one long-winded sapsucker, ain't he?"

Which was how the day went until my momma showed up on the last hole, dragging with her the half-dozen other ladies who were members of her Social Committee. Close behind was Sheriff Whitey Le Duc. "Out of our way," Momma barked, pushing through the folks circling the green.

Mr. Cruse was standing over a putt which would win the match, his club between his teeth like a sucker. Yogi Jones looked like a stone that could talk a little. He was doomed, he knew it; indeed, he'd known it when TRC introduced himself at the first tee as a man named Saladin and showed a business card with reapers, all grim, printed on it.

"Arrest that man, Whitey," Momma ordered, her pointing finger shaking. Her hair was windblown, standing out like a storm cloud. The sheriff looked confused, one hand on a pistol he'd never use. My momma said there were forces at work here, the darkest of them that man Tommy Reese Cruse, whose immediate incarceration would be a service high in the social order. "Well?" my momma said. "Cuff that smarty-pants!"

I was trying to look twelve ways at once, a million noises in my head. I could hear my own heart, like Daddy's, going lub-lub, lub-lub.

"Can't," said the sheriff, explaining that no law had actually been broken, the man being an invited guest and from what anyone could tell the only one here actually enjoying himself.

It was then that I caught Tommy Reese Cruse muttering into

his fist, his eyes empty of all but the darkest lights: "Ten-four, Capcom, this is Eager-Beaver, do you copy?" His voice was as inhuman as lead. "That's a roger, maxom. Repeat, we are go for vector at one niner three, we have a bingo. Affirm, do you roger, we have sin. Sin is everywhere."

—

You know the part where the hero takes it in the ear—where the meek sod-buster or proud Apache brave or sheep-ranching widower has his face ground in the muck by a guy with a week-old beard and gray teeth? Well, this is that part, the hero being my daddy, the guy to be loathed the one calling himself the Apostle of Doom. This is the part Lori Ann hates, saying I concentrate too much on the links play and not enough on the spectacle. She says there's nothing that satisfies the delicate and fine in my extended descriptions of thwack and pock and wham; that the contemplative spirit demands subtlety and shades, not sweat and lip noise; that my telling would improve some were I to focus on the slight, not the gross. Okay: I shall try, beginning with my daddy's preparations the morning of the match.

I brought him some cotton, told him to stuff it in his ears, the story being that TRC was now in the company of several females, sirens every one, whose specialties were humming to distraction.

"Nope," my daddy said. He was wearing shorts and a Julie Boros sport shirt.

"How 'bout dark glasses?" I asked. Johnny Red Shoes Dugan had claimed that TRC was coming in full body paint, a Soviet design of mooky and sump-views.

"Nope," he said. He was standing at the bathroom mirror, evidently self-absorbed. He said, "I am a gentleman, am I not?" I agreed. "When was the last time I whipped you?" It had been a couple of years ago when he caught me smoking Pall Malls in the laundry room. "I've done everything right," he said, "I've been respectful, abided even those laws I despised, paid my bills."

I looked at him, hard: He was, he had and he did.

"So how come I feel so shitty?"

I know now I should have slugged him or told a joke about teeth and hair, anything, this being one of those well-chronicled moments of jitter and self-doubt. I didn't and we rode in silence (in his new Biscayne!) to the club, where we were met at the first tee by TRC and by a mob of those citizens who turn out for fires and dog races. Immediately, I learned that TRC had slept in a sand trap on the fifth fairway, dreaming (the story went) of plains and amber waves of grain; that day he looked like the sort of human you'd send to a far place to do a chore that involved peril and lead to despair. He was wearing what the lady from the *Sun News* described as the spread from the bed of a woman named Inez.

"My apologies, Colonel," he said. "I'm sorry I got to whip your ass."

"Me, too," Daddy said.

I was holding my daddy's clubs, feeling select and proud.

"Hey, Lamar." He winked at me. "What you think of my outfit?"

I had the idea I was looking at one of those Goths Mrs. Tipton is always lecturing about.

"Say howdy, Lamar." Daddy had me by the ear. "We Hoyts are polite."

The Colonel teed off first, an effort preserved forever in a glossy photograph by Club Historian Eldon B. Epp. It shows my daddy bent like a peasant to his task, his face a poem about the pleasures of knowing and doing.

"Nice shot, Colonel," TRC said. "I admire it, truly, as I admire all failed things."

A million contrary and still perplexing things happened when TRC addressed his ball. Among them: a sparrow, an instant before in merry song, gagged, sputtered, then flopped into the trashcan under its tree, dead.

"Citizens," Tommy Reese Cruse announced, wiggling over his ball, "I have been everywhere, but ain't lived until now."

Beside me, I could hear the Colonel breathing: "Pissant, dingleberry, snotface."

(These are some of the same words, Momma tells me, the Colonel was saying only a few days before he died last year at William Beaumont General Hospital at Fort Bliss. She'd been with him the whole time—"I loved him, Lamar," she told me, "I just couldn't live with the sumbitch." Every five minutes he'd shoot up in bed, eyeballs bright with fury, and shout, "Dog spit!" or "Toadlicker!" He could see the end coming, a thing of twilight and considerable cold. You'd try to perk him up, she told me, mention a shared pleasure or a good moment, and he'd holler, "Fart-face, grunt!" The last she saw of him, he was lying, grayfaced and buried in bed linen, his face poked out like a mole's, saying, "Poot, poot, poot." You just knew he was thinking about sport.)

By the fourth hole, TRC was telling folks that he was moving among the quick and inspired, blight a condition for those of low habit. Once, during his backswing, he stopped, still coiled, eyes fixed on his ball, and told Boot Taylor to take one giant step backward. "You hear it?" he said.

Mr. Taylor looked around guiltily. "What am I listening for?"

"Lilt," TRC said. "Little happy tinkles."

Then, with a groan, he uncoiled, smashing his driver, the ball describing an arc so perfect it met industry specifications.

"Shit," I said. It was a word I'd learned from Oscar Tweego and meant it to convey contempt for out-of-town show-offs.

On the fairway, TRC told the many of us that he had a new work in mind, one of sweep and drift. "Know what I'm thinking about right now?" He was looking straight at me, his face most unfamiliar. I felt a thought go through me: it had to do with fear. "I'm thinking of discipline," he said, "plus how I'm gonna celebrate."

When we finished the ninth hole, my daddy's expression had become virtually theological. "Lighten my spirits, Lamar," he said, "I'm beginning to fade." He was sweating so much he looked like he'd been in the shower.

We were tied, I reminded him. He was hitting the ball short, yes, but well down the heart each time. He was doing it with shrewdness and experience. Plus, he had me and everybody else—Turner Dale, for example, and Dickie Tidwell and Jackie Dunbar—for moral support.

"Daddy," I said, "I got every confidence in you."

Smiling, as if he'd heard a rueful remark, he held out his arm. He was cold; it seemed his insides were dry-frozen, fractured.

"Know what this is?" he said.

I did not.

"Neither do I," he said.

It was then, as I hung on to his small hand, that the noises in my head stopped, and I understood that, no matter what happened, he was already beaten, up against a fact as vast and permanent as death itself.

The end came on the fourteenth, the green surrounded by such spectators as Homer called minions. We were still tied, and Daddy was already in the cup with a par, TRC standing over his own putt as watchful as a tiger at a water hole. I could hear with a supernatural clarity, as if I had radar dishes for ears.

"Gimme a name for this," Mr. Newell was saying.

A few paces away, Judge Sanders mumbled, "Yup, yup, yup."

Next to me, Daddy breathed heavily, more like an animal than a colonel and a superior human being. Baking us was that sun favored by Mr. Wordsworth, a shine under which deeds are done for love and glory. On the highway, in the distance, cars flashed by silently. I remember feeling calm, as if I had survived the unhappiest event life could offer, and I was wishing misfortune on TRC.

"Here, take this," my daddy said, handing me his putter.

I could see it in his face: defeat and loss.

"Don't." The word did not come out the way it ought, strong and certain.

"Take the club, Lamar."

It should have turned dark then, but didn't.

"You're feeling bad," I said. "I'll get you a Coke."

"Lamar," he said, "grow up. I'm feeling fine."

Then he was moving, his walk measured and relaxed. I could tell from his shoulders that whatever had been weighing on him in the way of expectation and hope was now gone. An older kid than I would have had sense enough to cry. Maybe yell.

Nobody else was moving—not an eyebrow, not a pinky, not a lip—only my daddy, Colonel Lamar Hoyt, Sr., his spikes making squishy noises on the green. Things were giving way inside me when he reached Mr. Cruse, the bottom out of all my organs. This was my thought, exactly: Uuurrgghh, aarrgghhh.

They shook hands and, an instant later, my daddy was past him, head level, walking as if he'd been moving forever, casual and tired, his face—Momma tells me—blank and strange as if there were nothing at all inside him. When he got home, hours later, he went by my mother in the kitchen without speaking, going directly to his room, where he threw off his golf outfit, climbed into bed, pulled the covers to his chin and slept, without dream or waking need, for nearly eighty-five hours.

—

Tonight, an evil wind is blowing, the dust from the mesas a violent spray like shotgun pellets against my windows. It is well after midnight and, as I told Lori Ann hours ago when she phoned, I feel like one of my clients, guilty but defiant.

"What're you gonna do now?" she said. The girls were fine— some disturbed, to be true, over the change in living circumstances—and she herself was okay as well, though lonely in the night hours. "How 'bout I come over in the morning, make breakfast?" she said.

That was fine.

"Lamar," she said, "what're you drinking?"

There was liquid in a jelly glass. It was brown and possibly bitter, but I couldn't remember having tasted it.

"You go to bed now," she said. "I'll be over after nine."

That was hours ago. I have sat through the news—none of which surprised me—Johnny Carson, and an old movie which showed me ugly villains and a handsome but closemouthed buckaroo, comic relief provided by a dog named Shep. Over the years, I have kept track of Tommy Reese Cruse. He has played hither and yon, winning many, losing a few. He has changed his name several times—from Moloch to Laughing Eye to, most recently, the Big Bad Wolf. He has played lefty, with one arm tied behind his back, and from a folding chair; and along the way he has told people about mysteries and miracles, delights that daunt, and how to avoid wist. He favors ladies' evening gowns now and was seen yesterday in dark eyelashes and Spanish comb.

I won't be here tomorrow when Lori Ann comes over. I'll be miles and miles away, in Olney, Texas, positioned squarely on the last hole of the golf tournament, waiting for the appearance of Mr. Tommy Reese Cruse. I'll be reasonable, as distant from lunacy as my daddy is from this narrow world. TRC will be the one in the dancer's tights, his chest bare except for the gaudy epaulets he's had tattooed on his shoulders; and it will give me much and lasting pleasure to tell him—surely in the voice of Tweety Bird himself—that what is coming to him, as it came to my daddy, is, yes, wisdom: the inevitable disappointment, ruin and failure that is age. Then I'll leave, my heart light, and won't mention any more of this again.

ROLLING THUNDER

Around 1500 hours Baby Huey announced he was finished, crapped out. Huey's real name was Marvin Foody, and in the year most of this takes place, 1968, a week after the Tet Offensive when our home was a bunker we called the Inferno in the Khe Sanh Combat Base, we were best friends—him a nineteen-year-old spade from an unpopular crossroads in Rochester, New York, that had been removed to make way for I-490, and me a Roswell, New Mexico, farmboy with two letters in varsity basketball and a 1350 on my SATs.

"I'm done," Baby Huey told Krebs, our gunnery sergeant. "Here and now, I'm quitsville, Gunny."

The story was that Gunny had a standing offer from a Hollywood TV preacher—Billy Graham, possibly—to be a bodyguard or round-the-clock houseboy. Plus, we jarheads had been led to believe that he'd attended Rice University for several semesters of astrophysics before taking up combat business. I liked him. He was spiritual.

"Ears," he said to me, "you know what the hell he's talking about?"

In his rack, Huey was smoking the Laotian weed he'd scored in a deal with an A-Team Special Forces noncom for a pallet of meatloaf C rations.

"This is news to me, Sarge. Honest."

"How long you been in-country, Foody?"

Baby Huey was wearing his outfit again, smoking jacket like Hugh Hefner has and Hong Kong cravat, and he was trying to light a heat tablet under a tiny, blackened stove he'd made from a ration box dessert can.

"Nine months and seventeen days," he said.

"And now you're bailing out?"

Marvin Foody, my Baby Huey, had a Munchkin's marvelous smile, liquid and wise.

"Right on, Sarge," he said. "I am finito in your place."

I could hear a C-123 circling the airstrip. In a minute it would hit the tarmac, and the NVA would begin dumping on us again. Charlie wasn't nothing, we were told. These aggressive yellow troops were regulars, they had Soviet light tanks—T-34s and -76s—and they owned every valley, ravine, plain, gorge and ridge in the deep, spooky jungle around us. We were to be impressed, and I was.

"So what're you going to do?" Gunny asked.

"I'm thinking about visiting Charlie med. Get them to declare me loco."

"You ain't crazy, Foody."

"So maybe I'll hitch a ride out of here. Go down to the trench, see what's available. I got some pals in the engineers, guys you can do business with."

Gunny's posture, his cocked head, his slowly tapping fingers, reminded me of the less dramatic ways anger shows up in folks.

"That's AWOL, dickweed."

"No, it ain't, Sarge," Baby Huey insisted. "That's just me taking matters, so to speak, into my own hands. This is deep stuff I'm dealing with here."

In our semidark, closed-in hovel, I got a look at Huey's eyes, which seemed to be having nothing at all to do with his face, and I had the desire, felt in the gut, to be on the other side of camp somewhere, maybe the beer hall.

"I got my mind right, Sarge. I wish you could see inside it."

"You going to help me out, Ears?"

Gunny had his sixteen on his lap, holding it in a way that embarrassed me.

"I told him you might kick his ass," I said.

"Truth to tell," Gunny told me, "I did think about that."

Baby Huey and I had been pals since Quantico, when we

discovered all we had in common: affection for teenage living, common wanderlust, and an inability to motivate ourselves as our parents wished.

"Tell you what I'm going to do," Gunny said. "I'm going to visit the Old Man, see what he says about dipstick Marines. I might take an hour to do this, after which I could be back in a real nasty frame of mind."

I could hear rocket fire, NVA RPG-7 models, and it occurred to me that a walk to the officers' club could take two hours, maybe more.

"Foody," Sarge was saying, "I knew a guy like you one time, up in Poli Klang. I considered him a friend. We'd been Kappa Alphas back in Houston. Real smart fellow, turned down a TA in chemistry to see this part of the world. We were tight, man, Mutt and Jeff."

"What happened?" I said.

"He disappointed me," Gunny said. "A half hour later he was just a bad memory."

—

After Gunny left, I didn't say anything, just took in again the decorating Baby Huey had done for our bunker. We had water beds from a TuDo Street whorehouse, French wrought iron, Joe Tex and Wilson Pickett posters, two paintings Marvin had stolen out of a Manila Holiday Inn, and chute silk from a dozen magnesium flares that were supposed to have been dropped on Hills 881 North and South. This was our home and, under the circumstances, an absolutely superior expression of how we stood to each other as low men on Uncle Sugar's totem pole. One wall of sandbags was a collection of special weapons: a Cochiselike war lance Huey'd cadged off an E-6 in Nhua Ha Province, a club I'd paid 500 P for from a naked Montagnard hipster we called Mr. Pitiful, and an assault rifle we'd slipped free of a Friendly colonel in III Corps. We even had several Psyops tapes on loan from an

Army warrant officer named Cooter Brown. Often we'd rack out by listening to this woman telling Charlie, and all other murderers, to do the smart thing—give up. Hers was a language of clicks and singsong that, at loud enough volume, seemed even to overwhelm the whomp-whomp-whomp of distant Rolling Thunder—arclight bombs dropped from eighteen thousand feet by flyboys who would be back at Udorn or Guam within hours.

"You're serious, aren't you?" I asked.

"I am, Ears," he said. "I truly am."

"They could throw you in the brig."

"You're probably right, my man."

It would be dusk outside now, monsoon mists rising out of the valley, and soon you wouldn't be able at all to see the red dust that laterite breaks down to. Night would be a thing, as it always was, that put you in mind of ghosts and comparable horror said to walk the land thereabouts.

"What if everybody felt like you do?" I wondered.

"Then we could all go home and goof off there."

He had made meatballs and beans, offered me a dish.

"This is political, isn't it? You been talking to those Panthers in Philly Dog's company, right?" Now I don't know what I was hoping to hear, but I do remember having no appetite and being tired in a manner utterly inappropriate for a fit, youthful American.

"Ears," Baby Huey told me, "this is personal. I ain't against anyone in particular."

I nodded three or four times, aiming to be less baffled when I spoke again. "You're not chickenshit, I know."

"I ain't anything," Marvin Foody said. "I can dance, like to sleep when I can, and there's a woman in a two-story house in Brockport I'd like to know better. That's all I am, good buddy."

I wondered what my daddy would say, were he here. He was five feet ten inches of Southwest common man, and I had no problem seeing him and his pals—Sam Monge, Bob Swetman, the Harrison brothers—using Baby Huey's shiny black head in the cruel way drunk cowboys find so laughable.

"You want any of this stuff?"

He had piled most of his personal articles on his bunk—stuff I'd seen him trade for, buy, cajole or swipe. He had several issues of *Zap Comix,* as well as a very British pith helmet and a handful of Tokyo pornographic playing cards. He had a Kohner D-flat harmonica and the sheet music for "One-Eyed Woman Crying."

"You can take anything you want," he said. "Except my matchbooks. Promised them to Mayhew over yonder."

"What'll your father say?"

I was looking at the empty bangalore torpedo we used for an ashtray.

"You won't leave it alone, will you?" he said.

I shook my head, clung to the thought that he was my best friend and I loved him.

"I expect that my pop will bust my tail," he was saying. "I expect my brother Morris will bust my tail. I expect everybody in the family to line up and just have at me, that's what."

He was trembling, not doing a Marine's good job of keeping his emotions private.

"So everybody's going to get a shot at me," he said, "except Uncle Ho and those pissants working for him. That's the difference right there. I'm gonna be alive and roughed up some, and you're going to be right here."

I had my weapon and backed up, excusing myself.

"I'll get some air," I said. "See you later."

—

Outside, I had a smoke, a Lucky Strike. Four kilometers northwest you could see .50-cal fire on Hill 861. The 1/9 was up there, the most displeased people I'd ever met. I was thinking about my sweetheart, Millie Tanner. This was her sophomore year at Hardin-Simmons University, a business major, and we had been together since the sixth grade, but standing there, outside my hooch, fire on every high ground from here to the CoRoc ridge eleven kilometers away, I couldn't remember what she looked like. Was she blond, I thought. Or just light brown? I wondered, too, if I could still drive my Mustang or would somebody—my sister Joyce, say, or my mother—have to teach me.

I could see the airstrip six hundred meters yonder, and I tried to imagine Baby Huey out there in the morning trying to flag down a C-47. These were prop flareships, but some carried .762 Mike-Mikes that could fire three thousand rounds per minute; I had no trouble seeing him aboard one as it banked and pulled south, and I believe now, sixteen years after these events, that I may have put my hand in the air that night to practice my good-byes.

Here it was, then, that Baby Huey came outdoors. He was dragging something.

"Where you going?" I asked.

He gripped a shelter half by one corner, virtually everything he owned tossed inside. I could see the good-luck CAT hat he'd gotten from an Illinois concrete contractor we'd had a Wild West fistfight with during our R & R in Honolulu last August.

"Over there," he said.

He was heading for the dump where we burned gear and uniforms nobody needed—flack jackets, ponchos, fatigues, crates and boxes.

"Be careful," I told him.

"Natch," he said. "I am the carefulest man on this earth."

He walked away, and I tried to turn my mind to the good in me. I intended to conceive of the sort I'd be eventually, but I believe it fair to say that I did not come up with the Dallas, Texas, bank officer I am now. I did not see the large Buick I drive, nor the Christian wife I have nor our two daughters. I saw, I think, only four or five months henceforth and that I would not be percepti- bly better or more fine.

"You could go with me," Huey said when he came back. "We could eat chicken wings and hang out. In the winter, we could see about Miami. I hear Puerto Rico is worth the trip."

"Where are your clothes?" I asked.

Except for his issue skivvies, he was naked.

"Torched them," he said. "Got my new outfit all picked out."

I was listening for one VC we knew. We called him Don Ho and he liked to yell at us over a bullhorn from his hiding hole in the woods. The jungle would go still and you'd hear him, his voice shrill and outraged. "Too damn bad, Marine," he'd holler. "Hard rain going to fall." He knew Bob Dylan. And Charlie Pride. Even Henry David Thoreau. One night he read to us from Jean-Paul. "Sartre say go home. Have babies. Avoid nausea."

"Baby Huey," I said, "I am real disappointed in you."

He was two steps away, but fast, and for a second I thought he might cold-cock me.

"I got some George Dickel I was saving," he said. "Maybe you'd like to get wasted with me."

"In a minute," I said. "I'll think about it."

—

It had turned cold, as it could in that strange land, and I wondered where Sergeant Krebs was. In his spiritual mind, he might have arranged to forget all about my pal. Or he might not.

A Vietnam dog had wandered by, and I thought to ask how it was going, dogwise. There were perhaps fifty of these animals inside our two-square-mile perimeter, but this beast had one intelligent eye and an orange mange that would look good on certain protesters I knew of.

"Well, how about this?" I said. "Ain't this a crock?"

I could hear music somewhere: James Brown, the godfather of the soul I liked, singing about the brand-new bag Poppa had. I closed my eyes, considered the creature I was. I was Presbyterian but knew few Bible stories that had much to do with the current moment. I was fit and not much of a screw-up. I had a need to obey, which those who gave orders found becoming, and once upon a time I could run very fast. Plus, I understood enough Spanish to get around border towns like Juárez and Tijuana.

"You don't know nothing, do you, dog?"

That beast gave me a distinctly gyrene look, then snubbed me by wandering west.

"I guess I'll see you around," I said.

Our night was only semidark, so every shadow, inside and outside the wire, had a human or mechanical shape. I could see no-account fires on the Cam Lo-Con Thien road and mortar rounds disappearing into the stream below the plateau of our base. There was eye-stinging smoke and light diffused into odd, netherworldly swirls, a murkiness you'd expect to find underwater, and instantly it made sense to be more indoors than out.

"Hey," I said when I went inside, "I didn't mean it, Huey. I was just running off at the mouth. You gotta do what you gotta do."

He was impossible to find in our home, him another shade of blackness, but that was okay. I'd had several thoughts, all warmhearted and having to do with a reunion we should plan.

"Don't turn on no light," he said.

His voice contained a note which did not thrill me. Either he had cried or he was about to.

"Baby Huey, where are you?"

"This is humiliating, Ears," he said. "I'm in my rack with the covers pulled up to my goddam neck."

This would be over in the morning, I realized. We'd go topside and worship sunlight for a while. We'd visit Philly Dog or the Detroit Pistons or King Albert Lear, maybe drop Blue Cheer acid and have an in-body vacation.

"I am scared, Ears." Self-esteem was being fought for here, and not won. "Jesus Christ, I may have wet my pants."

I was across from him now, a giant step away, and my heart had flopped over the way it did the afternoon I learned where Uncle Sugar sought to send us.

"Damn," he was saying. There was a lot of home loss in his voice. "Damn, damn."

"Marvin Foody," I said. I felt somewhat like that dog which had spurned me.

"I ain't ever gonna amount to anything," he said.

I reached out, grabbed an arm to shake.

"I don't want to hear about it anymore," I told him. "Just shut up, okay?"

I imagined his grunt's face and how brave it might look in daylight.

"Give me a drink," I said.

And then we were quiet.

YOUTH ON MARS

I N the latter eighth of the century, Kirby Puckett was our most famous revolutionary. He was renowned, particularly, for his verse, which was arch as death itself. In De Funiak Springs (in the old Republics of West Florida), hours before battle, he read from his second publication, *The Unity of Philosophical Experience*. He alluded to avatars and privation. Flanking him, clad in skins, stood his lieutenants: Al-Ali Khadary, his expression suggesting squalor and sloth, was from Dallas and was said to be crafty with poisons and large numbers; the other, Ernie Witt, his hair wild as winter, was expert in woe.

"What are we," Kirby was saying, "but a plucky material that yammers and haunts from below? Rise, people. Join me in advocating rapture."

Around him, their sweaty hopeful faces lit by dozens of flickering torches, were his guerrillas. They cradled ancient Uzis and M-16s and Jetfire .25s, plus weapons which had once belonged to Vandal and Ostrogoth. Kirby saw cudgel and club, broadax and arrow. Many of his followers, including the women, had been with him since Little Rock, the months in the steamy deltas; they had been wooed by sentiment, as well as by metaphor and a senator's voice. Dozens had adopted names from his works: Plexor, Telugu, O City of Broken Dreams; all had ambitions to be the vaunted objects he put into poems: mottle, rifts, angels that ate.

"This is 'Flesh for Fantasy,'" he announced. "It is a sonnet and you may sing along." It recounted his experiences among the Mung, the GDF, the Kansas Khmer.

Yonder, beyond this clearing and the woods, he could hear his enemies. Occasionally a word came on the wind: "epicure," "je-june," "ectomorph." Twice a phrase: "outcry and clamor." Once, in a moment grave as those which used to attend money, he heard a complete sentence whose theme was the origin, nature, method and limit of human knowledge. Clearly, they were a choleric people—disobedient as weather, single-minded as insects.

"My people," Kirby said at last, "this is my last battle."

He waited for the wailing to cease.

"I'm tired," he said. "I am through with foment and our disgruntlement. I intend to roam about and lie up in places free of discord."

There were tears and displays of self-scourging, but Kirby hushed his people with a smile. He felt nothing, as if his organs were dry-frozen and fractured. He ordered his vehicle brought to him, a Buick from the olden days, substantial as the earth itself, its grillwork bright as daytime.

"Go," he directed, "vanquish and be free."

There was another roar, this in concert and serious as thunder.

"These men will lead you now," he said, embracing his pals Witt and Khadary. "They are like me, updrawn and always busy."

———

In his travels, he met the many who were afoot in those days: the Virgins of Albuquerque, datu bikers, a tribe of females allied with the Clytemnestra cults, the itinerant and gelatinous, carnivores, essentialists, purdahs and moujiks, knaves and their libertine masters. They wore plastics and leathers, some disguised as furniture or states of mind achieved in sleep. Their headgear fascinated: feathers for ideas, rickrack and crewelwork, metals that had meaning.

Near the ruins of Baton Rouge, a group of black men on horses stopped him. They wielded barongs and identified themselves as the progeny of several running backs for the old New Orleans Saints.

"What is the Grammar of Assent?" they demanded.

They had wounds and appeared intractable as perdition.

"It is folly," Kirby said. "Your dispute is with the scoundrels of Pittsburgh."

"And Cleveland," they said.

Kirby reminded them about the pashas of Ford, their ermines and many mates.

"You must be Kirby Puckett," they said. "What is your advice?"

Kirby studied their mounts, their artful hairdos. The air in this part of the world was thick, heavy as history itself.

"Go willingly to the end of a thing," he said. "Be jocular. Avoid the wistful. Practice horseplay. Reproduce. I recommend human delights. Remember, being is not different from nothingness."

They seemed to agree.

"These are dark times, white boy. *Adios*."

Toward midnight, in a densely wooded rest stop on the old I-10 east of Dallas, Kirby was ambushed. There were six, including two teenagers dressed like rinderpest, and they made him squat with his arms overhead while, snarling and laughing, they sacked his Buick. They carried stones and had faces the color of parboiled beef.

"I wouldn't do that if I were you," Kirby said.

A woman eyed him with interest. She had a toothy smile which suggested rot and what it is to fly. "Why not?"

Kirby had two reasons.

"I had a mother, too," he said. "I was her nursling and made these noises: Goooo, gaaaaa. I appeal to you in the name of our common debt to biology."

Behind her crouched the teenagers. They were eating Kirby's favorite apparel, the smock with the stars and the far-off frosty moon.

"What's the other reason?" she wondered.

Kirby waved his hands. "These."

He possessed the coordination and temper of a welterweight, and in an instant his bushwackers lay in a pile neat as cordwood.

"There is a moral to this," he said. "It has nothing to do with weal or shared uplift."

In Dallas, Kirby endeavored to establish residence in an abandoned movie theater near the shell of the old Cotton Bowl. Though dusty and crammed with refuse, the place still seemed as ornate as a doge's palace. Names were scribbled on the walls: Vico, Octavio-V, Dante, Dr. Filth. In the balcony lived refugees from the PAC 10. They spoke the patois of many western provinces, including the San Fernando Valley and Las Vegas, a tongue in which it was impossible to be either explicit or too profound.

"We heard you was dead."

One inconceivably pale man had edged forward. He was wearing jewelry said to be favored in these parts by citizens named Ike or Spoon. They were a clan, Kirby knew, subject to the same ills as farm life: splints, ulcerated eyes, wolf teeth, spavin, founder and worms.

"I am in retirement," Kirby said. "I have forsaken the killing arts."

A chair was being burned for light, and among the flickering shadows were beings to which the word *ruin* might apply.

"How do we know it's you?" the man said. He held a weapon Kirby had never seen; its name was Boy, and it had the bristly pelt and wet teeth of a cur. "Read us a poem."

Kirby felt his heart squeeze into his throat. There were too many to fight, too few to die for.

"I have many poems," he said. "Which one?"

There was a debate. Some wanted "Baby Green's Evening in Paris," a tirade that ripped through the truth like grapeshot. Others wanted rhymes which addressed their current condition of disarray. In the back, noisy as nightmare, a fistfight broke out between those who desired poems of cognition and those preferring coitus. A barbed spear whistled through the air. From the darkness, someone was shouting, "Aaarrrggghhh," and a garment red as sunset floated near the ceiling.

"May I suggest something for the rearmost of us," the man said. "Among us are the wrathful and mirthless."

Kirby held a sheaf of papers clotted with writing which looked like what fowl might write.

Boy, the weapon, was making a strangled sound—part whimper, part growl.

"We like carnage," the man said, "and stuff that whizzes around making chatter."

Kirby sorted through his papers. He had everything: verses which mentioned toxins, puling from the ruling class, what the hearty hear when wishes wilt.

"'Familiar Usage in Leningrad,'" he began. It was his best work. In it, citizens frolicked and gamboled. Garlands were mentioned, as were greenswards and naughty trifles. Its hero—more than a little like himself, Kirby imagined—was called El-Dor and he had come to our planet from a more advanced civilization; he used words like "ilk" and "vault" and sought to deflect us from pain.

"Lovely," the man said. "Give us all a hug, please."

Later that hour, in tribute, his host sent him a woman.

"My name is Lana," she said. "I had grandparents who went to the University of Iowa. I once believed in grains and such advancements as iron and long-distance communication. Now I believe in haste, plus the places chemicals take me."

She had hair like straw and the thighs of a Hittite.

"What is it you do, Lana?"

Her outfit split open and she showed him. It was a male-female principle involving sweat.

"Very good," he said. She would be in his next work, which would have the shape of sense and make the ears bleed.

—

Through the autumn—six months of storms and rent heavens—he drafted his third book, *Puckett's Ontology, Cosmogony and*

Physics. In it were insurrectos and the fumble-witted, those bois-
terous as riot, those gaunt with belief. He told the members of the
Universal Remnant Church of God, who sometimes bunked in
the balcony men's room, that it was like having the same child
twice.

Once Lana asked him where he came from. There were many
rumors about his childhood. Parents named Flo and Buster, for
instance. An immaculate conception. Several miracles.

He didn't know. An image came to mind: a house, a yard, a tail-
wagging lapbrute that knew its name.

"They say you speak to bushes," she began. "You had a wife,
we heard. There was mention of loaves. Of penury."

He was thinking of the beasts he'd seen in picture books: their
matted fur, their scales, their blind pink eyes. He'd seen a fish
once—a trout, Ernie Witt had said—small and desiccated, murdered by a hundred holes. He'd seen a bird too. It didn't soar, as
he was told it ought; instead, weighing over a hundred pounds, it
lumbered and was cloaked in the outerwear of a nummulite.

"I hear Kirby isn't your real name," Lana was saying.

Quite possible, he answered. In the northern wastes—the old
towns of Minneapolis and St. Paul—he'd been ice itself: rimy and
everywhere. In the deserts of the West, he tried to be like the
indigenous flora: thorny and shriveled, a hook for hair to hang
from.

"I like it when you're mystical," Lana said. "Here."

In a second she leaped atop him, heedless and moist, and the
world was wealth again.

Later that season, Kirby was one of several speakers at the
Cotton Bowl. In the full light of day, the crowd looked numinous
and pulpy, food that could amble and say hello. There were rep-
resentatives from all the sciences: disquiet, malice, lamentation.
The delegation from Corpus Christi—where fires were thought
to be still smoldering—wore foil on their ears and argued in
behalf of a contracting universe. In the air you smelled the scent
of these times: pitch and sulphur, a rain that glowed.

"Perhaps you have heard of me," the first speaker said. His name was Fork and it was claimed he had turned to philosophy from a related discipline, terror. From his neck dangled a sign, PLEASE STOP, and he wore rusty dropshank spurs. Kirby thought him the most serious man he'd ever seen.

"I have a number of observations to make," Fork said. He had a voice like a cat climbing a window, as well as apparent pain under the wishbone. "First: Things will grow less intelligent as time wears on. Second: The next era will be like the last—a cycle of assertion and disjuncture."

Kirby liked desperados who knew their own minds.

"Third," Fork said, "like ground fog, our confusions will disappear. Something has a plan for us. I hope it is good."

The next speaker, a man named Saint Teresa of Avila, was as broad-backed as a bear. He affected the outfit of a monodist and spoke of felons and nightsoil.

"I too have had other lives," he said. "A king knew me; likewise the maids of his court. I may have been a sailor, as I find myself quite festive near fluids. I have always been holy."

There was a weak sun somewhere—perhaps directly overhead, but Kirby couldn't be sure.

"In the afterlife," Saint Teresa continued, "my aim is to shimmer and flit about, being cheerful."

Thoroughly polite applause greeted Kirby when he reached the podium. There were thousands at his feet, all hollow-eyed and semigorgeous. Some looked familiar—perhaps from the campaigns in the Tennessee hills. Kirby felt he could have been gazing at ash or comparable vermiculite matter.

"In the old days," Kirby began, "I was bombed and paid meat to shoot back." His voice echoed into the yellow, parched geography beyond. "I was a youth then, living elsewhere with people named Butch and Congressman Red Sorrell, and impressions were made. I shunned inquiry into the spirit of things. I had two cohorts, Witt and Khadary. We learned to crawl and fake stupidity. We read books about venery, about edible grasses. All

night our lanterns burned. We were taught the assassin's skills—
the walk, the gesture that says little is amiss. We learned dis-
guise—plant, old-timey farmer, agreeable states of mind. We became familiar with loathsomeness, with chills. We fashioned
weapons from the impractical and the discarded. Footwear, texts,
credulity. We could imitate certain fowl, as well as habits of
thought. When we left, Butch gave us sloppy kisses and memen-
tos. Mine was the moral and political authority of literature."

In the east rose darkness and unfriendly noise.

"That is how I became a cutthroat," he said. "Goodbye."

—

That week, a woman knocked at the door of the projectionist's
booth Kirby often used as an office. Her costume, webbed belts,
large snaps, mail and coarse hair, had all the charm of peonage.

Kirby felt a muscle snap free in his chest.

"I know why you've come," he said.

He'd had a dream: decline, goo that once looked sapient.

Witt and Khadary, she said, were dead. Balazos, falling sky,
night.

"When?" Kirby asked.

Weeks ago. Maybe a month.

"Where?"

Florida, she said. That place he'd left.

"How?"

Bile, she said. Skulduggery, underhandedness.

That evening, Lana sought to comfort his head and lower
parts.

There was a code of honor, he said. The code applied to every
feature of daily activity: betrayal, calumny, piety, etc. It was pre-
scriptive, detailed as needlework.

"What will you do?" she asked.

On this issue, the code was usefully specific. He was to purify
himself. Abstract into the realm of fact. Keep the weep out of his

voice. Make his cerebration simple as the four winds. When this was completed, he was to gather an army and—in the argot of the deep past—kick ass.

Within hours, fighters had begun assembling. They were what he expected and deserved: the otiose, hooligans from the hinterworlds, a group of Bay City Orientals quiet as cats, those with the deportment of fifth-century pirates, many from the netherparts of natural worship.

"They're beautiful," Lana said.

Kirby selected one to interview. He had the absurd and painful-looking bones of a pulsator.

"Why have you come?"

Dust fell from the man's shoulders. He knew Kirby's publications, he said. Their sweep, their purl. Besides, there was doing this or, worse, dying slowly.

To a second, the same question. In another life, this hombre could have been a stone. "Me too," the volunteer said, "sweep and purl."

To a third, the question again. This time with additions: "Think of the ways you yourself could die—puncture, lacerations, heartbreak."

"What can I tell you?" the man said. "I heard the story, I got aroused."

By daybreak, they were on the road, hundreds of them, nearly as formidable as that regiment he'd driven into Birmingham years ago. Once again, Kirby was amazed at the shapes we came in: portly, robust, craven, slumped. There was a principle in this, he knew. It concerned the spirit and where hope lurks.

"I have in mind another work," he told Lana. "It will be true and last forever."

All morning they marched. Some of the old songs went up: "O Youth and Beauty," "Just Tell Me Who It Was." Few were in automobiles. Some rode scooters. Dozens had scrambled aboard an airplane without wings. Eyewear was popular: goggles, glasses, sunshades, sleep masks with holes. Many had modeled themselves after the legendary heroes of the former orb: Agamemnon, Batygh the Tartar, Captain Ahab. Those with beards were regarded as blissful, in touch with a more earnest mission.

"I had a vision such as this," Kirby told Lana. In this vision, there was menace overcome, and plunder. Sacrifice led to reward, love to joy. People spoke and were listened to. Respect extended from mammals up and down the chain of being. Gobbledygook was considered piquant but harmless. The lightsome was preferred to its opposite, and everyone moved at very high speed.

"I had that, too," Lana said, "only more so."

At bivouac, a brilliant wind came up. A cold, balsamic smell was in the air. Rubble was near and yon. Kirby remembered his history. First was the age of burdened beasts—quadrapeds and willing man. Then an age of cleared land: water flowed where it ought. The machine age. Then, most recently, the age of sadness and throng.

"Now," he told Lana, "is the time of the self-fortified and those the victim of shame."

Toward midnight, a spy was discovered. He looked like something which might eat its young, and it took four brigands to subdue him.

"What is your name?" Kirby asked.

The man had the disposition of a hammer. He used a vocabulary of graphic violence, then endeavored to break free to maim them all. His name was Jerome and he had ridden with the Redlegs, an ad hoc group of mongers from Missouri.

"I have heard of you," Kirby said. "I'm told you have good sense and a way to do mayhem painlessly."

Jerome was parts scorn and arrogance. He had a way, he said, of doing it gruesomely and often.

"Bring him closer," Kirby commanded.

Howling and wriggling, Jerome was dragged forward. At this distance, it was possible to smell him. There was a sweetness, like decay, which could have been fear. Or ignorance of it.

"How had you hoped to hurt us?" Kirby asked.

Jerome delivered a wonderful speech. It concerned disrepair and puddles the crushed viscera make. It drew upon documents from the lost age—*The Critical Heritage, The Drama of Human Relations*—to fetch up a world of small deeds swiftly performed. There were subtleties too: time and what mortifies. He offered to be to Kirby what pestilence had been to our forebears. He could be blight, a plague of frogs, murrain. When he finished, defiant and outraged, he was less than a foot from Kirby.

"My specialty is massacre," Jerome said. "I aim to be like you, but without all the chitchat."

They were at that point where one man is inclined to slay another.

"You're in a bad position here," Kirby said.

Jerome used the words "perdurable" and "wreckage," then showed everyone his wet, pointed teeth.

There was an exchange of earnest expressions. Kirby thought he saw something familiar in Jerome's eyes. Kindredness, perhaps.

"Let him go," Kirby ordered. "I feel generous tonight."

As Jerome plunged into the wilderness, Kirby had one question: What is man? And one answer: Three or four colors, an instinct to breed life, plus remorse at the loss of it.

—

Near the end of their trek, Kirby had occasion to lecture his people on combat. Even in death, he said, war was about living.

Clouds like flatirons rose out of the distance, and in the breezes hung particles gritty as granite. The terrain was a dreamscape of precipice and butte, bluffs and thawed tundra. In the formations of boulders could be seen faces and what the previous generation of addlement had achieved. One rock in particular, tilted toward the horizon and mammoth as a building, resembled chaos itself: split and gouged, with little to cling to.

Kirby remembered one firefight especially. His first, he said, in the leafy country in what used to be northern Arkansas. Like those that followed, it trafficked in tumult and shudder, rupture and din. With him were Khadary and Witt, youths as well. They wore the appropriate garb, camouflage, tight as skin; they were to be conifers, erect and healthy. The secret words were "chapel" and "moonbeam," and they fell upon the bad guys like night itself.

"We were stealth," he said, "as natural as calamity."

In his audience now were those dressed as a wise, scurrying species. Bushlamps gave them all a rapt look.

Chief among his weapons that night had been a righteous frame of reference. Plus foresight.

"We anticipated everything," Kirby said. "Who crept where, what to ponder when it was done, how to exit."

Kirby recalled his thoughts—the few which could be uttered: fall down, shoot, jump up, be sufficiently furious, shoot, flop down again. Intensely aware of his body, he had addressed his innards as you would slaves you depend on. Heart, beat on; brain, be serious; guts, be still. There were feelings too—ponderous as tides, and rampant: alarm and shock, tremors which were thrills.

For a time, he remembered, mere panic prevailed. Foliage was shredded. These were the sounds you heard: thump, whack, wail and profound disillusionment. Light spun in chunks, splinters, shards. Hoots, laughter, the groans the fragile have. The night had heft; thoughts, hue. Then order was found. A voice barked "Go" and several humans lurched to obey it. You heard clatter, steady as breath, and brigados scuttling beneath it. Hysteria, stampede, pleas from beyond—these were noted. Once something ragged limped by, waxen and mumbling. It was a thinking meat, now thinking less. "What do I know?" it said. "I am foolish and just want to be old." Kirby heard a wet cough, and another fellow was hurled headlong into an outer, eternal darkness. Then the ground quit trembling and the night was quiet as a tree stump.

Kirby thought he saw shapes—possibly those common to nightmare.

"Chapel," he whispered, "moonbeam."

A second later the proper reply: "We have divinity. Light is everywhere."

It was Witt and Khadary, and Kirby had flown to them in a flash. They were wet-faced and grinning.

"Such is battle," he now concluded, "crunch and a great drying up in the interiors. Then there is joy."

Stinging rains fell the next day. And the next. Machines sputtered, failed. Several pack animals toppled over from exhaustion. A few fighters deserted, in one case leaving behind a note, conceived as a fairy tale, which addressed indolence and how, in the context of the discarnate, one was to live.

"I am cold," he told Lana one night. "Squeeze me."

She was strong and had knowledge of the tender joints.

The next day, the sun came up bleak and distant as heaven. Kirby remembered old, odd things: spades for digging, voluptuaries for being kind to, dank climes to leave. By afternoon, it had begun drizzling again, constant and fine as needles. Words came to mind: *tissue, crater, melt.*

"Lana," he said, "what would you do if I died?"

She had the posture of a queen. Mourn, she said. Then go elsewhere, for another.

"How long would that take?" he wondered.

"A week," she said, "possibly less."

That night he suffered dreams—of plains and such seas as heroes ply. He remembered being small and hungry, an orphan. He had learned a lesson from his mentors, Butch and Congressman Red Sorrell. It concerned demise, what it is to flee this mool. One aimed to have an idea, Butch said, then act immediately upon it. He provided examples—humility, cleverness, the usual vices—each a method for affecting one's circumstance. Congressman Red Sorrell advocated the direct approach: wrath, radical demeanor. Reflection was for those who followed, not for those who stood apart and screamed.

In the morning he dressed in gold, a textile shiny and slick as glass. A title had come to mind: *Youth on Mars*. It was himself, he believed, removed, indifferent as truth.

"On the one side," he told Lana, "is swill, an accumulation of objects, dismay."

"What's on the other?"

He smiled. "Me."

That day, his tropas marched with dispatch. He encouraged them to concentrate on the zany, the subversive. "Avoid nostalgia," he counseled, "it trivializes and saps the fighting juices." As his partisans moved through southern Alabama, he visited with small groups, shaking hands. He liked their costumes—their skins, their whichaway plumes and chestgear. "Convert," he told them, "have a notion, then realize it." Once he spoke through a bullhorn. Standing atop his Buick, he watched them trudge past. They were an array, motley and euphoric like a mob. "Be muscular of mind," he said, "exercise against the inert weight of the past." In this part of the country, the sky was orange, as if filtered a thousand times. It was a fine sky, vast and parlous as themselves. "Be proud," he advised, "you are ooze which speaks and often renews itself."

From his final bivouac, he sent out scouts.

"Be a shadow," he told them, "be a root."

They made affirmative sounds, stood at attention.

"Be dust," he said, "be a cloud."

Hours later they returned. Kirby could hear his enemies clearly now. Sprawled like one of the old cities, they were noisy and near.

"What are they?" Kirby asked.

His foes were the usual sort, one scout reported. Stiff with rage, eyes frenzied, unreconciled minds. They had a million disguises: glory, promise, lower states of mind.

"What weapons have they?"

Another fighter stepped forward. He had watery eyes and the expectant look of a pet.

They used noxious vapors, he said. Plus coils and slings, contraptions which flung stones over sizable distances, a command of fire, fertile imaginations.

"And what have we?"

The man drew himself up with pride.

"Humbug," he said, "and ire."

Through the twilight hours, while Kirby labored at his verses, there was a star shower, glowing streaks flashing thither. Beside him sat Lana, toying with her pistol and its four slugs. Names from his past reached him: Pesto, the Great Humongous, Virgil. These brought forward yet more: Butcher, Nod, X. It was a trail which, if followed, would lead backward into yore, a time of mists and smoky nights and swamps and the kind of misrule which sped hithermost on two legs, its shaggy head crowded and heavy with fear. Yore, Kirby knew, was a time like this.

"I am not scared," Lana said.

"What is the matter?"

"Nothing," she insisted. "I can't get my leg to stop shaking."

She looked delicious—an accomplishment with teeth and rare talents. He would miss her one day.

"What should I do after I slay them all?"

Do as he did, he confessed. Hie away and celebrate.

His musicians woke him at dawn. It was a thrill to hear brass and string in the service of peril. Rain had fallen during the night, and everything—beast, human, invention—was sheathed in ice. The hill in the distance, behind which his enemies were massed, glittered and sometimes looked like fire.

"This is a good omen," he said.

Lana was in the back seat, sorting through his outfits.

"What will you wear?" she asked.

He could be anything: pantologist, bronco buster, gent with a god.

Raiments, he said. Robes and many vests.

"In honor of this event," he told his people as they assembled, "I have written another lyric. Later will be the time for singing." He felt calm, as apart from this adventure as Witt and Khadary were apart from life. He could be standing meters away, he believed, his arms crossed and most amused, saying, *Kirby Puckett, my-my, you have come some ways since infancy.*

"For now," he said, "let us go forth and slaughter."

—

Early into the battle, after his people had tumbled screeching and yammering down the hillsides into the encampments below, Kirby believed he heard a loudspeaker or a radio. There were few in operation in these days; of those which did operate, most dealt in zealotry and affliction. This one now was speaking of sluts and man's due in discontinuous times.

Through his spyglass, Kirby watched his legions swarm and trample. He saw a turmoil of chair legs, fence posts, machetes. He saw one of his fiercest fighters—identifiable by his rictus grin and evident need to please—charge headlong into a group. He was a tornado, furious and lashing. Close by stood Lana, in a Calabar frock and bandana. She was shouting, too, and making flesh heave over in a heap. Kirby could read her mind. *Flee me,* it was saying, *I am Kirby's product and not at all merciful.*

"This is perturbation only," the voice on the loudspeaker was saying. "Repel and trounce."

Kirby surveyed the opposite hills. Cudweed, shrubs, char.

"Worry them, citizens," the voice was shrieking. "Cause them to drift and cry out."

Kirby could see little but ravaged trees—twisted and uprooted and blasted—and clogged earth. Perhaps they had a poet, too, he thought. A man like himself: slender and determined, but empty on the inside.

He spun his attention to the right: over there was flame and terror composed into men. On the left, Lana, hair like a storm. He read her lips: *This could be over in minutes, or maybe days.*

"Be not forlorn," the voice was saying, "hit, hit, hit."

Kirby held the spyglass steady. Slow, he reminded himself. Anxiousness is for the slack-brained. Breathe, he told himself. In. Hold. Wait for insight. Count. Listen. Out. A fireball shot up, like a sun in collapse, and for an instant he was blinded. Wait, he thought. Relax. Concentrate. Think. Life is meet. Think again. One, two, aaaahhhh.

So there it was: a ramshackle house trailer, painted green and dirt brown and set into the slope. Very cunning.

"What are you?" Kirby whispered. He knew the voice, its whine, its furor.

A second later he had located the loudspeakers and between them, mostly hidden in a lacework of shadows, the speaker himself. Jerome.

"How nice," Kirby said, "I favor things which come to an end."

His organs turned over, shook. He could feel his heart slamming into his ribs, the stomach tightening like a fist.

"Rise up, my people," Jerome was hollering. "Hurl yourselves into them!"

There was an idiom for this, Kirby knew. It was swift, vulgar, and true.

Struggling down the slope, his footing made treacherous by mud and debris, Kirby remembered his first woman. She had been much, much older, with a name which suggested beauty— April? Linda?—and it was said she had been a girl in the years of Heat and Great Darkness. She had scars and hair like mold. Loving her, Kirby decided, was like knowing the world's first primate.

In the valley itself—between, in fact, a shack of beaten corrugated tin and a breastworks of sandbags—Kirby's Orientals, grinning mysteriously and babbling, went racing past. They were dragging mattresses and buckets, old-fashioned grips and weathered luggage. "Shit," they were muttering, dispassionate and sullen. "Shit."

"What did you find?" Kirby asked.

"All goddam stuff," one said.

They showed him: petrol cans, a desk, toilet articles.

"What will you do with it?"

The man spit. "Who goddam knows!"

Off they scrambled, pointing and grabbing.

Nearby, a scout, the one with the dark eyeballs and the tragic aspect, was spinning in ragged circles, arms fluttering. "Pillage," he was saying. "Displace." It was an A-B-C recitation like that which schoolchildren had once upon a time to sit through. He nodded, thoughtfully, began anew: "Hobble, incrust, wander."

Kirby noticed that the voice, Jerome, had stopped. All that could be heard was Kirby's former host at the abandoned Dallas theater scolding his weapon, Boy. "Growl," he was saying, "charge, leap, bite, snap. Do it endlessly."

Kirby had a thought: turmoil. And another: uproar.

"This is my philosophy," someone was saying. The voice hailed from a long way off, perhaps a kilometer or more. "We should surrender ourselves to the underhalf of our natures. Eat and sleep, then find another venue to savage."

Kirby waited.

A motor was running: clank, thud, clank, thump.

A poplar tree disappeared in a whooshing geyser of flame.

"I have a philosophy, too," another voice was saying. It was distant as well, and most reasonable. "There ain't no complex nature. Just such rigamarole as us."

Kirby watched three men pedal by on a bicycle. They seemed happy, undisturbed.

Behind him, an animal was loose and in pain.

A gun went off—pssst, pssst, pssst—and then a man dashed up to Kirby, grabbed his hand. He was frenzied, a glaze of tears on his cheeks. The hem of his caftan was crusty and torn. He kept pointing to himself and spitting. He panted. He hollered for another minute, then vanished into the woods.

"Who was that?" Lana was positioned on a rock nearby.

"Fork," Kirby said, "from the Cotton Bowl."

"What did he want?"

To go home, Kirby said. People were trying to hurt him.

Lana nodded and bounded out of view. Again, Kirby stood alone, waiting. An image came to him: himself flopping about and heading rearward in time.

He touched his verses in his jacket pocket.

He wanted something to happen very soon and to be very important.

Ten giant steps away squabbled two men. "Yes," snapped one. "No," said his confederate. They slapped each other, hard, then hurried off, mumbling.

There was another principle here, Kirby knew. It addressed dither and such hugger-mugger as the fear-wrought make. And then came the familiar voice.

"Well, lookee here."

To one side, not a dozen paces away, stood Jerome in the outrageous sleepwear of a prince. He was wearing a fez, and with him were a dozen equally dark-minded attendants.

"I was expecting you," Kirby said.

Jerome executed a bow he was clearly proud of.

"These are my elite," he said. "Let me introduce them."

They had not names but states of consciousness: Envy, Torpor, Vigilance, etc. They all excelled at behavior appropriate to disorder. They had bony, massive hands and appeared to enjoy their work.

"They must love you," Kirby said.

"I am loved everywhere. I inspire serious affection."

So this is how it will be, thought Kirby. I am to be slain by a youngster in love.

They had circled him now, Jerome in front, his eyes glistening. He had an ascetic's face: gray and blank with need. War, evidently, was food to him.

"Why are we doing this?"

A combination of reasons, Jerome said. Ennui, rigorism, the riffraff we are.

The sky was dark once more, like a bruise. It would rain in an hour. Nature, Kirby knew, could be especially impressive during clamorous times.

"I am told you were a real son-of-a-bitch." Jerome was using his hands like cleavers. "I used to have great admiration for you, truly. I was impressed, specifically, by your mongrelism and where it got you."

The battle proper was shifting away, into a glade several hundred meters distant. Hectoring and praising, Lana was directing his warriors. She looked jubilant. She was resolve and fury, plus such forces outlaws feel. Good, he thought. She will be the son-of-a-bitch now.

"Would you like to hear a poem?" Kirby brought out his manuscript.

"I think not," Jerome said.

"What is it you want to do to me?"

As before—now years ago, it seemed—Jerome told him. It was an entertaining five minutes. Havoc was discussed, as were the concepts of disunion and crypt-life. He mentioned melancholy and longing, firmaments and what creatures seem from a higher point.

"Now?" Kirby said.

Jerome nodded and his henchmen closed in like a claw.

NOTES I MADE ON THE MAN I WAS

I N the times before what my new wife calls "the troubles"—
before Vicki, the teenager I'd married in college, began living
with the A-Card golfer over in Las Cruces and when my home
seemed as composed and felicitous as any heaven could in this
desert town—I was what the disc jockey on KOBE the other day
said was a good listener, which means you sigh regularly and
shake your noddle in the pitiful parts. My friend Newt Grider,
whose own story is well known hereabouts to the six thousand
folks we are, used to tell me everything, particularly details from
what he said was his soft inner life. The glossy, blissful aspect of
the mystic would fall over him, and wherever we were—drinking
a Coke at the Triangle Drive-In, say, or on the practice green at
the Mimbres Valley Country Club—he'd grip my elbow in a hand
more fat than meat and drag me aside as if to a private corner of
this nosy world. He'd tell me the damndest stuff: how in high
school, years ago, he'd once touched the erect pecker of Coleman
Baker (who is as queer now, which is the word he uses, as talking
fish); or how once, semidrunk and blue-hearted, he'd worn the
underclothes of his wife, Alice Mary; or how he wished his
daughters were boys and therefore unlikely to be preyed upon by
the horny youth-sort he'd been.

One time, only weeks before he fled this town forever (disappeared, in fact, as completely as if he'd vanished into the misty
afterworld—the place Reverend Turlock advises us to believe is
parts snow cloud and string music), he stormed into my showroom (I sell Chevrolets for a living) and thrust at me a list so
scribbled it could have come from a blind person. It was two
pages of names, many strange but some—including Irene
Puckett and Betty Lou Bates—familiar as my own family.

"These are women I slept with," he said, his voice mostly air and throat.

He had that look again: eyeballs without focus, the shiny peaceful cheeks of a sleepy man. There were seventeen women in all, he said, a few with last names he couldn't remember, and most of them had been made love to while he was a married man. As was my habit, I nodded and aimed to report what my Uncle Red had once told me about relations between men and women, an observation which addressed the animal parts we are; but Newt, who could be as single-minded as a bird, was already in motion. He scooped up his pages, rolled them like a baton and, without the hesitation I think the moment called for, set them aflame. They made a smoky, eye-stinging blaze, which he dumped into my trashcan. He was still grinning, the way he did when we played tackle football together and thrashed the daylights out of everybody.

"Fenton," he began, "I've done some thinking about this."

Through my glass walls, I could see a pair of my employees staring at us as if we were pound-bred canines in Florida sport-coats and lace-up wingtip shoes.

"I'm putting this phase of my life behind me," he announced. "I'd like to be good, plus I love Alice Mary."

Then he left, shoulders squared as if he'd just slain a cutthroat who'd been using his name for years.

I tried once, some while ago, after Newt had gone away, to tell Alice Mary something of this, but she only said, as if starved of patience and related hopes, that it was a fallen world (made grimmer still by betrayal) and that if I knew anything about Newt—"or your own self, for that matter!"—then I could just as well shout it down a wellhole, or keep it to myself.

Which, until now, I've done.

*

Months later, near enough to Vicki's departure to be memorable, E. Bishop Pike, from the parts department, invited me to his

place, which was a house trailer on Yucca Street with what a
realtor might tell you is a sultan's panorama of the mountains
(but which I have always thought of as merely acres of scrub-
weed and those shrunken, twisted trees we'll one day find on
Mars). Pike's real name wasn't Bishop but Eddie, the nickname
slapped on him by a daddy who thought his youngster too sober-
minded and perhaps sissy. Pike's real problem, he told me that
afternoon, was that he was a goddam learned man—a victim, he
said, of living in the mind in a place which asked so much of the
flesh. His face, I think now, had all the evidence of what such
learning can do: hollow-eyed as a dog and pasty-lipped. He was
thin too, sixty percent shoulderblades and kneecaps and, somewhere between hips and head, the ribby, slumped chest of a boy.
Sometimes, in fact, I didn't think of him as a twenty-year-old,
employed for the summer (because his daddy had asked), but
as the oldest, and third, of my sons; and sometimes, because
I truly liked him, I let him call me "Pop," which at middle
age made me feel as feeble and wrinkled at the neck as my own
old man.

That day I am talking of, we sat on his Wal-Mart lawn chairs,
aluminum and rickety, and looked mostly east, where the sun
was shining to and where, so many miles away it can't be seen at
all, my Vicki lives now and is, as far as I can tell, happy. Bishop
told me that he hadn't had any of the adventures his peers had—
no motorcycle riding on the flats, no athletics except six months
of bowling at the Thunderbird, no fist-fighting, nothing but what
you know of bookworms everywhere. "Which," he said, "is reading, thinking about it, then reading it again." That day, as a
matter of fact, he was reading *Ivanhoe,* which fetched up to my
mind knights and armor and snorting steeds to ride, but which
brought to his, he said, the upper half of life. He was talking
about derring-do, he told me. Peril and escape. A world in which
people used such language as "dauntless" and "stalwart" and
meant them the way we, in ours, use "pissant" and "chickenshit." His was a rare habit of mind, I learned, as useless in this
New Mexico desert as tits on a teacup, and sometimes—in his

dreams, mostly—he found himself drifting loose of this world, little in real life as shaped and clear as what he read.

"Pop," he said, "I'm thinking about dropping out of school, what d'you say?"

He had, you ought to know, the same expression Newt got when his mind was made up, but I told Bishop, as I ought, that his parents, his Baptist daddy foremost, would be much disappointed and, well, I'd be some empty-hearted too, as I believed in school. I was trying to be wise, I remember, but uppermost in my brain was a picture of Vicki at SMU, an image that was as colorful and love-laden as the best from Walt Disney.

"What would you say," Bishop began, "if I told you I was going in the Army? I got to get me some excitement."

This was 1968, and what came to mind was the only place our Army was going, Vietnam, and what a death Bishop's might make over there. I could see him, though he sat next to me eager and keen-eyed, as just more of that despair which was entering our living rooms every night.

"This isn't rash," he said. His thinking had risen to rumination, and did I understand? "Jesus," he was saying, "I'm not doing anything in this dump."

He was up now, pacing and looking westward where hope is thought to lie. He had a vision, he said, of that life he wanted. He mentioned meaninglessness and those ideas you find in rhymed verse. He walked past me then, and I put my arm out.

"I wanted to be other things too," I said. "I wanted to drive race cars, hang around with Mario Andretti or those Unser brothers."

It was a wish, I told him, which appealed even now; it was nothing for me to sit back, after Mr. Cronkite told me how events were among my kind, and feel myself strapped into a vehicle which left our world reeling behind. I could even see myself in a political life, a white-whiskered state senator, in my hands the welfare of trusting citizens. Bishop was stopped in front of me now, his expression contrary and mixed, lips almost purple, and for an instant I thought he would either hug me or knock me silly with his scholar's fists.

"Mr. Riley," he said, "maybe you ought to go home now."

Silent as a monk, he worked the rest of that summer; then, far as I knew, he went back to UNM to be that zoologist his daddy wanted. I didn't hear from him until two years later when a picture arrived: it showed E. Bishop Pike in almost biblical sunlight, dressed in the grubby work clothes of an oilfield roughneck, smiling as if possessed by the secret knowledge witches are said to have. He was standing atop sands that looked as hot as any we have here.

"This is Arabia," he had written on the back, "and when you watch the news tonight, think of me in it and running amok with my joy."

—

This is the old world, and it is gone—as are the folks who lived there. New people from Ohio and Michigan have moved here to take the place of ours who have gone to California or Oregon or even death. With them, of course, have gone secrets I once knew. Scooter Le Duc, for example, has taken with him to Boise, Idaho, his tale of terror and flight and what moral it had. Jimmy Bullard has taken with him his story of the bottle and its charms. Gone are all those stories I have heard—of gloom and of wist and of the disarray that attends male grief. Even I, who am still here and thinking of it, am gone from the other person I was: I am fatter, losing hair above the temples and have lately switched my allegiances to such straight-shooting Republicans as Abraham Lincoln and Governor King. Curiously, this change has to do with the last time I saw my Vicki, who appeared one Saturday, with my boys, after driving back from the Phoenix Open (where her Yogi had finished seventeenth and had made pals with Billy Casper).

They were driving a Chrysler, plush and in the 12K range, and seemed to climb out of it as if from a boat, gingerly and looking around for menace. My boys, Taylor and Buddy ("Yogi calls me Brad," he said), were taller and heavier by seven years, all the innocence gone from their faces; they didn't give me the hugs of offspring, but shook my hand like those raised by the military.

"You look good, Dad," Taylor said, "maybe you ought to send a snapshot."

Yogi, awkward as an African, said he was pleased to meet me and there were no hard feelings. He was florid, with a sports-man's squint and blond arm hairs; plus, he gripped your hand as you do a putter, firm but cautious.

"I'm pleased to meet you, too," I said, meaning some of it.

And then Vicki herself came up my walk, her hair like that I see in commercials, windblown but exotic. Her legs, as well, went to the heart of me and for a moment I thought she had sprung, say, from the vast, turbulent mind of E. Bishop Pike himself; she seemed less like one I had lived with than one I had read about in the barbershop.

She gave me the cheek kiss you get from aunts you don't much know, then she said, "We thought we'd bring the boys by, say howdy."

That afternoon we sat out back by the pool I'd built for her. Life was dandy for them, they said. Yogi was playing a dozen tourna-ments a year, not making much but taking trips to pricey places like Dallas and Palm Springs. The boys were well, too, Taylor average in school but Buddy ("Brad," Vicki said) hot-tempered enough to be gifted. I made drinks—vodka, I believe—and they wondered how I was and what I had been doing. Yogi was sitting on the other side of Vicki, and you could tell he'd once thought I might shoot him or otherwise become the ugly person she'd told him I could be. They held hands—hers on top—which I thought was okay.

"I built a new showroom," I said, "and hired a few more."

I told about who'd died and what babies were new and those I'd met at the Wildcat twenty-fifth reunion, but mostly, from the shade I sat in, I was watching Vicki. I was wondering about the cherry mole she had on her breast and that tiny scar she had on her rump from falling off a horse; I wondered, too, if she kept his

place as tidy as she'd kept ours and if she was still having a
menthol cigarette after orgasm. I mentioned some names—J. E.
Odom, Chuck Gribble, the Clutes (Mickey and Jane)—and she
said that the only one she was in touch with regularly was Alice
Mary Grider, Newt's wife, and that life seemed the same hereabouts. It was hot, I remember, and I longed to be inside, alone,
air-conditioned and watching the Dodgers on cable TV. You
could hear the boys in their old rooms, hollering occasionally, and
once Buddy came out, holding a stuffed pig I'd bought him at the
Grand Canyon; he said, "Taylor wants to know, was this his or
mine?"

Here then, noonlight weighing on us heavily, those people
talking to me and the desert lying endless and blank as it ever
has, your hero felt that old world fall away from him. I felt it and
them burn up as completely as Newt Grider's list of women he
would not sleep with anymore.

"Buddy," I said, "it's all yours."

The silence among us had heft and some emotion to it. "Let's
go out for dinner, okay?" I said. I was thinking of the Ramada
Inn, its steak house. I had it figured this way: We would drink
some more, I'd get to know Yogi Jones, they would leave and I
would be free at last to go out into that new world I had heard
about, where I could find the wife I have now—who is Eve
Spalding and who believes, as I do, in the always current moment and what it means.

THE VALLEY OF SIN

NEITHER Deming's best golfer nor its worst, Mr. Dillon Ripley was, as the six thousand of us in these deserts now realize, its most ardent, having taken to the sport as those in the big world we read about have taken to drink or narcotics. Almost daily, you'd see him on the practice tee, elbows, knees and rump in riot, his fat man's swing a torment of expectation and gloom. With him would be Allie Martin, our resident professional, and together, hip to hip, faces shaded against the fierce sunlight we're famous for, hair flying in the breezes, they'd stare down the fairway, as if out there, waiting as destiny is said to wait, stood not riches or happiness, but Ripley himself, slender and tanned and strong as iron, a hero wise and blessed as those from Homer himself.

On the weekends, noon to dusk, he'd be accompanied by his wife, Jimmie. He had bought her the spiked shoes and loose cardigans of the linkster, and he tried teaching her, as he was being taught, how to grip the club, what "break" was, and what enchantments came to mind when the ball soared, as it ought, or plopped into the cup on its last revolution. Golf, he told her, was bliss and bane. Holding her by the shoulders, as earnest about this as others are about religion, he would say that golf was like love itself. He used language like "passion" and "weal." He mentioned old terms for the equipment: mashie, niblick, spoon. He knew everything about the game, its lore and minutiae, and his weekday playing partners—Watts Gunn, Phinizy Spalding and Poot Taylor—had often heard him remark that one day now, when he'd squared his affairs at the Farmers and Merchants Bank, where he was a vice-president (Loan Department), he, Jimmie and the four children would vacation in Scotland, specifi-

cally near the Old Course at St. Andrews, home of the Royal and
Ancient Golf Club. He imagined himself, he told his partners,
among the ridges and hillocks, cheerful at the sight of meadow
grasses and sheltered dunes, knolls and hollows and whins as
dear to him as money is to some. So profound was his affection
for the sport that once, at the fourteenth tee, already set over his
ball, scarcely any traffic at all on the gravel service road which
paralleled the fairway, he announced—a week before Jimmie ran
off with Allie Martin—that he knew what best tested the kind we
are: It was not death or travail or such woe as you find in newspapers; it was the hazards of unmown fescue and bent grass, or a
sand wedge misplayed from a bunker known as the Valley of Sin.

It happened in May, the Sunday before Armed Forces Day. We
suspect that Dillon was too involved in his forthcoming round to
notice that Jimmie, erect as a hat model, brighter in the eye and
cheek, leggier, seemed nervous or rather too beautiful that morning. Dressed in his so-called Cuban outfit (red NuTonics, pink
slacks, black polka-dot shirt), he felt superior. Eating as if
starved, he told his oldest boy, the teenager Brian, that today was
an anniversary of sorts: on this day in A.D. 508, Dillon claimed,
King Clovis had established Paris, formerly Lutetia, as the Fran-
kish capital, following his vanquishing of the Visigoths.

"So what?" the boy grumbled.

There was evidence—Dillon had the boy by the ears now,
smiling like a clown—that golf, which may have been suggested
by the Dutch game *kolven,* was already being played in Scotland.

"Oh," the boy said, "great."

To the youngest girl, Marcia, Dillon described the ancient
burns and thickets that were extant when our forebears—
smaller, hairier, ruder—ruled a world flat as a cookie sheet.

"Jeez, Dad," she said, shaking her head. "You know some
awful dumb stuff."

Looking as if he'd slept for a century, Dillon arrived at the first
tee before noon. He did not use a cart, instead hiring as his caddy
Tommy Steward, a Wildcat football player thought to be the most

wayward AA right tackle in Luna County, New Mexico; and through the front nine, which he played well if not stylishly, Mr. Dillon Ripley had the stride of a general, as well as the amused expression of a citizen worth seventy thousand dollars a year.

"I feel young," he told Phinizy Spalding.

He recounted an anecdote about his Lambda Chi days at SMU, a boozy, melancholy escapade about women, which was embarrassing enough to be true; then, at lunch in the clubhouse, he revealed that this July he and the family would be visiting the British Open. He mentioned Watson, Nicklaus and Trevino, plus such legends as Old Tom Morris and the vaunted Harry Vardon. He mentioned Strath Bunker and Hill Bunker—the Scylla and Charybdis of the 172-yard par-three eleventh. And, after buying them all, including Tommy Steward, a Bloody Mary, he marched his foursome to the tenth hole, quoting Sir Guy Campbell on "the thick, close-growing, hard-wearing sward that is such a feature of true links turf wherever it is found."

Hard for us it is to know our fate—or grace or, for that matter, our doom—when it appears. For some, it has a hue; for others, a sound. For Dillon Ripley, as for most, it had a face and a name and it swept by him—on the fourteenth fairway, of course—at upward of forty miles per hour, a silver '79 Volvo sedan.

"Hey," Tommy Steward said, waving his chunky tackle's fist, "ain't that Allie?"

Yonder, gaining speed, its horn whining, the car flew toward them, dust boiling up in the wake. Dillon, his wood balanced against his leg, was washing his Maxfli, watching the Volvo swerve. Light glinted from the windshield like sparks. It looked as if, though you couldn't be sure, there were two people inside, the passenger lifeless as sculpture, the other thrashing to and fro as if overcome with ecstasy. For a time, Dillon's foursome had a single organ of understanding: they looked and shrugged and opened their hands to say that, well, what'd you expect? This was old Allie Martin, Mr. Cut-up.

Tommy said, "Is he drunk or what?"

Poot Taylor recalls he had no thoughts at all, just the notion, felt like ice in the heart, that something—our planet, its moon, the hithermost stars—was awry.

Watts Gunn believed he smelled rain in the west, where clouds had built into a pavilion high as heaven, and he wondered if the windows in his Monte Carlo were closed.

Next to Dillon, Phinizy Spalding, a fast driver himself, was thinking of chaos, and a question came to mind regarding babble and sloth. He saw, as well, a pall falling between him and the future.

And then, when the Volvo came abreast, horn blaring, throwing up road filth behind, Tommy Steward hollered, "Hey, Mr. Ripley, ain't that your—?"

Zooming past, looking headlong, was Jimmie, indifferent as truth, her shoulders pearly, luminous and bare.

"Lordy," Tommy said, aghast, "she's naked!"

There was a noise, choked but awful as thunder, and when our linksters turned around, stricken Dillon was in collapse, his lips a disheartening shade of blue.

—

After three weeks in the Mimbres Valley Hospital, his heart mended with diet and drugs, Dillon Ripley returned home. His instructions from Dr. Weems said to avoid difficult physical activity. No lifting, for example. Walking was fine. But no golf. Not yet. A housekeeper, Mrs. Fernandez, who lived on Iron Street, had been hired to tend to the children; and, though few saw him, the rumor was that Mr. Ripley was well, reading his chief diversion, not mournful. Many spouses, we were learning, had been abandoned by their mates, and Mr. Ripley was being as stalwart about his condition as, say, the fish is about its. Life was a jungle, it was said in the clubhouse, and we, its upright creatures, were no more noble or charmed than thinking worm or sentient mud. Hereabouts, in fact, heartache was compared to history; both had to do with time and inevitable sadness. Many people, moreover, accepted the view offered by Dr. Tippit at St. Luke's Presbyterian—a view which held that ours was a fallen orb, burdensome indeed, but bound to improve, to yield itself to the wish of an enlightened master. Yesterday, it was argued, man was only an ape; today he was more upstanding, to be sure, but hardly far enough from the trees he'd sprung from.

That winter, Dillon Ripley attended the Christmas and New Year's parties at the club, turning a cha-cha-cha with Millie Gunn and doing a modified twist with Grace Spalding. He looked hale, thinner by thirty-five pounds, and everyone wondered when we'd again see him at the practice tee, his spine stiff as a sentry's, his powerful and collected gaze fixed on the horizon.

"Soon, soon," he'd answer.

Though no one said as much, people were still keenly interested in Jimmie and Allie. Poot Taylor had heard they lived in Florida, Allie trying to qualify for his A card so he could compete on the satellite tour. Dr. Weems understood they were in Honduras, Allie in a field which included all manner of felon and vagabond duffer. Watts Gunn thought they had fled to Cincinnati, as Jimmie supposedly had a younger sister there. If Dillon knew, he wasn't saying. Instead, he danced—the Cleveland chicken, the rhumba, a naughty knee-knocking mambo Jackie Gleason would have envied—and proposed a champagne toast to what his daddy had called fortune. "Which, as I understand it," he began, smiling at us whom he had known all his life, "is part pluck, part guile and part sense of humor. Happy New Year!"

In February, the month Dillon put his house on the market, Tito Garza, who handled the night watering at the club, found the flagsticks on the tenth and eleventh holes twisted into impossible shapes—one, it was said, an idea of horror made steel, the other a loop a drunk might make falling down, the nylon flags themselves scorched. We had the sense, felt like an icy current of air, that something parlous, of claw and cold blood, perhaps, had invaded our course, its vast mind consumed by a single thought of rage.

Three weeks later, we Sunday linksters began finding notecards stuffed into the cups on several holes on the backside. Each card was margin to margin with handwriting so fine and peculiar it looked like crewelwork practiced by a lost race of tiny, nearly invisible people. Under the magnifying glass Mr. R. L. Crum kept in the men's locker, you could tell the writing was either complex as knowledge itself or witless as mumbo-jumbo. "The world is almost rotten," read one. Another: "We are a breed in need of fasting and prayer." On a third: "Porpozec ciebie nie prosze dorzanin." His face blotchy with passion, Abel Alwoody, who'd been to Vietnam, insisted it was all gook to him and called forth for us a vision composed of fire and ash. Judge Sanders suggested it was a prank, probably from the Motley brothers, whose shed adjacent to the twelfth hole he had recently condemned.

"Hold on a second," Garland Steeples said. The air in that locker was close, heavy as wool. Steeples was the high-school counselor and it was clear he was bringing to our mystery his professional training in the human arts of hope and fear. He pointed to several words, "want," "venery," "vice," and a phrase, "the downward arc of time." His face, particularly around the eyes, was dark as winter. It was a moment to which the word *ruin* might apply. "What I see is this," he began.

He was speaking of misrule and bolsheviks when we began edging away.

Through April and May, a season glorious in our arid clime, there were no disturbances, other than several late-night calls to Yogi Jones, the new pro, who felt he was listening either to a ghost or to a very arch infant. Then, the first week of summer, near midnight one Wednesday, when he was necking with Eve Spalding, Phinizy's daughter, on the fourteenth green, Tommy Steward, fuzzy-minded on red-dirt marijuana, thought he spied a figure, possibly human, darting amidst the cottonwood trees. There was a new moon, pouring light down like milk, and the high wispy clouds that mean a wind is up from Mexico. While he held Eve, he spotted it again, loping like a low beast but wearing the togs of a sportsman, and his heart shot to his throat like a squirrel, all claws and climbing. Words came to mind: *flank, cranium, haunch.*

"Eeeeeffff," he groaned. "Aaarrgghh."

Even from a distance, the thing appeared murderous, a creature of carnage and outrage like those scale-heavy, horned, thick-shouldered figures he knew about from nightmare. In an instant, tumbling Eve aside, he was dashing in a dozen directions at once, shirttails flapping.

"What's the matter?" Eve was saying, almost frightened herself. She had her blouse open, her breasts—like Jimmie's, months earlier—firm and white.

Tommy sputtered: "Naaaaaa, naaaaa."

His arms, as if jointless, whipped the air. He felt he was breathing sand. A thousand ideas came to him, none concerning humans. And then, in a way more swift than flight itself, the thing, wretched as a savage, leaped in front of him, not ten giant steps away. It was in skins, yes, and dirty as orphans you see in French movies. One fist was shaking overhead, and in the other, like a cudgel, hung a golf club heavy with sod.

"Goddam," Tommy was yelling, "Jesus H. Christ!"

There was noise everywhere—roars wrathful and morbid, both. The ground had begun to tilt, and Tommy, dry-mouthed and trembling, felt he was staring at the hindmost of our nature, its blind pink eyes, its teeth wet as a dog's. Then, dragging and pushing and carrying Eve, Tommy was gone, running elsewhere—anywhere!—in a fury, too addled to scream.

—

That month, until too bored to continue, Poot Taylor and Watts Gunn, riding in an electric golf cart, patroled the country club at night, each armed with a .22. The night the lookout ended, someone sneaked onto the ninth green and, using a shovel (later found in a mesquite bush), dug several pits, the deepest in that spot from which the great Willie Newell had once sunk a chip for the Invitational championship. In the morning, signs were discovered. They had the theme of heartwork and dealt with such concepts as travesty and blight. "Pray and your life will be better," one read. "We are base," another said, "and nothing can be done."

In August, Dillon Ripley sold his house and moved his family twenty miles farther south in the desert, to Hatchita, where, as we understand it, there is no sport at all save hunting and where the winds, infernal and constant, blow as if from a land whose lord is dark and always angry.

WHERE IS GARLAND STEEPLES NOW?

EVERY time Garland told the story, which, according to his sister, Darlene Neff, was so farfetched and shifty an item that it couldn't be true, he gave its hero, the dog, a new name. Garland's first week back after discharge, those medals of his—the Army Commendation Medal, the Good Conduct Medal, the NDS medal, and that unit citation for valor from the Republic of Vietnam—still untattered, the dog was called Chester Sims, supposedly after a spec four known to Garland up in the MR3 with the 18th ARVN. In April, however, a month after Garland had begun working at that 7-11 which was practically in sight of Arlington Stadium, the dog was known as Mr. Eddie and had only three legs, the absent one reportedly blown off clean in a place identified as the Crescent of Fertile Minds. In June, before Garland started the bank-robbing he became famous for, the dog was Spike or Marvin, and its story—from the time it was met and loved and then murdered by Garland—took nearly thirty minutes of telling. Ivy Parks, Darlene Neff's neighbor, heard that the dog was named Nick Carter, after Garland's favorite reading matter, and was supposed to be as big as the enemy itself and, what with toothsome grin and mange, probably rabid. In July, on the day he brought home the gleaming roadmaster, its engine a masterpiece of brightwork, Garland told his boss, Mr. Hemsley, that his dog was named Tiger and that, like all stories, Tiger's was part joy and part trouble, the whole of it unhappy as Xmas in Russia—not a word of which Hemsley believed on account of Garland's goofy grin and the way his eyes turned dark whenever he reached the passages about being able to speak canine, a fact he illustrated by going "Aarrff" and "Woof" and "Grrrr" until the story was not English at all but only bark, ardent growl and gesture that looked like four-legged distress.

After a time, though, everybody, from Darlene's husband, Virgil, to Ike Fooley who lived down the street, to Bonnie Suggs, the First Federal teller to whom he told it while pointing a big old cannonlike gun—everybody knew it as Garland H. Steeples's story, "The Dog of Vietnam," a narrative he told a thousand times in 1971, always mentioning how he was on loan to the 1/26, Hotel Company, in particular a fivesome of ethnic savages who billed themselves as the Detroit Pistons (because of their affection for basketball and place of national origin), who high-stepped around Firebase Maggie dressed up in these abso-fuck-ing-lutely outrageous tailored outfits they'd gotten on Nathan Road in Hong Kong (black leaf-patterned camouflage suits so tight they were skin itself, with matching boonie hats). "I was truly happy," he told Darcel Worthy, a man who'd come into the store one night looking for ginger ale and Cheez Whiz. "I had me a mission in this life," Garland said, "and folks around to help me do it. Plus, I was eighteen, which means I was permanently optimistic." He had his mind right, he said; he was not terribly aggravated by peacecreeps nor otherwise upset about the down-scale living and dying that took place when Victor Charles sought his destiny and Uncle Sugar aimed to resist. Truth to tell, he was some excited by all that NVA bang-bang and the hardware by which, including CAR-15 and beautimous Claymore mine, he endeavored to hush it. "I was gonna do my two years, get loose of that place and go back to the world an adult."

Anyway, Garland would say, having established time, place and central character, into Firebase Maggie one day walked this dog—here G's eyes would get all misty and quite unfocused from the memory of it all—with mussed hair like a twenty-dollar streetwalker and an expression that said, "I could be forty thousand years old, but screw you anyway, GI." That animal, someone said, brought to mind such words as *scourge* and *mishap*. "It was a Vietnam dog, all right," Garland told his brother-in-law. "It had floppy ears, one practically chewed right to the bone, and you could tell it just loved being around the smells and wealth of us. I

knew right then I had to have me that animal." It took nearly
twenty minutes for the beast to take the pressed meat Garland
offered, what with its disposition being more wary than trusting;
then the two of them went back to G's hooch and shared a corn-
flake bar while the human one introduced the animal to the CO
and an E-8 master sergeant named Krebs; Garland pointed out
that beyond the bangalores and perimeter wire and artful maze
of land mines lay an almost impenetrable jungle in which lurked
a shitload of high-principled cutthroats who rode bicycles and
who would like nothing more than, given their usual diet of rat
and rice, to feast upon haunch of dog or backbone filet. "So what
do you say, Vietnam dog, how 'bout you and me becoming pals?"
While the animal appeared to debate the question, Garland cast
about for more convincing arguments. "The way I look at it,"
Garland said, "you are alone and I'm alone, which means that we
ought to be together having fun. Loneliness ain't for the kind we
are." Whereupon that critter, so the story went, lay its muzzle on
its forepaws and seemed to ponder for a time; then, with an
affirmative noise, it leaped aboard our boy, leaving sloppy lick
marks all over his cheeks.

It was, according to Darlene Neff's recollection, the sort of love
as was had between Pancho and Cisco, Tonto and the Lone
Ranger—Garland and his grungy sidekick as inseparable as
white on chalk. They went everywhere together—latrine,
commo tent, even on a dark-of-night extraction near Hill 199
when a Chinook warrant officer, trying to evade heavy ground
fire, almost pitched them into outer space. "I told that dog everything about me," Garland confessed to Billy Pickering, the boy
who delivered the *Times-Herald*. "I showed him pictures, too: me
at Disneyland, me at high-school graduation, me pissing into the
Grand Canyon." He even read to that dog, its favorite passages
being those when Marc Bolan, the Executioner, blasted the bejesus out of the lowdown evil other guy. He taught that dog how
to sit up, how to roll over like a drunk, and how to cross its front
legs like a Frenchman named René. He taught him how to beg

like you were being done a favor; and once, after some three-star
action in Recon Zone Hood, he got that furry creature high on
Cambodian weed and they staggered off to eyeball the stars and
make up miracles to astound the in-country gangsters they had
occasion to deal with.

"Oh, that was some smart animal," Garland used to tell the
other clerk, a wide-hipped Big Springs woman named Colette.
Why, he took that dog one time into the big airbase at Da Nang,
made it walk right up to Mr. Bob Hope and shake his Hollywood
hand, Garland later coming up on stage to take a bow for having
such an intelligent and well-mannered companion. Yet that dog
could be plumb feisty too. One time, so the story went, it bit the
rear end of a larcenous Friendly, which prompted a blizzard of
directives up and down the chain of command—which resulted,
so rumor had it, in MACV itself, in the estimable person of General William Westmoreland, saying it favored and did encourage
man–pet love as a morale booster, as essential to a given
hombre's welfare as letters from home or exotic R & R.

The trouble started, Garland told the ticket-taker at Six Flags,
when his dog—then called Buster or, if female, Sally—chewed
through its leash and somehow found its way to Garland's side,
forty klicks into the murk-filled hinterlands. The TL, a Philly
delivery man who liked to be called Bigfoot, was all for shooting
Buster. He said "Shit" and "Goddam" and "Ain't this a crock?"
and twice flicked the safety off his Sixteen with the full intent of
vaporizing the entire hair and teeth and scrawny, pest-ridden
hindquarters of him who was one man's best friend. Garland was
outraged: "You don't touch my dog," he yelled, "Touching my
dog will get you killed many times!" A COM/SIT report which
surfaced after the war said an hour's discussion followed, during
which it was reported that because LURPs in II Corps were
supposedly bringing along skivvy bar girlfriends (not to mention
those Highway 14 Rangers who'd taken a Saigon rock 'n' roll
band named Teenage Wasteland into the Ir Drang Valley), it
seemed okay to bring along old Shep or whatever the hell his

name was. "He's got to watch his ass," the TL said. "I don't want to hear no squealing or nothing."

According to EYES ONLY paperwork out of the GVN, the murder and Garland's subsequent ill-will began the night he went into the bush with the Detroit Pistons to bury several Black Boxes on a so-called high-speed trail down which Charlie and his ilk were conveying ordnance so sophisticated it was feared that Uncle Ho himself would soon be following in an AirStream house trailer with Bar-B-Que and Magnavox color TV. Garland said the night was pure Alfred Hitchcock: pale moon, inhospitable flora, fauna such as might have been invented by Dr. Frankenstein, not to mention an E & E route they all believed led right past the open door of the Hanoi Politburo. Buster was there, too, half dipped in lampblack to give him that dangerous Hell-I-don't-care evil look it took humans only twenty minutes to acquire over there. Everything was fine for a time, the good guys being sneaky and expert, the six of them, men and dog, stopping for a while to eat and catnap, then there was a crackling noise in the woods, a six-sided shiver of recognition, and the TL tumbled over in a heap, a big hole where his chest used to be, which was followed by scrambling, jumping and diving. According to the Governor of Texas, who'd heard it from the TBI, who'd gotten their information from the Tarrant County sheriff whose deputies had interviewed the guard and two tellers at the Citizens' Bank on Cedar Street, the ATL took it in the neck, and one by one, in a storm of tears and rendered hearts, all the other Detroit Pistons fouled out, there being now in the whole wide world only two creatures to worry about: a dog that could have been named Butch and a Van Nuys (CA) PFC named Garland H. Steeples whose insides and sense of self were all scrambled on account of fear and a handful of U.S. Army methamphetamine.

"I didn't move for an hour," Garland said in the holdup note he gave to the girl at the Quik-Mart in Richardson. It was a seven-page document in which, his handwriting cramped with hysteria, Garland said he and his mutt huddled in a hidey-hole while

all about them flocked deadly sons-of-bitches got up in gray pith
helmets and regular greens. "That dog and I were doing some
heavy communicating," he wrote. "I was saying *Scoot down,
scrunch up, pull that branch over you;* and that dog was saying
in body language *Stop leaning on me, let go of my neck, watch
your elbow.*" The man at the Texaco station, which Garland
stuck up the last time he was in the state, said that Steeples and
his dog had a real primary thing going in that hole: they were one
breath, one heartbeat, one desire. They could see little, smell
nothing but their own stinks and hear nothing but Haiphong
gobbledygook. "I could sing to you," Garland said. That dog gave
him one dark eyeball and the chin tilt a rich man uses to convey
impatience and distaste. "How about this?" Garland wondered,
doing several lines of—almost inconceivable in this situation—
"Soul Xmas in Bethlehem." His voice, a whisper really, had all
the charm of dirt. "I know some others," he said. Around them,
they could hear crackling undergrowth and native chitty-chat.
"Dog," Garland began, "I believe we're gonna die." He felt the
animal looking at him with intense concentration, its eyes like
tiny wet marbles; it was then, Garland swore, that he plainly
heard that dog talk. It said, "Steeples, why don't you just shut up
for about five minutes and let me think." If they had been somewhere else, Garland proposed, that canine would have been
smoking a Havana cigar and wearing La Dolce Vita sunshades.
Old Bowzer then said, "How'd I get myself into this pickle?"

   (This was Darlene Neff's favorite part, wherein her brother
and this humanoidlike dog crouched face to muzzle in a jungle
mud pit, exchanging opinions. "Garland said that dog sounded
like Walter Cronkite," she told her neighbor one day. "Said that
dog was smarter than some teachers he'd known. Said he had no
problem seeing that dog driving a Buick or opening a Sears account." Even after he was long gone, Darlene liked to describe
Garland's face every time he came to this spot in his adventure: it
was a miserable, fraught-filled expression, what it was, as if he
were again in that distant world, a place of darkness and terror

and heat in which it was entirely possible that persons much influenced by loneliness and imminent doom might indeed strike up a relationship with rotted tree stump or far-off fleecy cloud.)

Here it was, then, Garland remembered, that his amigo, Old Yeller, actually barked—a sound so loud and alien in this place it was like a spotlight shining in his eyes—and he found his hands clamped immediately around that dog's snout. "You're trying to get me killed," Garland said. Through the leaf growth, our boy could see the enemy frozen with curiosity. "Steeples," that dog said, "What the hell are you doing to my neck?" Garland brought the dog's face to his own. "If I let you go," he whispered, "don't yell no more, okay?" The animal seemed to take a long time to consider. "Boy," the dog said, "you ain't learned much about me, have you?" Yet as soon as he was released the dog started to take off, the racket he was making loud enough to be heard on the moon. Garland grabbed him by the throat. "What're you doing?" The dog eyed him suspiciously: "I am leaving here and you, 'bye." Garland clamped his hands over the jaws again. It was a moment, he remembered, as still as death itself: two creatures, one with a big brain and no hope, the other with eons of instinct and four legs for running. "Honest," Garland said once, "I was inside his brain. I knew where he came from, which was Long Binh, and that its old momma was the dog equivalent of a three-dollar business suit." It was thinking dog thoughts: bone and hank, piss on bush and fly on out of there. Garland could almost see himself through the animal's eyes: a skinny work of American manhood, some pimpled, its cheeks completely tear-ravaged. "You're about to do something mean, ain't you?" that dog said. "Dog, you are some first-rate animal, you know." The dog affected the aspect, yes, of supreme disinterest: "I could've been a lot of things in this world." Garland could see the bad guys pressing in from nearabouts, all of them evidently waiting for the next peep or telltale howl. He tried explaining that there was nothing else he could do—life was a pisser, it seemed, ignorant of him and his desires. "I'd like to live, plus you're an orphan—and a dog besides." Whereupon that dog, Garland had to admit, tried to talk him out of it, tried appealing to our boy's sense of fair play, of loyalty; said it aimed to go on down to My Khe, heard there was a whole pack of poodles down there, all named Fifi or Babette, with painted toenails and French-cut hair; said it was scraggly, sure, but in the long view offered by such as Monsieur Descartes just as valuable as Lassie or Rin Tin Tin himself. Garland shook his head; he was truly sorry. "Well, then," the dog said, "go ahead and do it, you old son-of-a-bitch." Whereupon that dog composed himself into a sterling example of insouciance and turned on in its eyes a light such as might emanate from that vast afterworld they both knew about.

"So I started squeezing," Garland wrote in a letter to the Dallas *Morning News*. He threw his whole weight, all 176 pounds, into his grip, one arm around the head in a Kung Fu–inspired move the Army had guaranteed to incapacitate utterly. That dog, Garland reported, was thinking airy thoughts the whole time— about getting a bath with GI soap, about having commisary chopped steak in the Philippines, about having maybe even a Washington, D.C., backyard to cavort in. It didn't squirm or struggle or shiver a bit. Though it was still dark, Garland could sense the NVA folks milling about like customers at a circus; and he could feel, as old Buster got short of breath and his eyes rolled up partways, things giving loose inside himself as well—his heart thudding, his stomach doing a flip, his lungs filling up with some awful liquid he assumed was related to having to do unfortunate deeds for the best of reasons in the worst of times. "I don't know how long it took," Garland wrote, "'cause the next thing I knew it was morning, the enemy had melted away like mist, and I was holding this limp, crushed friend to my chest."

After he was gone for about four months, you heard this story often and with considerable conviction, it now having entered

the popular imagination. It was told by a KINT DJ and appeared
in the CB cross-talk on I-10 or up around Odessa. Darrell Royal,
then coaching the Longhorns and in Houston for a cookout, told
a high-school running back named Scooter that it, the story, was
pure-D invention—wish and whine from those of mashed spirit.
You heart it in Goree, at the VFW hall in Heron, at Mildred's
Diner. It was heard at the Flying R dude ranch in Big Bend
country once, all its grit removed, the story itself as slick and
unfelt as glass. You heard it gussied up or nude as an oyster.
Were it woman, a legislator from Huntington County once said, it
would be named Sheree or Debbi-do, a being that looked good
with a cocktail or a water bed. Once, Cappy Eads, a one hundred
percent look-alike for Santa Claus himself, heard it from the My
Sin saleswoman at Neiman-Marcus who'd heard it from her
neighbor who'd heard it from her nephew who'd gotten it from a
wild-haired East Dallas youth. Cappy said that old Tramp's story
was only cheek and shinbone, the bulk and organ of it removed,
the murder itself taking place in a thousand middle-class bed-
rooms, Garland no more than a shade or Vincent Price ghoul
from the netherworlds. Sometimes, in fact, Garland wasn't in the
story at all, his place taken by an equally unfulfilled round-eyed
youth; and sometimes it wasn't a dog which died, but a crawly-
grimy piece of work which looked like a vision drunks weep over;
and sometimes the story itself took a whole day and much whiskey to tell, its moments from getting to losing spirited, mean and
epic enough for silver screen or drive-in movie.

After a year or so, it left Texas for the rest of North America. In
Florida, you heard it as "Another Story of Fate and Circumstance," the human no longer a boy but an adult named
Dalrhymple or Poot, the dog a specter called forth from the lower
waters by tribulation and shared failure. In South Carolina, it had
a dozen episodes, including one in which that canus familiaris
took up a Parker Bros. ballpoint and, after some cogitation, wrote
its name and several sentences of the complex-compound vari-
ety. At Frank J. Wiley Junior High School in Chaney, Nebraska,

it produced a dozen essays, foremost of which was written by Oogie Pringle, Jr., who, at the honors assembly, recited the whole thing, devoting particular attention to those sections in which the dog, some cleaned up for this telling, and on the verge of everlasting darkness, was saying "Okay" at the very instant the protagonist, Garland H. Steeples, was crumbling to dust in his frozen, desperate and wracked heart.

The story was told last, it appears, by the famous West Coast psychic Charlene Dibbs, in the studios of KNET Phoenix, who informed an audience of St. Vincent Gray Ladies that she, at this precise instant, was in mental contact with the notorious felon and veteran, Garland Steeples. It was a moment of dire expectation. She could visualize him now, she said, as if he were sitting across from her, his face darkened by three days of bristly beard, his clothes shabby and loose. "I see him as a hobo," she said, there being in her voice a lilt such as used by those fetched up by UFOs or victims of out-of-body travel. It was Garland H. Steeples, she said, who was living in reduced circumstances, most probably in a trailer park, him the uneasy guest of a woman named Rae Nell. "At this time," she announced, "I will try to invade his mind." There were many oooohhhs and aaahhhs as Charlene Dibbs set herself to this task, her eyes squinty with concentration. "May I have quiet, please?" she said, "I am getting interference." You could see she was doubtlessly picking up the troublesome thoughts of several naughty people, among them those in pain or about to be. "He is miles away," she said. There were mountains in his distance, she said, but mainly he lived in a flat, barren place—a place of winds and wild climates. "My, that boy is unhappy." It was here, everybody would one day remember, that Ms. Dibbs's face suddenly took on a strained, unlived-in look and she pitched forward in her chair until she had arranged herself in a crouch, alert and suspicious. She made sounds, too, throaty and wet, as if what was to be said was best put in grunts and groans. And then, in what came to be known as the climax to this story of man and dog, it came to pass that an army of viewers from Yuma to North Tucson saw Charlene Dibbs, as if by magic, transformed into one Garland H. Steeples, and you could see that he was out there—anywhere, everywhere—long of tooth and gleeless, as if he had centuries to wait, as if he again were in a deprived venue and again faced with the impossible choice between life and love.

I'M GLAD YOU ASKED

IKE Fooley wasn't doodley-squat when I knew him; he was a II Corps dipstick with what the CO termed a Frenchified way of getting in and out. The war, Ike used to say, was a parochial enterprise—in that shadowy place between crime and tease. He had a Sixteen with the phrase "Nothing To Be Saved" carved in the stock; dressed in inspired night-fighter cheek paint, he looked like a seashore watercolor by who's-it. "Wet dream," he'd holler in the hot spots, LZs and such. "Moil and grope, boys!" That's the breed of grunt he was.

He took a PX Panasonic into the bush near the Do Long bridge one time. Taped the bunch of us doing our deadly duty with Victor Charles. Ike was the gleeful one, the other sounds being random riflery, whirling rotors and a whump-de-whump you knew to be the heart in stress. Mine was a whine, training abandoned for the comfort of a damp hidey-hole.

A tape might go thusly:

Ike: "Get some, my heroes! Ours is the vanquished Lord—dander and the like! Lay some over here, Amp, I believe I know that dink. Hear me, slope—I am the quote menacing, driven stuff of this life unquote! Flee, you motherfuck."

Al-Ali Jackson (a Cleveland spade whose usual retreat was a dry-heave of footwork and frenzy): "Nigger, you diseased. I'm gone! Look for me someplace else. 'Bye!"

The CO: "Mother Goose, Mother Goose, this is Chickadee, come in." (The CO was Nam one thousand percent; he'd told us that Nhua Ha Province was the locus of—what? Glory, maybe; a concept which evoked the shuddery arts. He was blessed and wondrous, and I respect him still.) "Mother, please speak to your boys at the front. We aim to serve only."

On another, I spoke:

"I'm thinking of another place," I was hollering. My heart was in a bush, up a tree, flying like a football overhead, bouncing like a tire down a hill.

"Buck up," Ike yelled, "Nothing To Be Saved" going blurrp-blurrp. "Convert woe! Think of that which uplifts, and get some!"

You could hear trees exploding, ordnance shredding the heavy leaf growth.

"This place I'm thinking of," I said, "is peaceful and lacks rot."

Ike told me he liked to play the tapes for B girls. "It's an aphrodisiac," he claimed. "All that mortality brings them to a sweat and something heavenward. Trust me, Jeeter. Yours is the voice that puts them in a dervish spin."

He played me selections—the parts where upside was down and several indecencies were committed, plus the effort I made to shrink from it all. You could hear me, in a voice I'll describe as anticourageous, appealing to my Daddy Vincent and my Momma Tammy. You could hear Ike too, arguing the virtues of selfhood and Plato's whatchamacallit; Ike was intellectual.

"I got the dope on truth," he said. He described it as the ineffable, that which ain't till the bloods flow.

"Fooley," I said, "I have an impossible affection for living long."

Then Something-Burning-from-Above floated in like a huge orange sail, and he disappeared into the bush, making a merry mating noise, his face a wash of afflicted joy.

—

Next time I saw him, I was at China Beach, taking three days of in-country R & R. He was driving a vehicle identified as Friendly, with him an Air America villain sporting wild Mennonite hair. Fooley was dressed like a greaser named Insipid—leather and convict's sideburns, an infant's dismal grin.

"Come with me, Jeeter," he said. He had sergeant's stripes he might have stolen.

We went to a skivvy bar where several luminous females met our specifications. The AA spook hunkered by the door, eyeballing the scene.

"I'm fighting the evil crap," Ike said, "which accounts for my manner and special methods. I need bodies for a unique undertaking. Yours would do nicely. This is a venture into smut."

I told him I had a day left here. I intended to find luxury and squat in the lap of it.

"I'm impressed," he said. "They had hard cases like you at Tulane where I went. I was a dork among them. I studied everything—Pilpay to Heine. I was that weak creature in the stacks. My girl was Lois De Rosa, very beatnik. I had this urge to achieve for her. There I was a dufus; here I am Old King Cole. I've found my mission in this world: I like to crawl around and murder."

"I appreciate the appeal." I told him that in four months I would be gone, to Heron, Texas, there to work and be content. "Think of me with a yard, a brick barbecue and five dollar whiskey." It was a scene I'd cut out of a picture magazine. I had kids' names already picked: Buck, if a boy; Debbie-do, if not.

"I'm known to the brass as their favorite personality," he said, rising. "I go out in the bush, smell it, track it to its dump or hooch or tunnel, leap upon it with a howl, and love it to death. I've begun to approach allegory."

—

When I was a month short, he called me on a radio hookup later called unconventional. It involved a stealthful and intermittent transmission.

"See it my way," he said, his voice crackly with static. "I could be in your hamlet in three hours. We could be Sylvester and Tweety Bird. I admire the natural in you. The untutored. Why, in two days I could teach you the essentials about having it and keeping it."

"Where are you, Fooley? I hear giggling in the background."

There was a storm of interference, noises galaxial and empty, then he came back on the line: "Al-Ali Jackson said you'd gone over to our POV. He was wrong, huh?"

"I've gone over to nothing," I said. "I heard from my girl. Ike, that letter was nasty. I'm going home to it and more."

He said he had a boy up there in the hinterlands named Large. I could be his boss. I could say 'Boo' and he'd be Easter Amok Itself. At my bidding, he'd stomp, spit fire, roll his eyes till quarters spilled from his mouth. Large was straight out of *Battle Cry*.

"I'm a lieutenant now," Ike said, "field promotions and rewards. I'd be happy to share this fame."

"Sorry," I said.

"You're like my own daddy," he said. "I couldn't please him either."

—

I saw him the last time when he stopped by my house in Heron. This was '74, the bad times only a memory. I'd put fear and dissatisfactions behind me.

"Jeeter, you look as lovely as ever."

He generated a Venus glow around his temples that said, *I am full of myself now, well fit for the future of doing right and having my share.* He was a captain, too—his body the mold, it seemed, for those of similar wants. In addition, he had about a week of barbiturate in him.

"My wife's out," I said. "Her name is Dorene, and she's beautiful."

You could almost hear him thinking about it.

"We're not profound," I said. "Just citizens like several others. My favorite beer is Lonestar, and I appreciate the many efforts made in our name. I have enough money for the things I desire, plus elaborate plans for spending. Dorene's taking a course: preparing it and serving it. You ought to live here, Ike. You'd make out swell."

He looked at me like I was a rock that could tap-dance.

"I suspect you're still bloodthirsty, right?"

"I've talked to Lois De Rosa," he said. "She's married now. Mentioned there was room for something free on the side. I played her a tape of you and me. 'Damn,' she said, and went into the other room to dress up. I sicced Large on her, which he later thanked me for." His breath was an odor that put you in mind of the past. "You want to listen to them?"

Then Dorene came home, and we didn't speak for an hour.

Yes, I hear from him sometimes. Says he's affiliated himself with many, among them Cherokee Bill, Porky and a surly study with no interests save deceit—men of uncertain race and up-bringing. Said they were going to a place that respected vigilance and wreakable havoc. It was profound.

Otherwise, I know not another thing about him. Except the way he signs his name—which has all the subtle pressure of a being abandoning the swoons and sighs of grief for the higher cries of well-being.

"Look for me in the mirthful spots," he wrote.

THE WORLD OF APPLES

IN my days as a drunk, years ago, Jane Clute was the woman with whom I performed a whirling, arm-whipping tango in the produce aisle of our Piggly Wiggly. I was thirty-three then, twice divorced, on temporary contract as a high-school civics teacher; and, on the afternoon I bowed in front of her (like everyone else, I learned my manners in our desert cotillions), I was the fuzzy-witted victim of six hours of Scotch whiskey and a lifetime of apathy.

The store was crowded, as if all our six thousand citizens were famished that day. In the cereals section I stood, my basket laden with potato chips, Swanson's frozen dinners and every sugar item Nabisco makes as treat or finger food. Here and there I saw many known to me or my family. Mrs. Willie Newell, the wife of my daddy's best friend and golfing partner, was yonder, making a decision against Cocoa Puffs; nearby, Dr. Weems's oldest girl, Beth Ann, was holding forth on the virtues of Comet; and then, my soaked brain occupied by a debate between lard and oleo, over the intercom burst Muzak which, with the force of magnetism itself, transported me beyond the current moment to the times I used to sit with my mother, listening to her ancient LPs.

"Lordy," I said. "Geez."

I heard, filtered through one-hundred-proof hooch, "Moonlight on the Ganges," "Carolina in the Morning," and a modern melody by the Platters, the principal part of which was an "oohh-oohh-oohh" that sent me vaulting heavenward. My heart shifted, much tilted in related organs, and I found myself, light-footed as an elf, tiptoeing toward tissues, arms aflutter, face aglow, the world before me vast, lightsome and nearly perfected.

"La-la la-la," I sang. "Do-do-do!"

In produce, between bananas and lettuce, I frolicked, dipped as aesthetes are wont to do, and ended with a flourish of legcraft those in paradise could learn from. Beside me, trembling, stood a woman, nearly my own age, her cart filled with edibles as forlorn-appearing as herself: roughage, Chicken-Stix and a melting quart of vanilla ice milk.

"May I?" I meant my voice to be music itself, lilting and heading forward toward joy. "We will cavort and be beautiful."

In her eyes flashed none of the lights you see in the blessed or those with especially toothsome secrets; so, impatiently, I grabbed her wrist, startled though she was, and, gently, I wrapped an arm around her waist.

"You smell wonderful," I said, inhaling at her neck as if she were more flower than beast. And finally, to the ooo-wah-ooo of "I'm Forever Blowing Bubbles," we shoved off, gliding and turning—two headliners in the Deming, New Mexico, Ice Capades.

She was, at first, reluctant, but, while I spoke of her grace and nimble toes, she relaxed, stopped mumbling, "Wh—? Wh—?" and let me lead her this way and that, our cheeks attached, her pelvis brought almost ardently to my own.

"I am Scooter," I said, "and I feel like a butterfly."

Nervously, she looked around, as if this were TV and she the butt of a New York wisenheimer's lame joke.

"Jane," she said, "Jane Clute. You know my husband, Mickey."

I felt something but ignored it. Mickey was a guard on the Wildcat football team I had been the scatback for, but right then, while Jane and I whipped like dervishes into housewares, I stood as far from the past as I was tight against her. I spoke of her throat, which was delicate, and her soul, which was brave. My mind held aloft by lyrics from Tin Pan Alley (was it "Louisville Lou"?), I told her how special she was—to me and to the planet itself. I praised her modesty, celebrated her tact, urged her (as I was doing) to spurn the wanton among us, and concluded, after several dizzying whirls, with language in reference to wonder.

"Jane Clute," I said, setting her loose in frozen foods, "you are ever a bride. Be not disappointed in the dark thing we do. *Adios*."

"Huh?" she said. "What?"

I skipped toward the exit, cut free from the workaday world. Panting just a little, I remained at the electric door. Shoppers were flabbergasted, like infants. Mrs. Newell was slapping the air as if fending off bees. One checker, slack-lipped and whey-faced, was stammering my name, and way off, up in his tiny manager's office, shook Chester Pomeroy, aghast.

"God bless you all," I shouted. "And to all a good night!"

―

In the days I'm writing about my life was held together by booze alone and it in great quantity. Every month I'd trot down to the Farmers and Merchants Bank to cash my granny's trust check (believe me: no small thing it is to be heir to a cattle ranch in southern New Mexico), and announce to everyone, customer and capitalist alike, that these were parlous times. These were times, I told them, which were best survived in the place I climbed toward each night: a beerhall Dreamland constructed atop the soft depths of sleep.

The day after I danced with Jane, I confessed to Dillon Ripley, Daddy's personal trust officer, that, given our era of alarm, we humans ought now, this very goddam minute, pitch off our fallen, craven selves and cleave to a new code.

"What would that be, Scooter?" he said.

His eyes were tolerant and sparkly, and I thought to haul myself into his rich man's lap to hang on the way the truly frightened young do.

"Dillon Ripley," I began, "I don't know what the hell I'm talking about."

We were one contented, well-fed man in a shiny suit and another, me, who looked like the dark-minded used-car salesmen they have on late-night California TV.

"Well," I said, "I'll be going now," and soon I stood outside, rich enough again to afford another month of maudlin reflection.

In June I wrote letters, filling them with philosophies I'd stolen to pass off as my own. To my first wife, Vicki, who was living in Albuquerque with my two youngsters, J. E. and Alton, I said, "Love, like change, occurs on the edge of destruction." I reminded her of our UNM days and what grief did in those the victim of it. I said howdy to the white-collar American she lived with and included $250 for the grade-A meats he was said to like. To my second wife, Darlene, a nurse in El Paso and especially gifted in our healing arts, I addressed the subject of history, which is made at night. "I am as you knew me," I wrote, "red-eyed and unbalanced in spirit, but now that vacation is here, I have undertaken a program of self-help." I included a picture, too, of my Frigidaire and the eats I lived on: greens, yellows and what industry provides us in fancy packages. "You be good," I concluded, "and one day I'll meet you in the wet Eden Dr. Hammond Ellis, my Episcopalian, talks of. 'Bye."

I also used this time to draft documents our Deming *Headlight* would not publish. I stormed into their offices every Monday, in my fist a sheaf of papers. I made proposals about school redistricting, coming up with a novel way of filling youth with virtues we picked for them. I believed in book learning and aimed to make it as dangerous as firearms in a mob. My curriculum featured lectures on underhandedness and heartache, as well as what to do when the glands call. In another open letter, I argued for anarchy, a clean sweep of our republic. I said that Mr. T. C. D. Wales, our city manager, was a fine though limited man whom I expected to see the next morning in front of my Olive Street duplex, broom in hand, clearing the rubble from the muffler shop parking lot across the way. I ended with the dream I'd had: There were stairs, a trek through mists and thrashing waters, then a wise fellow who resembled Humpty-Dumpty whispered to me, "Losing faith is complicated and takes time; there are no epiphanies. Go back to sleep."

The day before I saw Jane again, I attended a meeting of the Luna County Democratic Party, of which my daddy, spry though seventy, is still the chairman. During the speech-making I leaped from my chair to make this pained but effective noise: "Eeeeffff!"

It was a smoky place, to be true, but it was Daddy's den, familiar to me as my own bed. There were his golf trophies, snapshots of what he looked like in WW II and bric-a-brac my momma had fondness for.

"What you all think about agony?" I wondered. It, like calumny, was an old theme with me. "I think it's a fine idea for the lazy hereabouts."

Beside me, Eugene Puckett, our clerk of courts, was breathing hard and gazing hither as if paralyzed. Next to him, Al Borders was shaking his shopkeeper's noggin, mumbling words with menace in them.

"Scooter," my daddy said, "why don't you go in the other room. Mother has treats in there."

I said no, thanks. This was an open meeting, I said. I was a citizen, plus a party regular, not to mention generous with donations and a free agent.

"Okay," he said, "what's on your mind?"

I was woozy, hollow-minded as a bell; and for a second nothing came to me except what a spectacle we adults were. I found a thread on my sport coat that needed plucking, then said, "You remember that time we played those Las Cruces High Bulldogs? This was '65, I think."

You could see all thirty-five of them think, then accept the exasperating item I was. The wind had come up, blowing hot out of Mexico, and it was possible to believe that outside, turning and howling by our Esther Williams swimming pool, was nightmare itself.

"This was the third period, and they were killing us. They were animals, those boys. They were carnage." I had no idea where this—or anything—was coming from, but knew that between them and me, as between bird and reptile (or past and present), there was a connection. "I got the ball one time," I said, "and went yonder." I showed them, shooting from the three-point stance into a cleared space near the billiard table. "Those animals were after me, I say." Wheezing some, I feinted now as I had then. "Mr. Puckett, sir, scoot your chair a mite, will you? I feel the urge to hurdle." And I did, flying over him and Del Cruz as if beyond, in our dining room, lay victory and young people to share it with.

I shook my hips, rolled my shoulders, and did a two-step I now find impossible to describe; then my father pinched my ear. "Scooter, this is plain embarrassing. Go home."

I gave them my smile—which is teeth, twinkling eyeball and the thrust chin of Joe Palooka himself. "Wait a second," I said and dashed left till I couldn't anymore. "Sorry," I said. It was Mr. Borders with cheese in his lap.

Then, as in '65, I went down. *Supine* is the word.

"This is how they had me." I gasped to show how it hurt. "They were brutal, I say, and they crunched me."

These were Democrats—well acquainted with the unwholesome, shabby things we sometimes are. They eyed me good, indeed, not one of them delighted. Del Cruz, for example, looked partly rabid, and Red Sorrell, our district representative, was having trouble with the sneering half of his face.

"What do you think?" I said. "Isn't this the way it is in our times, some hugger-mugger followed by demise?"

Somebody had a wet cough, and one tummy was rumbling to my left. My father had his cigar going, the upper half of his white head lost in clouds. My head, too, was in a foggy place, and it seemed that in the next minute, or the next, I would be asleep.

"Let's adjourn for a bit," Al Borders muttered, and an instant later they were gone, marching out one by one, me leaving this vale for another; and what I remember is waking once or twice and, over my collapsed self, listening to such sentiment as I expect to hear in the final hours of clatter, dread and folks.

—

Sober now for several years, I can tell you I believed in those spirits which brought us, say, Pinocchio and polite Sir Lancelot, spirits to daunt the creature in us. Drunk—on gin or Buckhorn beer or exotic liquors, it didn't matter—I was the Mad Hatter himself or Don Quixote or another whose job it is to meet woe with a sword or a sharp remark. But on the day I saw Mrs. Jane Clute on the fifth fairway of the Mimbres Valley Country Club— it was a Sunday—I didn't know who I was. I had been at St. Andrew's that morning, drunk but uplifted as are the worshipful hereabouts when Dr. Ellis lets his mind go. Ears still ringing with talk about angels to harken with in a paradise verdant enough to shame any resort you know, I was in the pro shop, on the edge of a group of men who gathered every Sunday noon to speak of grave, disheartening issues. There were seven regulars, all ruling-class gents but old, with leather armchairs and some eloquence on matters of consequence. They had opinions, which you heard at often painful volume. They argued about war and the peckerwoods who caused it, love and those beleaguered by it, as well as the loftymost half of lust; but I was content just listening to them and the faint music coming over the PA system which linked all the buildings—caddy shop, locker rooms, ballroom and men's bar—and, by an elaborate speaker system, virtually every tree on the course. Plus, I was dressed in my linkster's outfit of reds and pinks, feeling myself grand as any species which has brain and heart and many years yet to live.

Lord, I thought, gazing at our glorious outdoors. How nice to be from here and not elsewhere.

They were discussing sloth when I went into the adjoining room where our clubs are stored and cleaned, and even as I took a swallow of the rye I hid in my golf bag I could hear one—Mr. Dalrhymple, I think—sputtering, laying out his insights like poker cards.

"No, goddammit," he was yelling, "you live, you suffer, *then* you die!"

Standing at the window, I considered our course and the hardy scrub which is our flora. Everywhere was sunshine, bright enough to be the envy of the rusted, dark states up north; but in that room, which smelled of dead turf and human sweat and dirty water, I sensed only that gloom found near car wrecks and other calamity. I felt something—doom, or the fate I believe in— tugging at me. Mr. Dalrhymple was addressing wist in beasts ("You know what dogs think about?" he said. "Food and where to put their dong, that's what!") when I saw Jane Clute in the fairway with a threesome of club ladies.

Geez, I thought. Holy moly.

My heart had pitched sideways and toppled. This time—and the way it usually is in stories I like—she was beautiful: a work even villains could be proud of. She was also, thank the Lord, the worst female golfer I'd ever seen, her swing like turmoil itself: haste and violence that produced dither.

Eeeeffff, I thought. Eeerrrggghhh.

With her was Mrs. Hal Thibodeaux, my ninth-grade biology teacher. Drinking and feeling special again, I watched them bang, swat and flail their way hither. It was not the carnal I felt, but that notion Dr. Hammond Ellis had preached about: human fettle and what it tends toward in creation. In the other room, Dub Spedding was defending envisceration, while in the distance Mrs. Thibodeaux, grim like an Elks Club wrestler, settled over her ball, waggled her ample rear end, then had at it, lashing out as if clutched by panic. Breathless, I saw the ball fly forward and slice, dribbling into the knottiest rough we have.

"Dang it," I said. There was a lesson here, I thought. Maybe I would one day learn it.

I took a deep swig, thought of waves in paradise and the white beaches leading from them. When Jane Clute stood over her ball, I conceived of the goodness mankind itself stands for.

"Smack that thing," I said.

As before, she wound up, paused, looked everywhere but where she ought, then exploded like a Juárez firecracker. While behind me the learned of my region were taking up the topic of finitude, in front of me, a hundred yards away, Jane Clute was watching her ball soar like that perfection described in *Golf Digest*. Things—bone, muscle, fibers—rattled in my innards. I saw her mouth working and knew she was exclaiming, "Well, how

about that, Marge? Isn't this something?" She high-stepped as
the fortunate will, shook herself with glee, and there was a moment when I expected trumpetry or other celestial fanfare.

A minute later, Jane and her partners plunged into the rough
to hunt Mrs. Thibodeaux's ball, and I stopped resisting the need
to be heard. Switching on the PA, I grabbed the microphone,
blew into it as Allie Martin, our pro, does when he starts our
Four-Ball Championship, and said howdy. I was speaking not
only to Jane and her pals, but also to the dozens of others who
were spread about our 565 acres.

"Mrs. Hal," I said, "this is Scooter, how're you?"

The effect was instanteous as slaughter in a public place: people were frozen or ducking as if bombed. Mrs. Hal herself,
crouched and tense, wielded her driver like a war ax.

"If you peek in that no-account mesquite to your left," I said,
my voice rolling like thunder, "I believe you'll find your Maxfli."

She spun around twice, eyed the clear heavens. It was a miracle she was looking for.

"Moreover," I said, "roll that right hand a bit and you won't be
putting yourself in any more hazards."

Two holes away, on the seventh, I saw my father and said
hello, you old geezer. "You get on in here," I told him, "and we'll
have some beer, what say?" He was stomping his wedge in the
sandtrap when I told Mrs. Hal that she should, as well, spread
her stance some, for balance, so her partners could observe the
fine whacking she's capable of. "Tuck that elbow in, too, okay?"

I had another swallow, then spoke to her who had inspired me.

"Mrs. Clute, you're looking lovely today."

She was the picture of poise—radiant as what I'd like to paint if
I had the talent. I wanted her to know what pleasure I felt to be
within hailing distance of that which seemed the best of hope
and affirmation.

"I tell you," I told her, "that whatever you need—money or
help cleaning up your backyard or a letter of reference—you just
let old Scooter know, okay?"

I had another swallow, cranked up the volume. Way off, a

plane was making its way westward, and it was possible to believe in things bigger than ourselves and how we are in time.

"What's your middle name, Mrs. Clute? It's Betty or one equally fine, like Rose." She was smiling now, listening as intently as I do when intuition utters. "You ought to have children," I said. "They'd be great, spirited but not rowdy. I could fetch them presents and stuff."

I was having airy thoughts of what the future might be, and paying no mind to those who had gathered like a posse to charge my way.

"That Mickey of yours," I said, "he's a lucky guy. Not much of a football player—too heedless, mostly—but not dumb as I thought." My heart was big as pride itself. "I'll be going now," I announced. "Maybe if you've got a sister or a cousin, you could tell me about her, all right? It's my belief that you're a special breed. Bye-bye."

Full of sweetness, I flicked off that machine, emptied my bottle, hitched my trousers the way heroes do, turned around.

"Howdy, fellas," I said.

Standing before me were Wrath, Dismay, Disgust—all the untoward ideas we have; and you could tell that when I left, lurching some, the topic henceforth among these codgers would be lunacy and what it looked like wearing togs.

—

What I'm writing about is tragedy, which comes to us here in the arid Southwest as a private, unspectacular force. In the time this takes place, while the big world was occupied by murder and riot and high crimes in office, we hereabouts were discussing the divorce between Eugene and Irene Puckett and what was going to become of Del Cruz's Triangle Drive-In. In our wind-beaten, often broiled geography, we were debating truancy and where the new city well would go—all issues full of doom for the narrow kind Dr. Ellis says we are. At the center of my world, however, because I had nothing else to brood about, was Mrs. Jane Clute.

Though I hardly saw her the next month, I learned plenty about her and Mickey. From Buddy Spillner, the bartender at the Thunderbird, I learned that Mickey was having labor trouble with his beer distributorship. Somebody at Woolworth's told me Jane was visiting Dr. Weems's office a lot, and a couple times, when I drove my Fairlane by their place on Iron Street, I saw Buzz King's heating and air-conditioning people on her roof wrestling with the swamp cooler. One time, parked in the Hitching Post lot, drinking for cheap what would in another hour cost me a lot, I saw Mickey's pickup turn down my row and ease into the space in front of me. It was another hot night, our moon ghastly for its size and light. I could hear well, too, particularly Uncle Roy and his Red Creek Wranglers, who were loud and ambitious. At the moment Mickey switched off his motor, Uncle Roy—a stringbean cowpoke whose real name is Newt Grider— was singing of misery and the blight it leaves in the heartspot.

This is something, I thought. This truly is.

For a while, Mickey just sat, as I was doing, and I imagined us as we had been years before: him, bulk you know as Disquiet and Gruesomeness; me, the sort who takes the easy way out. I remember liking him a great deal, especially for the way, in our locker room before a game, when Oscar Veech, our coach, used to describe the mess we'd make of our foes that night, Mickey would growl and bark and thrash, working himself toward a frothy state of being; then, at a signal from Coach, he'd say, "Hats off, men," and the fifty of us would go to one knee, asking for inspiration, protection and courage. One minute Mickey would be yammering about pissants and dingleberries; the next, eyeballs inflamed by faith, he'd be talking about, oh, manna and morning dew. You just had to like a delinquent as soft inside as he, and I did. I liked him for his thick neck and his brutal-appearing forearms, as well as for a grin that once upon a time could have belonged to the Big Bad Wolf. Most of all, I liked him because, notwithstanding his hulk and what it might do to the frail who offended him, he was on the inside a creature of tenderness and unrealized hopes.

So when he finally got out of his pickup, it took me no time to lean out my window. "Hey, Mickey! It's me, Scooter!"

He was confused for a second, but I rushed up, grabbed his lineman's meaty hand and shook it the way my daddy taught, which is related to looking the other guy straight in the eye.

"How you?" I said. "Me, I'm splendid. You going in? Let me buy you one, okay?"

His eyes shifted in and out of focus, then he knew who I was and snatched me up in a lineman's smothering embrace.

"Well, piss on me," he said, "just dump all over me."

It was that usual scene of reunion between old pals: cheerful and awkward; but it was over in a jiffy and soon we were inside, waving to Uncle Roy and telling Miss Pettibone behind the bar to sell us beaucoup drink. Oh, it was grand. We took a table by the dance floor, and the hours flew by as they once did. Uncle Roy sang "All Hail the Power," and we fell to tapping our feet and harmonizing. Everybody was there—Nell Jean Sanders, Billy Jo De Marco, Ida Fitts, the bowling team from Franklin's Auto Parts, some cowhands from my granny's ranch—and the mood was gladsome. I told Mickey about me, how I was semirich and a boozer who loved Thomas Jefferson and rabble that makes government; and he told me about himself, how he was still crosshearted but some in love, too.

"I'm pleased to know that," I said.

By ten-thirty we were drunk, and more than once I had charged to the dance floor. I had his wife, Jane, on my mind, I think, when Uncle Roy went into his Merle Haggard imitation; I scooped up Dee Dee Harrison and flung us into a tornado of arms and legs. When "Loving on Back Streets" came on, Mickey himself took to the floor—for the most part alone—and did hootchy-koo with his rump that earned applause from the bar. He had his grin again, and I could tell that this too was prayer for him.

"Lord," Mickey hollered, "I do love to frolic!"

But then—by black magic, perhaps—the mirth vanished and we found ourselves, toward midnight, slumped at a booth in the corner and speaking about despair.

"What you think about women?" he asked.

Around us was a scene worthy of Mr. Dante—litter, sharp odors, human yackety-yack.

"I think they're wishy-washy," Mickey said. "I think they're the worst thing that ever happened."

I was dying to ask about Jane, but he was preoccupied by the underhalf of things: selfhood, mopery and time. He was gray-faced, his hair slapped across his forehead, and every now and then he'd bang his fists on the table and make our bottles hop. As it sometimes does, unhappiness had gripped him hard, and I wanted to hold him by the cheeks and say that home, where he ought to be right now, was marvel and wonder and wish, Jane Clute.

"C'mon," he said. "I want to show you something."

For an hour, we raced around in his pickup. He had a pint of 4 Roses we shared, but not much else. One time, driving fast past Buzz King's Chevron station, he mashed the brakes hard and we screeched to a halt in the middle of the street.

"Scooter," he said, clearing the clutter from his lap, "what you think about love?"

He looked as serious as he did when he was about to ask his partisan gridiron God for vanquishment.

"Mickey," I told him, "I think it's the finest damn thing in the world."

He looked like that youngster in those *Sunset* magazine ads for a military school where are taught only death and the defying of it. He jammed the stick into gear and whipped us forward.

"Love ain't nothing," he said, "but time and the money it costs."

At high speed, he talked about glory, of which there wasn't nearly enough, and other topics which obsessed him. He used the words "mooky" and "diddly-squat," and once, flying around a corner, he said he was a direct descendant of Vandal and Ostrogoth.

"No, you're not," I insisted. "You got to accept the goodness you are."

I was stupid and he told me so. "You're drunk," he said, "shut up." For another hour we roared and squealed through many neighborhoods, twice clipping off mailboxes.

At last, in what I know to be the end of this episode, he stopped on Fir Street. He was mouth-breathing and I thought, with some fear, that he was going to pass out, order me to walk, or choke me.

"You know who lives there?" he said, pointing.

We were two blocks from my own house, and suddenly I knew exactly who lived in the meager place he meant.

"My girlfriend," he said. "My outside woman."

Everything about her residence said danger—its faded stucco, its undramatic yellow porch lamp, its pair of scrawny evergreens; and I felt good fellowship leave me then as swiftly as I one day expect to lose my soul.

"Her name is Ronnie Louise Suggs," he said, "and I do honestly hate her."

———

The next day, like a private eye, I began trailing Jane Clute. I saw myself as part Lone Ranger, part Spiderman, part Zorro—the figure of justice your children root for. Earlier than usual, I'd get up, make myself presentable and inconspicuous, and drive to a corner near her home. I had binoculars and a bagful of snacks— Snickers, Cheetos, Jiffy peanut butter. I followed her to the cleaners, the hardware store, everywhere. I learned all her habits—which were marvelous, too. She was, for example, a determined teeth brusher and a believer in public libraries. Her favorite book was *The World of Apples,* which is poetry that puts you in mind of weal, plus what it's like to live free. On Mondays, she cleaned house, lugged the garbage to the curb. On Tuesdays, she had her hair done at Ida Fitts's beauty salon. "She don't like frosting or bleach," Ida told me. On Wednesdays, she went to the club for her lesson and a round on Ladies' Day. Sometimes she took a swim afterward.

She kept appointments, was punctual and would not abide mischief when it led to sore feelings. From the janitor at the Baptist church, I learned that she sang in the choir and would fill in at Sunday school if the lesson concerned a struggle that came out right. She wore White Shoulders perfume. She had been for two semesters to SMU, where she met Mickey, then worked at a Dallas Mode O'Day after he lost his scholarship. Her mother, Ella Mae, was living, I found out, but her daddy, Fred, who'd done something in oil, had died two years ago from bacteria he'd caught in Venezuela. She was thirty-one, a Libra, shopped out of catalogues and liked to eat at the Ramada Inn. I dug through her trash, peeked in her mailbox, gossiped when I could and more than once put my ear to a closed door. One day I discovered she smoked when she drank Gallo wine, and used Benzagel on her neck blemishes; another day, I learned she hated charge cards, as well as news that comes out of Europe. The more I learned, the more I desired to be near when the ceiling fell.

In the third week I was discovered. We were in T, G & Y, me in housewares feigning interest in tiny kitchen appliances. I was in my customary outfit: fedora Mr. Spillane would like, Hawaiian shirt (palm tree and cunning animal that thrived there), Bermuda shorts to relax in. I had Tyco's cookie cutters in hand when Jane popped up beside me.

"Scooter," she said, "what're you doing?"

Instantly, I was plunged into abashedness. She wasn't at all pleased.

"Shopping," I mumbled. "Party. Friends. Cooking. Eat."

We made eye contact, and I was first to look away.

"You're following me," she said. "Take off those glasses, you look like a beatnik."

She was giving directions and I obeyed: the dough cutters spilled from my hands and I pulled off my shades.

"Does Mickey know you're doing this?"

By the school supplies Mrs. Irene Puckett was eying me like a well-done cutlet. I waited for my noontime drinks to kick in and further soften my spongy brain.

"I am not doing anything." I was on my knees now, trying to tidy up.

"You've been lurking about all week," she said. "I saw you at the Rio Grande theater and the Weems's barbecue and the Pick-Quik this morning."

She was tall and worth being below again sometime.

"Explain yourself," she said.

In that moment I noticed many things: flickering fluorescent bulbs, scratches in the linoleum, a shaving nick on her calf.

"Accident," I said. "Honest, pure luck is all."

She looked unconvinced, so I explained my world to her. It was a place of peril, I said. Or good fortune. There were wonderments, I said. Think of physics. Think of cures, and how the brown are living nowadays. Of course, there were also, uh, forces at work. Pestilence. Greed. Blips in the cosmos.

"Good Lord," she said. "What're you talking about?"

Chance, I said. Emanations. Inanimate objects which speak. Thieves and ill-will. People who fly, pets that count.

"Are you trying to make fun of me?" she said.

I spent a long time studying her eyes, which were big and pained. I put blather out of my mind.

"No," I said, "no." Hoping it would not break, I put all I knew about morality and authority into my voice. "I am doing nothing but keeping you happy."

Irene Puckett was getting an earful, and I fought the urge to grab Jane's shoe.

"Well, don't follow me anymore," Jane said. "I'm grown up and can be satisfied by myself."

Then, like a lady, she excused herself and withdrew, nodding hello to Mrs. Puckett.

"Serendipity," I hollered after her. "Just being in the right place at the right time!"

Thereafter I lay low. I borrowed Daddy's Biscayne, parked at the other end of her block. I kept to the shadows, ducked into doorways or pretended to find fascinating what you see in Amer-

ica's shop windows nowadays. Then, as if struck by sickness, her
routine changed and the world wobbled, from high heaven to
deep blue sea. I felt a quake, profound as any truth, as if I were
standing atop a mantle of earth fractured like glass. She stayed
indoors, kept the shades drawn. She didn't pay the paper boy, nor
snatch up the waste that had blown across her lawn into the
hedge. Every morning, Mickey would leave for his warehouse,
and inside all the lights would go off. Once Mrs. Levisay from
next door went over and rang the bell for ten minutes. She
knocked, tried looking through the window. "Jane," she called,
"you in there? I have that seed you wanted." Nothing. Mrs.
Levisay banged on the screen, put her bag on the steps and went
home.

That night we had rain—pretty rare for September—and in
the morning the bag was still there, soaked and droopy. In the
afternoon, I pulled the Biscayne closer, my spyglass ready. Occasionally, I'd see a shadow, insubstantial as a ghost, and the heart
would tumble right out of me. I ate Twinkies and was vigilant.
On Friday, Sheriff Gribble rolled by, asked what I was doing.

"Thinking," I said.

He was older and knew me as a responsible, if odd, citizen.

"I was thinking, too," he said. "My subject was trespass, what's
yours?"

In the evening, I paid Billy Taylor five dollars to pick up her
yard. "Remember," I told him, "anybody asks what you're doing,
you say this is part of the specialness you are." He took forty-five
minutes and two trash bags before going inside for supper.

Near sundown, Mickey pulled into his driveway. He looked
forlorn, beaten; and I came within an eyelash of running over to
him. My mouth was dry, my lungs like paper sacks. The streetlights had flickered on when Mickey let himself in. I had a bottle
of Johnnie Walker Red and some Buds, who were my steadfast
companions. As you speak to those you live with, so I spoke to
them; we had, yes, a conversation. Was there mayhem in that
house? I wondered. Disarray? I imagined tumbled furniture and

rent fabric. I heard a door slamming and conceived of the ruin a bad God might make. I had these words: *befuddlement, mistake, ingratitude*. Plus the sentence they fit in. Twice I grabbed my door handle, hoping to jump out, but felt only weakness inside. What will you do? I asked myself. Look at you, I thought. You have the fists of the leisure class and no boxing skills. Plus you believe in peace. I took an inventory of what I had: legs like you find on cheap tables, a belly that Charles Dickens puts on his fools, wits addled by modern times; and, shaking like a simpleton, I thought of life as Mickey himself saw it: a long thing of lies and blue-heartedness.

"Okay," I said to myself. "Get up now."

I didn't move, not a bone, though drier links gave loose inside.

"Now," I said. "You just can't sit here no more."

I consulted the moon, the stars and the rest of heaven I could see.

"Please," I said. "This is really important."

And I did it: put into action all those words I believed in.

"Well, how about this?" I said to myself. "Aren't you something after all?"

Creeping like a robber, I sneaked into their backyard, heading for the kitchen windows. Having been back there many times, I knew that yard as well as I knew my own—the rosebushes, the creaky part of the flagstone patio, where the lawn chairs sat; my trip would have made those in charge of combat as proud of me as they are of their own cutthroat commandos. Way off, a dog was barking—the Newells' boxer, I think—and the sky was not black enough for me to get lost in. Jesus, I thought, what is it I'm doing? Hunkered beneath the windows, I knew: Peeping-Tom is what.

Mickey and Jane were eating—mashed potatoes and roast beef—and what had passed between them was not what used to pass between Ozzie and Harriet. They were glum, each bent over the table like the self-denying monks I've read about. I was enthralled. Clearly, they were strangers—from different and contrary planets. He, weighty and bedraggled and low-browed, was meat, heft that was nearly thoughtless; and she—because she's the one I want you to celebrate—was that familiar princess haunted by the familiar woes. Once he tried speaking to her, and it was fun to imagine the language he used. (He did not, I believe, say what we should be in our times—which is upright, fed often and blissful by choice.) As he had done with me, he spanked the table for emphasis, flipping the flatware. Maybe he was talking about his world with Ronnie Suggs. Maybe, as he had been when we roared down our streets, he was full of the rigamarole we humans were: muscle and the means to stick it anywhere, loathing for his own failures. He went on banging and speaking; and Jane's face was stone. I don't think she even blinked, just considered him as, from ten feet away, you watch an angry dog on a five-foot chain. Then Mickey was moving, grabbing his jacket. He was going to say more, thought better of it, and I heard the side door bang open and bang shut.

"One-Mississippi," I said, "two-Mississippi." When I got to forty, his pickup was squealing in the distance.

I could hear a TV somewhere, a drama about police virtue and life in Miami Beach. I heard, too, a citizen in the Taylor residence yelling about something he would not put up with. But I was frozen. Night was complete, daylight was another world away, and I was on tiptoe, nose to glass, my breath held for all time. I had one thought, possibly warmhearted but slight as thread. And a second.

"Go on," I said.

I offered myself further encouragement and became wise enough to accept it. And next, in a way those in Hollywood might like, I was pushing against that window, raising it.

"Howdy," I said.

Slowly, Jane looked my way and I am still delighted she didn't howl or brain me with a saucepan. All she said was "Scooter?," nothing in her voice but amusement and what I wish to call relief. I jammed that window up, looked innocent as Peter Pan, and undertook the athletics of dragging myself in. She was in control, indeed, as if in our era this was the only way for folks to meet each other.

"Don't say anything," I told her, and flopped into the sink.

Her house was immaculate, with little to hurt myself on, and I told her so.

"Scooter," she said, "what do you want now?"

It was a room of a million shining surfaces, me foremost among them. "Only this." I had flung open my arms the way parents do. "C'mere," I said.

She was wearing a housecoat and the fuzzy slippers grannies like; she looked wholesome as milk.

"Hurry," I said, "my arms are getting tired."

She had her arms folded and a schoolteacher's expression of suspicion.

"Why would I want to do that?" she said.

I looked at her kitchen table and thought about eating what they hadn't. "I'm kind of hungry, Jane. What do you say?"

"Well, only for a second, okay?"

Her little smile had weight and warmth, and a second later she was leaning against me.

"Thanks," I told her. "I was going to fall over, I'm sure."

She didn't weep and I didn't weep and for a long time our expanded universe was a swell place to be from. She smelled wonderful—flowery and what soap leaves behind—and I had no thoughts other than those associated with civilized life in heaven.

I spoke. "Let's stay like this, all right?"

She made an affirmative sound, and together, clasped, we hung on, hearing a tick-tock and waiting for the door to blast open again.

—

You're wrong if you think we fell in love and married. Fact is, in the following months I was well consumed by drink, finally arrested and later rehabilitated at my daddy's expense. When I returned to Deming, I learned that Mickey had sold his business so he and Jane could move, start over. I hear they're in Las Cruces, sixty miles east, and more than once I've thought about driving over to say howdy. But I'm a sober man now, ginger ale my strongest beverage, and sixty miles might as well be six thousand to the modest spirit I currently am. Plus, I'm dating a fine woman, Irene Puckett (Eugene's ex,) and am uncertain she'd forgive this part of my past.

Sometimes, as a warning, I tell my classes—I teach eighth graders now—about this period in my life, and invariably at the Twirp Week sock hop or on Sadie Hawkins Day I am asked to dance with Dawn or Jo Jo or Ann Marie as I had once danced with Jane Clute. We move to the center of the floor, a record or a teenage band making a fitting racket, and for a time, a young pointy bosom against my stomach, I am again in our Piggly-Wiggly, nimble and smiling in all dimensions, saying things about mirth and glee and gladness that I don't regret. Then the music ends and, chagrined, I say "Thank you" to my escort and take up anew my place in the real and sober world.